After
the
Rain

After
the
Rain

JANE LORENZINI

Published by Nest Press, Nashville

 Edited and Designed by Girl Friday Productions
www.girlfridayproductions.com

Editorial: Alexander Rigby, Amara Holstein, Carrie Wicks, Sharon Turner Mulvihill
Cover and Interior Design: Paul Barrett
Cover Image Credits: © Shutterstock/grop; © Shutterstock/Hulinska Yevheniia

ISBN (Hardcover): 978-1-7323248-1-7
ISBN (Paperback): 978-1-7323248-0-0
e-ISBN: 978-1-7323248-2-4

First Edition

Printed in the United States of America

For Hoda
My world got brighter the day we met.

Chapter 1

Several doors down from Duggan's general store, Belle Carson was spending her afternoon break in the company of sunrays on this still winter day. She'd chosen a bench with a back to lean against so she could sit comfortably with her eyes closed. Her hands lay folded in her lap, finally at rest after a morning of sorting store goods—buttons, pins, and needles. She turned her face slightly, tracking the sun. On the street in front of her, a buggy rattled by, its driver clicking at the puller. A day drinker war-whooped from inside the nearby saloon. Fort Myers at noon had signs of life, but on balance was quiet, townsfolk either eating lunch, serving it to visitors, or working straight through it.

"Wake up, Miss Belle."

She opened her eyes to see Augie Morgan smiling as he moved toward her, his hands jammed in his pants pockets.

"Well, hello, you." Belle greeted him with a head bob but sat perfectly still, her body relaxed and content to do nothing but accept the sun's embrace.

Augie took his place on the bench, always to her right, closer to the door of the local newspaper shop where he worked as a printer's devil. Fifteen years old, he was an apprentice to Stephen Fitzgerald, editor of the local paper, the *Fort Myers Press*.

"What's in the news today?" she asked, as usual.

"My fingers," he said, also as usual, and held out his ink-stained hands.

The pair sometimes sat together to chat a bit and watch the daily doings. This afternoon on Front Street an oxcart loaded with sugarcane was parked not far from their bench. A burly bearded man straddled the cane, rebalancing his load. From atop the mound, he hailed a passerby. "What about this year? What's the word?"

The passerby stopped in front of the oxen, sleeping on their feet. "Depends on who you ask, but my word is—they're coming." He winked at a young girl lying across the thick cane stalks. "That's two words, isn't it?"

With 1888 under way, residents of Fort Myers and nearby communities had begun to speculate if world-renowned inventor Thomas Edison and his family would once again spend a few winter months in their little slice of paradise, boosting community pride and exposure for the remote region. Last year, the family traveled south from New Jersey to vacation at their grand estate along the Caloosahatchee River. When Edison purchased the property nearly three years ago, he'd assured residents that he would equip Fort Myers with electricity, a luxury known only to privileged individuals and businesses up north. To date, only the Edison property had been wired for lights.

"What's your guess, Augie?" Belle asked. "Will the Edisons visit this year?"

Augie poked his thumb toward the newspaper shop. "Mr. Fitzgerald sure hopes so. The Edisons sell papers."

Nodding, she said, "We do love their doings, don't we?"

He smiled at her wordplay.

Belle always walked away from Augie pleased that they'd crossed paths. He was enthusiastic and confident, everything she wasn't at his age. His mother and father were hardworking and well-mannered members of the community and, from what she saw in their son, fine parents.

The two sat quietly for a few minutes. Across the street, at Duggan's rival store, people pawed at a prickly mound of pineapples unloaded right onto the ground. Next to the pile, a man stood atop a mammoth dead turtle, clutching rope reins looped through the reptile's shriveled mouth. A cow chewing greens from someone's garden wandered past.

"I've got some news of my own," Augie said, his shoes tapping the sandy ground.

Belle swiveled slightly on the bench toward him. "Good news, I hope."

"Mr. Fitzgerald said I could start writing copy for the business card section," Augie said.

"Well, now," Belle replied. "What do you think?"

"I think it's about time," he answered, "in fact, well past time."

The teen reached into a hip pocket. He pulled out a small piece of torn newspaper and read it aloud.

"The Palms Hotel: The popular hotel is situated on the bank of the Caloosahatchee River and has a wharf and all the conveniences for boaters."

He looked at Belle and feigned a yawn, patting his lips with his palm.

"Needs some work?" Belle asked, amused.

Augie ran his thumb and pointer finger across the air, creating an invisible business card.

"The Palms Hotel: Boaters and all who enjoy the best are welcome at this riverfront palace, where you will dine like royalty and want for nothing but perhaps another day in paradise." He poked the air, a period on his sentence.

Belle nodded in approval. "Much better. Now the Palms is booked solid."

Augie shoved the ad back in his pocket. "I just hope Mr. Fitzgerald sees that I can be a reporter one day."

Belle patted his knee. "You're on your way, Augie. Don't under-estimate how far even a small step can take you."

"Thank you, Miss Belle." Augie looked down at his inky fingers.

Belle turned her head to again fully face the sun. *It's time,* she thought. Well past time, in fact, that she took her own advice.

Chapter 2

The coffee on the side table was lukewarm, shown the same disinterest as everything else in the room. Belle sat cross-legged in the center of her bed, focused solely on the newspaper. Ignored, her cat napped against the pillow. Once again, she read the job description listed on page 2 of the *Press*.

"GARDENER NEEDED AT SEMINOLE LODGE!"

Thomas and Mina Edison needed help, and that was the good news. Her worry, though, was how many others were reading the very same words and planning their own perfect pitch to land such a coveted position? Probably dozens. Right now, neighbors were pacing in their kitchens, the paper tucked under their arms as they practiced singing their praises aloud. "No one will outwork me . . ."

And then there were the Baileys. If the owners of Baileys' Nursery showed up to the interview, everyone else may as well head back home and tend to their ho-hum gardens. Gus and Grace Bailey had taught her everything she knew about gardening. The Edison job was theirs if they wanted it. Belle pressed on her temples. If only, somehow, she could tear the listing out of every newspaper in town.

Butterflies stormed her stomach. Who would interview her? No name was offered. What should she say about herself? Should she bring along one of her plants or her gardening tools? Somehow, she had to make sure *her* hands would dig in the soil at Seminole Lodge. Belle closed her eyes and imagined standing up straight. She heard her strong voice: *I'm the right choice because I'm creative and efficient . . . the gardens are already planted in my mind.* Then, nothing. Her bold words spiraled downward, losing volume until they lay in a heap of silence. Her squared shoulders slumped. She opened her eyes and popped the paper with a flick of her fingers. Clearly, showing up and showing off would be daunting. But the prospect of waking up each day with a purpose—instead of simply yearning for one—was absolutely compelling.

"I've got to try," she whispered to the page.

At twenty-five, Belle was living under someone else's roof in a converted storage room, dabbling in her passion and silently managing ghosts—one a haunt, the other a distant wisp. She was ready for the wind to shift and carry the haunt far beyond the horizon.

She traced her finger under every word, reading again.

"GARDENER NEEDED AT SEMINOLE LODGE!
The distinguished Thomas A. Edison requires
an accomplished gardener to create a set
of dazzling flower beds on his thirteen-acre
riverfront property."

She stared at the capital letters and their urgent call to action. They may as well have read, "BELLE CARSON NEEDED AT SEMINOLE LODGE!" Finally, thankfully, her talent had aligned with a need. The qualifications listed described the best of her, especially "an affinity for all things botanical and a flare for artistic color combinations." Belle focused on the line that excited her nearly as much as the chance to get paid for what she loved to do.

"Whoever is hired will also receive complimentary room and board at Baker's Boarding in the cottage on the property of owner Abigail Baker."

Belle drew in a breath of musty air and looked around the room. Over the years, she'd transformed it from a stark rectangle to comfortable quarters, potted sweet potato vine and petunias spilling over the edges of wooden shelving, borrowed books stacked neatly under her narrow bed. A floral print curtain hung over a small window that interrupted the north wall. She'd done her best to disguise the room's true self—a place where pickles and kerosene lay in wait—but anyone could tell she lived in a storage area. While she was grateful for her makeshift room, the chance to move out of it and into a cottage of her own at Baker's Boarding was exhilarating and worthy of much preoccupation. She'd already looked away from the paper twice to cozy up the cottage in her mind. *I'll sweep and dust first . . .*

Baker's neighbored the Edison property, fully inferior in grandeur and one-third the acreage of the famous couple's winter retreat along the Caloosahatchee River. In 1885, Thomas Edison, along with his friend and business partner Ezra Gilliland, strayed from a family holiday in Saint Augustine to explore Florida's less developed Gulf Coast. After several days in Fort Myers, he purchased an expansive riverfront property where he could relax and work for several months, away from the public eye and frigid northern climate. The *Press* heralded Edison's miraculous decision to its readers: "HURRAH FOR MR. EDISON!" The Wizard of Menlo Park, an internationally recognized man with nearly six hundred patents, was now a part-time resident of Fort Myers.

From a boater's view, Baker's sat to the right of the sprawling Edison estate. Abigail Baker, a single woman, purchased the boardinghouse a decade before the electrical wiz happened upon Fort Myers. Now, Belle had a chance to work for the Edisons, live in her own cottage, and plant a seed of hope in her heart for a more meaningful life.

She stood, stretched, and walked out of her bedroom into Duggan's. Merle Duggan owned the general store, set in the heart of the town's business district on Front Street. One of the building's walls still had a mail slot carved into it from when he served as the region's postmaster. Much about Merle was oversized, including his broad smile. So large and numerous were his teeth that a person might be amazed that his lips, when closed, could conceal such dental abundance. His sizable hands matched his unyielding compassion. He routinely left baskets of necessities from his store on the doorsteps of struggling families, waving off gratitude with fibs like, "I just needed to make some room on my store shelves, Iris." Tall and stout, the fifty-two-year-old lived above his business in a small room chock-full in the evenings with tossed clothing, bulky boots, and heavy clouds of loamy cigar smoke. Widowed in Georgia before settling in Fort Myers, he was known as a prudent, fair businessman and a reliable, contributing member of the 375-person town.

"Merle?" Belle looked around the store.

A "yup" floated up from the floor behind the front counter. Merle popped up holding a penny and grinning.

"Got it." He opened the cash register and added the coin with a *clink*. "Hope you had a solid breakfast. We need to shuffle the bushel baskets, freshen up things on the porch."

Belle hadn't touched her coffee or oatmeal. "Agreed. I'll start with the turnips and eggplants." She tidied a stack of postcards on the counter. "So, I know Saturdays are our busiest days, but I'd like to take tomorrow morning off."

"Of course," he said. "Whatever you need."

Merle never missed a chance to support and encourage Belle, as he had for quite some time. Eleven years ago, on a rainy summer evening, he awoke to loud pounding on the front door of Duggan's. Standing on the porch was a drenched teenager, shaking despite the August heat and humidity. Her long hair was plastered to her face, which was swollen on one side, her lip split and bleeding. The girl's dress was ripped and she wore one boot, the shoeless foot covered to the ankle in sandy muck. Within seconds, Merle recognized the panting figure as Belle Carson, adopted daughter of Betsy and Nelson Carson. Over the years, she'd made countless trips to Duggan's to pick up sundries for the family: coffee, thread, sodium bicarbonate. He enjoyed having the subdued but curious girl in the store. She sometimes asked politely to shake the rattlesnake rattle on the front counter or quietly requested his dated *Old Farmer's Almanacs*. But on that stormy night, the fourteen-year-old's voice was loud and firm.

"I won't go back there." Her dripping fists were clenched at her sides.

Merle gently pulled Belle over the threshold and quickly locked the door.

"My God. What happened?" He glanced through the window into the darkness.

"No." Belle vigorously shook her sopping head. "No talking about it."

Merle fought back tears as he placed Belle's feet in a bucket of water and gave her thick cloths to clean herself off. He toweldried her hair, but she wanted no part of him touching her skin. After guiding her up the stairs and tucking her into his bed, he locked Duggan's and walked in the downpour toward the Carsons. Halfway there, he spotted someone calling out for Belle. He soon recognized the man as Nelson Carson.

"Belle's with me," Merle said. "What the hell happened to her, Nelson?"

"I don't know," Nelson said, his palms cupped around his eyes to divert the rain. "Not yet."

"She'll stay with me tonight," Merle said, his tone squelching any discussion. "I'll come by tomorrow, without her."

Nelson opened his mouth but didn't speak, exhaling instead. He nodded once and walked briskly in the opposite direction.

•••

The next morning, Merle knocked on the Carsons' door and Nelson answered. Betsy stood behind him, holding a small pile of clothes and a sack. Their twenty-two-year-old son, Julius, flanked her, his face covered in scratches, one eye swollen shut.

Nelson tipped his head back toward Julius. "I gave him what he had coming."

"For what?" Merle said.

The two men stood motionless. No one welcomed Merle inside.

"What happened, Nelson?"

"That's our family business. Like I said, I took care of it."

Took care of what? Merle glared at Julius. Over the years, he'd had little interaction with him or the rest of the Carson family, one of the more private in town. Nelson was frequently away for days at a time, tending to avocados upriver. Betsy kept to herself but did her part when it came to town customs—dropping off food for the bereaved or attending monthly meetings. Merle glanced around the Carsons' kitchen. Something had happened in the house to terrify Belle, launching her into the storm.

"All right, then. She won't be coming back here," Merle said.

Nelson nodded and motioned to Betsy. She walked to Merle and handed him Belle's belongings. "Should be everything," she said softly.

With that, the longest conversation Merle ever had with the Carsons was over.

Since then, for more than ten years, Merle had sheltered Belle and delighted in her company. Not once had anyone questioned their arrangement, to his face anyway. Early on, comments made their way to Merle: "That girl needs a mother," or "Why would the Carsons give away their daughter?" But he'd dismissed them all, long immune to the constant chatter in town. People traded gossip like recipes, hungry for even an ounce of intimate or unflattering news about a neighbor.

Merle ushered Belle through her teens guided by routine— three meals a day, store duties, frequent visits from his good friend, Abigail Baker. He came to realize that Belle wasn't a shy girl as much as someone who'd accepted herself as nearly invisible. He tried his best to slowly help her reappear, to view herself as a val- ued partner in the rhythm of their daily life. "Flapjacks or eggs for us this morning?" he'd ask. Or, "Why don't you hand out our fruit samples today?"

By her twenties, Belle had engaged more frequently with people besides just Duggan's customers. He could almost hear her think- ing, *I don't like this, but I can do this.* She'd grown better at accepting offers to have coffee in someone's home or even take an afternoon walk along the river with a man. Joseph Yount, who sometimes skippered the mail boat, got a "yes" for one walk, but that was it. Merle laughed with Belle when she returned from the stroll and said, "Joseph talks an awful lot about the mail when he's nervous." His pride in her evolution was outshined only by his gratitude for their close relationship.

On this Friday morning, inside Duggan's, the two continued talking about Belle's request to take off work the next day. She fiddled with wildflowers nestled in a small vase next to the cash register. "I hope to be at Baker's by nine o'clock tomorrow so I can interview for the gardening job at the Edisons'."

Merle was surprised but didn't show it. He'd seen the listing in the *Press* and knew Belle would be excited about the chance to cre- ate such special gardens. He wasn't sure, though, if she'd be willing to undergo an interview.

"I'll make us breakfast before you leave."

He smiled at her, but his stomach dropped. If Belle landed the job, she would move out of the store and out of his daily life. Duggan's would seem gutted of the very thing that had brought him joy for so long. And then there was the nagging truth—that he'd already let her go once, decades ago. His shoulders slumped as he turned away and pretended to work numbers on a pad.

•••

The next morning, Merle swallowed the last of a biscuit slathered in raspberry preserves and checked his pocket watch.

"Plenty of time, honey." He paused. "They'd be lucky to have you."

Belle gave him a tight-lipped smile, a habit that concealed a small gap between her front teeth.

"Thank you, Merle." She drew in a deep breath and released it. "Off I go."

She walked out and hoisted herself onto the seat of an adult treadle tricycle that Merle gave her when she moved in. It was always parked in front of the store's hitching post like a three-legged horse. Her long chestnut-brown hair was wrangled into two thick braids, and a straw hat adorned with assorted fishing lures shielded her face from the warming sun.

Belle spent many a morning aboard the cast-iron tricycle, traversing the town before work. The three-wheeler was equipped with buggy-like rear suspension, but the craggy streets of Fort Myers humbled the coil springs. A blue gingham seat cushion offered little relief from the jarring thumps and thuds that rattled her pail full of tools—a folding saw, hedging shears, and a hand hoe. Belle kept an eye out for small gardens that could use a light pruning or weeding, a small gesture welcomed by busy townsfolk, especially the business owners. Mr. and Mrs. Gibbs, who owned the Palms Hotel, always waved to her in thanks, sometimes with both hands.

"You're an angel!" they'd yell from the porch. A guest might wave, too.

Sheriff Frederick Clark was rarely home, so Belle took extra time beautifying his small pinery. The sheriff kept the town safe, so the least she could do was check on his pineapples. She had the same compassion for the Abbotts, who seemed to always be doing for others; plants were the exception. Their neglected garden was a regular stop. Dr. Richard Abbott was frequently out of town, performing surgeries in Key West for extra income. His wife, Maude, was left alone for weeks with three young children. Often, the Abbotts' yard was occupied by members of the Seminole Indian tribe who'd spent weeks trudging in from the Everglades to await the doctor's return for treatment. Makeshift chickee huts shielded them from the blazing sun. Belle would weed and smile at the colorfully dressed families sitting under the open-sided log frames thatched with palmetto fronds.

There were only two gardens that Belle wheeled right past. One was in front of Billy's, the town saloon. She'd witnessed too many cow hunters watering that garden with what they'd drunk an hour earlier. The other garden belonged to Ida Cravin. Her husband owned the town's rival general store, Cravin & Company, which currently housed the post office. Belle avoided both the store and Ida, who carried a Bible at all times and walked briskly, as if making a beeline for perfection. She always dressed in Sunday clothes and owned a stable of elaborate picture hats with broad brims. Each was festooned with garish plumes, and one with an entire stuffed bird. The hats were the worst of it for Belle. As a proponent of the Woman's Christian Temperance Union, Ida championed "total abstinence from all things harmful," yet her millinery addiction supported the slaughter of millions of herons, flamingos, and roseate spoonbills. Each year, countless egret rookeries were wiped out by plume hunters so "little snowies" could embellish fashionable hats purchased by the likes of Ida. To Belle, fishing lures were by far a more civilized way to decorate a hat.

As she rode toward the interview at the Edison estate, she considered what questions might be asked. *Why are you the best choice? What experience do you have? Do your hands always shake like that?* Nervous energy powered her spirited pedaling. She drew in the crisp air, inhaling the smell of sawdust from Ritter's Mill, tobacco from Varga's Cigars, bacon and coffee from every kitchen. A January morning was unfolding, and so was her chance to secure the perfect job, if you could even call it that. To Belle, gardening wasn't work. It was a slow, deliberate process that amazed and fulfilled her. She and the plants were partners. Their journey together began with her planting a seed. Next came watering, then waiting. One day, up from the dirt came a sprout, then a stalk, and finally, a brilliant bloom. They'd done it! To Belle, a bourgeoning garden was reassurance that she could—at least with nature—cultivate a healthy relationship.

A five-minute ride had brought her to the entrance of Seminole Lodge, the grandest property in town. A board fence ran along the front of the compound, which was lined with Spanish bayonets, hearty plants with dark-green, daggerlike leaves. *Press* articles in years past reported that Mr. Edison himself had hand-drawn an extensive landscape and gardening plan for his winter haven, but the bulk of the project had yet to materialize. In the family's absence, a New York man lived year-round on the property in a one-room caretaker's cottage.

Belle left her trike next to the fence and hung her hat on a handlebar. She nodded at Abigail, who was standing at the start of the long driveway, explaining the interview process to several women who'd arrived early. A loose line had formed, and Belle joined it. Several more women and a man were approaching, one carrying a trowel. No sign of the Baileys yet.

"Folks, prepare to sit for the interview for no more than five minutes." Abigail's hands were tucked into the pockets of a pale-blue cotton apron. "Mrs. Edison is in the area briefly on personal business. She arrived here from Fort Ogden last night and will leave on the *Patricia* at noon."

Gasps erupted from the surprised interviewees. The woman ahead of Belle in line twisted her head around and mouthed, "Mina's here!"

Belle sighed and dropped her head in frustration. Talking about herself was foreign enough, but a sitting with Mr. Edison's venerable wife?! *Calm down,* she told herself, but even the voice in her head sounded nervous.

At exactly nine o'clock, Abigail motioned for the first candidate to walk down the driveway to the Edison home. A woman holding a posy of evening primrose shuffled forward, and the process was under way. As the minutes passed and others chatted around her, Belle studied the faces of the just-interviewed as they walked back up the driveway and past the waiting hopeful. Some smiled as if they were now best friends with Mina. Others wore poker faces. One woman put her palm to the side of her mouth and whispered, "She's sitting on the porch." When Ida Cravin's daughter, Hazel—who Belle hadn't noticed in line—returned, she was visibly shaking as she retied her bonnet strings.

Within a half hour, Abigail nodded at Belle and said, "Go on down," touching her shoulder as if to gently launch her. Belle smoothed her linen dress as she walked, unsure of what to expect other than apprehension. Within a minute, she reached two stately butter-yellow homes with white wraparound porches. The setting was quite inviting, if you had the nerves to focus on something other than the boxing match between your heart and chest. Mina was sitting on the porch of the home closest to the driveway. Belle froze, uncertain about walking up the steps without an invitation.

"Good morning. Do come up," Mina said, smiling and pointing her upturned palm at the two stairs.

Belle offered a nod and made her way to the wicker chair Mina gestured toward as she remained seated in an identical version.

Oval cushions and pillows on both featured a sunny pineapple print.

"I'm Mina," she said, and held out her hand.

Belle shook it with a quiet reply, "Of course. I'm Belle Carson."

"As you know, I'm looking for someone to develop a set of spirited gardens in front of both houses on each side of the porch steps. My family and I truly hope we can visit this winter, and a burst of color would be a wonderful welcome back." She ended the sentence with a broad smile.

Belle stared at Mina's straight teeth. The *Press* ran frequent articles about the Edisons, and Belle instantly recalled references to Mina's "good teeth" and "olive complexion." Both were true. She'd seen Mina from afar several years ago when the Edisons held a town gathering at Seminole Lodge to turn on their house full of electric light bulbs. Belle had been transfixed by Mina's poise as she glided slowly across the porch like a great blue heron. Now Belle was close enough to smell her perfume, an aromatic homage to the gardenia.

"How long have you been gardening, Belle?" Mina touched a stray, wavy bang and coaxed it to rejoin the rest of her sideswept hair.

"Well, for as long as I can remember." Belle's mind went blank, but she heard herself say, "I think I may have been a plant in another life."

Mina grinned. "Kindred spirits." She recrossed her legs, shifting the silky fabric of her ivory dress. Thick, dark hair spilled across its collar.

With no question to answer, Belle remained silent, in awe. Mina was not yet her age, and at twenty-two lived a life far more advanced. She was a mother, a trained pianist, a socialite, and a loving wife to a world-renowned inventor.

"Do you have time to devote yourself to the project and maintain it until we arrive?" Mina's voice was warm with no hint of hurrying along the interview.

"Oh yes," Belle answered. "I don't have children or a family." Blood rushed to her cheeks. The only thing the two had in common was the color of their eyes: dark brown.

"And you can relocate to the Baker cottage?"

"Easily," Belle answered. Fearing she'd again revealed her few connections with people and possessions, she added, "I do have a cat. She's a good mouser should you have any need for that."

Mina folded her hands in her lap.

"Oh, but of course," Belle said, placing a palm on her chest, "I would *never* allow her in your house. And I'm sure you don't have mice." If she could have buried her face in the pineapple pillow, she would have.

After gently clearing her throat, Mina continued. "As you might expect, we value our privacy." She paused. "Our daily life up north is quite hectic and . . . observed."

Belle struggled with whether to simply nod or talk. She did both. "Oh yes. Our newspaper is quite interested in your and Mr. Edison's every move." She squinted, trying to somehow make everything smaller, especially her missteps. She added quietly, "I . . . um . . . don't read all of the articles . . . just sometimes."

Mina smiled and said, "It was a pleasure meeting you, Belle." She stood. "Thank you very much for coming by. I'll be sending a letter to the gardener I choose."

Startled the interview was over, Belle stood but didn't speak. She grabbed the bottoms of her braids as if to shake loose a sentence.

"Safe travels home, Mrs. Edison." She turned toward the stairs and on the way down added, "Thank you."

Belle made her way back up the sandy driveway, her eyes firmly fixed on the ground. As she passed people waiting in line, she could feel their gazes upon her, searching for clues as to how they might do better. Belle walked behind Abigail, who was busy answering questions about the cottage from the remaining six applicants.

"It has two windows, one that faces the river."

Belle mounted her trike and began the quick trip back to Duggan's. A knot in her stomach had strangled the butterflies. What a fool she'd been to think she could hold her own in an important conversation with a stranger, a luminary to boot. She cursed the bumpy street and squeezed the handlebars. Every push of the pedals took her further and further away from a more purposeful life, and she was to blame.

Chapter 3

The current batch of boarders liked one another well enough to linger at the dining room table in Baker's Boarding. That didn't always happen. Abigail had seen plenty of chairs quickly push back from a meal to escape a heated conversation or due to basic disinterest in the other travelers. Not this afternoon; bellies were full and bottoms were firmly planted in their seats.

"The birds here are simply swoon-worthy!" A woman named Colette brought her hand to her neck and caressed imaginary feathers. "We saw snowy egrets with wispy white neck beards."

"And the black skimmers looked like they were wearing white shirts with black dress jackets!" Her husband's voice was as animated. "Absolutely glamorous!"

Abigail entered the room to clear the dessert plates. "You two are a good reminder that we locals tend to take our beautiful bird life for granted."

The professor at the table spoke. "I'm a member of the Audubon Society, and I take pride in shooting photographs, not birds." He smiled as he turned to the man next to him. "How are you feeling, George?"

A sudden coughing fit shook the man's slight body. When it stopped, he laughed. "Forgive me, Professor Ricalton. I guess I just answered your question, though."

Abigail took George's plate, stacked it with the others, and headed for the kitchen's washbasin. George had assured her upon arrival that his illness was not contagious, but simply a case of wet lungs that his doctor said needed drying out. His young son had accompanied him from Pennsylvania.

"Every day I can draw a bigger breath, so I must be on the mend," George said. "Jamison, will you go ask Miss Abigail for some water for me?" The boy nodded, slipped off his chair, and disappeared into the kitchen. "I hope to venture into town soon."

"Irwin and I have. We took a stroll to the wharf the other day, and two men were fighting," Colette said. "I didn't want to bring it up in front of Jamison because I didn't want to laugh about a fight, but—"

Irwin interrupted. "But we couldn't help giggling. Two men in band uniforms were rolling around on the ground, pummeling each other while the rest of the musicians just kept playing, as if the composer had written a brawl into the score!"

Abigail entered the room, filled with laughter. She was holding a cup of water and Jamison's hand. "Oh, those two." She shook her head and gave George the water. Jamison took his seat. "They fight every single time they talk about our town coffers. The equipment Mr. Edison needs to light our town was expensive."

George tousled his son's hair. "Now, I'm the town cougher, right?"

Everyone chuckled.

"So, where are you all headed this afternoon?" Abigail noted two empty coffee cups. "I'm listening . . ." She turned toward the kitchen to quickly grab a pot off the stove.

"The boy and I are going to sit by the river and watch the boats . . ." George's voice trailed off, starved for air by his soggy lungs.

Professor Ricalton stretched his bony arms over his head. "I'm off to take a nap. I can't seem to close my eyes enough these days."

"Of course you can't," Colette said, her cup raised for Abigail to refill. "From what you told us about your travels for Mr. Edison, sleep must always be tugging at your sleeve."

Irwin accepted more coffee, too. "Thank you, Abigail. Are the Edisons planning to visit this season?"

"We'll see. We prepare as if they are." She wiped a brown drip trickling down the pot.

Jamison looked up at Abigail. "Will there be a parade?"

She smiled. "That would be fun, wouldn't it, honey."

"I imagine Mr. Edison would dismiss the idea," the professor said. "In my experience, he's a man who likes productive endeavors, not pomp."

"Well, you're right about that," Abigail said. "He declined the idea of a parade during their honeymoon visit. He suggested we focus instead on smoothing the bumpy road from downtown to their property."

The professor winked at Jamison. "A parade would be more fun, though, right?"

"It certainly would," Irwin declared as he stood and took his wife's hand, leading her off her seat. "C'mon, son. We don't need the Edisons for a parade!"

"You're right, Irwin!" Colette began to swing her bent arms back and forth and high-step behind her husband.

The others watched as the birders and the boy marched around the room, the professor pounding a beat on the table. George waved his napkin in the air and cheered until he coughed.

Abigail chuckled and banged a knife against the metal coffeepot. There were days she missed her life before Baker's, but this was not one of them.

Chapter 4

"Thank you, Belle." Mrs. Sally Richmond passed by with an armload of clean laundry, headed for her clothesline.

"Of course." Belle tipped back her hat and looked up from her squatting position. "Looks like I have the easier job today."

"Well, thankfully, once I hang everything, the sun and breeze do all the work." Her voice trailed off toward the backyard.

Belle was weeding the Richmonds' small vegetable garden that provided the produce they sold to Duggan's. Every other row was planted with flowers to attract lady beetles and lacewings whose larvae dined on garden pests. Much was ready for harvest—beets, broccoli, collard greens—but Belle was there simply to weed, a favor to a loyal supplier.

While she worked, thoughts of the botched job interview and living the rest of her life with Merle bounced around in her head. *Maybe that's for the best. I'm safe and sound there. Merle needs me.* Her poor showing with Mina was probably a good thing. With a sigh, she stopped weeding. How lucky she was to live comfortably in a place that, as a child, she loved to visit.

At school, she'd had few friends. Maybe she was too quiet, always huddled over a book. Other children talked and played around her but rarely included her. Even the teacher seemed to look past her. School was simply not a place where her sense of wonder or belonging was bettered. But thankfully, cherished spots did exist for her in town.

Behind the apothecary, discarded glass bottles lay in a heap, some with corks or stoppers, others with cracked necks. She loved to carefully rummage through the pile for her favorite tints and shapes. Off came the labels to ensure a collection that featured only smooth glass. At home, she'd set the handpicked treasures in an ever-growing row along a windowsill. She would track the exact time of day when sunrays brought the bottles' colors to life. No one noticed her bottles on the sill, so no one bothered them.

On the town wharf, she shared in the excitement of anglers without ever dropping a line. She'd sit on the pine planks near enough to the action to watch a flapping fish break the water, hooked for supper. Neighbors yelled "Hooray!" or "The biggest yet!" She enjoyed the anticipation and the chance to secretly root people on. The variety of species yanked out of the river was thrilling as well. She learned quickly which fish were expected and which were coveted. Nearly everyone threw back the inky eels. Always, people left behind a variety of fishing lures. If any were painted with bright colors or fashioned with tiny feathers, she claimed them, something pretty to call her own.

By far, though, her favorite destination in town was Duggan's. No matter when she visited, Belle loved the sameness of the noises and aromas in the store. Thick heels on the floorboards made the wood vibrate and murmur with deep echoes. The aroma of breakfast bacon always lingered well into the afternoon, mingling with the leathery scent of a two o'clock cigar. And there was no grandfather clock like there was at home, a towering brute that would sneak up on the hour with a startling *bong*. Everything at Duggan's was pleasant and predictable, especially its owner.

The biggest smile she'd ever seen belonged to Mr. Merle, and he welcomed her with it every time she walked through his door. She'd grin back and begin her trip around the store to look at everything, even though she needed only a few items, listed by her father on a slip of scrap paper. Her route began at the decorative crocks and ended at the glass cases filled with razors, barrettes, hat pins, and fans. In between were bars of soap, jersey overshirts, and cut-crystal cruet sets. She touched nothing, except what Merle told her she could: seed packets with their clever art, clay marbles in a halved coconut shell, and his prized rattlesnake rattle displayed on the front counter. She'd listen intently each time he described how the snake must have shed its skin eleven times, the number of segments in the rattle plus the nub at the end.

"See here?" he'd say. "Eleven sheds, then a button."

Every visit included food—a sweet or salty treat just for her. From behind the counter came an oatmeal cookie or a long strip of beef jerky. Other customers would watch him hand over the goody and smile lovingly at the gesture.

Over time she developed a sense of ownership at the store. Merle often let her make decisions and truly seemed to want her input.

"Should we stack the beans on top of the minced meat or the other way around?" he'd ask, his massive hands dwarfing the cans. And then he'd stack them as she suggested.

"What should be on special today, Belle?" If she said corn, then corn it was.

Her favorite task was helping him manage the mail. If the store was slow, he'd focus on his duties as postmaster, applying postmarks and cork cancels. She was in charge of the "fancy cancels," a unique mark the postmaster created as his signature design. Merle's was shaped like a diamond, carved into a cork bottle stopper. He taught her how to press the diamond into an ink pad and then onto the stamp, ensuring no one could reuse it. If she imprinted the cancel dead center, he'd declare, "Bull's-eye!" or "Socked on the nose!" She would grin and sometimes even giggle.

The worst part of the visit was when she had to leave, when she ran out of reasons to linger. The only good thing that remained was how Merle looked at her. He'd wink and wave and make it clear he'd be waiting on her.

"We'll see you next time, honey," he'd say, even if he was busy checking out a customer.

She'd nod at him and leave with her small bag of wares, listening to her bootheels clack their way down the porch steps. How she loved going to Duggan's, where she was always seen and heard.

"I'll bring in all those garden goodies to Duggan's tomorrow, Belle." Mrs. Richmond had returned, empty armed, drawing Belle back to the garden. "I'll see you around lunchtime."

Belle resumed weeding. "Thank you, Sally. I'll be there."

I'll be there forever.

Chapter 5

Merle charged into the store, holding an envelope in the air as if it were a gold nugget he'd just discovered under a river rock.

"Lookee here, Belle!" He used a sleeve to wipe his sweaty brow. "Come see."

Atop a footstool while dusting crockery, Belle looked down at Merle as he calmed his heavy breathing. When she saw what he was holding, her balance wavered. She grabbed a shelf to steady herself.

"That underhanded Ida Cravin hid it," he said. "I *knew* something wasn't right. When I reminded her that detaining mail was illegal, out came the letter."

Belle remained on the stool, frozen. Merle walked over and helped her down. As the two stood face-to-face, he held up the white envelope so she could see its front.

"Look at the handstamp, honey. See? West Orange, New Jersey."

Belle confirmed the stamp with her own eyes and looked back at Merle.

"Read the writing out loud to me," he said.

After two slow blinks, she said, "Belle Carson, Duggan's on Front Street, Fort Myers, Florida."

Merle flipped over the envelope. "What letters do you see stamped into the seal?"

Belle reached up and ran her finger over the red wax circle centered on the back flap. "M, E, M." She swallowed. "Oh my."

The hinges on the store's screen door squeaked, interrupting their inspection.

"Well, hello there, Eugenia." Merle handed Belle the envelope and walked over to his customer, who was cupping two heads of cabbage she'd harvested from a wood-slat basket on the porch.

"Hello, Merle. Cabbage looks good today." She set the produce on the counter and rummaged through her purse for change. Without looking up, she said, "Did you have a bee in your bonnet? I just saw you running up and down Front Street."

Merle and Belle exchanged a glance. She now knew why he was out of breath after retrieving the letter from Cravin & Company.

"Let's just say I made a happy lap, Eugenia." He beamed. "I'm happy today."

Eugenia continued to poke around in her bag. "Well, you did a fine job of hurdling that horse trough." She located the coins and offered them with a smile.

When Eugenia left, the bell on the door jingled a goodbye. Merle returned to Belle, who handed back the envelope.

"Please open it," she said, as if her shaking hands could somehow break it.

He did as asked, carefully separating the wax from the paper. Slowly, he pulled the folded note from its sheath and gave it to Belle. She lightly ran her fingers over the soft cotton paper and then brought it to her nose to see if she could detect gardenia. So many times she'd imagined this very moment.

"Here we go . . ." She began to unfold the note and then stopped. "Do you want to read it with me?"

Merle shook his head, watching her closely. "No, honey. You read it first."

Belle opened the note. Two lines were printed at the top of the sheet:

GLENMONT
LLEWELLYN PARK

Her hand flew to her mouth, muffling her words. "Oh my goodness."

The name of the Edisons' northern estate and community was followed by cursive writing penned in black ink.

January tenth
Dear Belle,
It was lovely to meet you and spend even just a moment in your southern sunshine. I trust you've been well. With pleasure, I am writing to offer you the gardening position we spoke of at Seminole Lodge.

Belle looked up, eyes wide, and threw her arms around Merle's neck, clutching the letter and pressing her cheek to his chest. Relief and excitement surged through her, an unfamiliar heady mix. Mina had chosen *her*! Gardens she'd designed in her head could now spring from the sandy soil. And a riverside cottage was hers alone. Merle gently patted Belle's back. Neither spoke until she finally let go.

"Let's read it together," Belle said, and stood beside him. She began again, this time aloud:

January tenth
Dear Belle,
It was lovely to meet you and spend even just a moment in your southern sunshine. I trust you've been well. With

pleasure, I am writing to offer you the gardening position we spoke of at Seminole Lodge. I do hope you are able to begin your move to the Baker cottage upon reading this, and when settled, start work on the set of gardens. I will rely on your creative sensibilities but would like two species to be included for certain: black-eyed Susans and a rose variety that blooms abundantly. If we can coax butterflies and hummingbirds to visit, that would please me as well.

In advance, thank you, Belle. We are eager to visit and do hope that we can this winter.

My best,

Mina Edison

Merle put his arm around Belle's shoulder and squeezed it. As she looked back over the letter, she noted the date. "January tenth? That's quite a while ago."

"Exactly." Merle pointed to the date marked on the envelope's handstamp. "The letter was delivered weeks ago, but Ida hid it."

"Ahh," Belle said. "I saw Hazel at the interview."

"Such utter hogwash." He continued to mumble harsher words under his breath.

Belle took the envelope from Merle and trapped the incredible news back inside. "How did you know to look for the letter? That I would get the job?"

Merle tugged at his minimal beard. "Because Mina's husband isn't the only genius in the family."

His answer was rewarded with Belle's unabashed smile, the small gap in full view.

•••

The distinctive chirp of an osprey cut through the whiny racket of gulls navigating the airspace over the Caloosahatchee. On the water, anything with sails was speeding past everything powered by steam.

"I'll bet this wind will blow in some weather," Abigail said as she looked up at the hazy morning sky. Her barrel-shaped body was always wrapped in an apron, as if she was just seconds away from preparing a meal.

This afternoon, she was leading a tour of her property, Belle and Merle in tow. Her vacant cottage would house Belle while she created the Edison gardens. Merle was familiar with the Baker grounds; Belle hadn't spent much time there over the years. The trio passed a large wooden cistern built on stilts and several barrels topped with muslin designed to collect rainwater. Geese and ducks waddled about the yard, oblivious to several chickens poking around in the sand for fleas and pebbles. Peck marks pocked every inch of low-lying wood. Abigail pointed to several small A-frame wooden coops layered with pine straw and sawdust. Cleverly hinged roofs allowed for easy access when bedding needed to be changed or eggs retrieved.

"I feed my geese figs in the fall, and then when they're four months old"—she made a slitting motion across her throat—"they're dinner. The figs make their livers rich and sweet."

Merle laughed. "You're ruthless."

The fun-loving relationship between Merle and Abigail had always comforted Belle. Their bond was solid, rooted in a friendship spanning thirteen years. She'd never heard the pair argue. Instead, they'd poke fun at each other or share what ailed them, everything from sore joints to business challenges. Years ago, Merle had explained Abigail's nickname for him. He said on her first visit to Duggan's she'd marveled at the vast inventory, saying, "You've packed every inch of this place with everything under the sun! I'm going to call you Squirrel instead of Merle."

As deep as her love was for Merle, Belle's fondness for Abigail was as unshakable. Over the years, she could always rely on Abigail to walk into the store and head straight for her. "There you are," she'd say. Twice Belle's age, Abigail would sit with her for a bit and talk about plants or look over something she was drawing or embroidering. And somehow, Abigail knew when her day was gray, even if the sky above was bright blue. The two would simply sit quietly snapping string beans or shelling field peas. The fact that Abigail never missed a chance to give Belle's cat, Coquina, a spirited stroking made her even more endearing.

The tour of Baker's continued, now moving away from the boardinghouse. As the three walked into the backyard toward the river, the *ting-ting* of a hammer striking nails rang out from next door.

"That's Boone working on Mr. Edison's house. There's always something leaking or creaking," she said, shaking her head. "He worked with the original crew that assembled both houses and the laboratory. Good man."

Belle turned toward Merle as they walked. "I've seen him around town but never in Duggan's. Why not?"

"From what I understand, Cravin & Company set up some sort of"—Merle wiggled his fingers in the air—"special account for the Edisons."

Abigail added, "Boone ships oranges and grapefruit up north to them so it's easier to also do his shopping at Cravin's. One stop."

They passed a large vegetable garden that fed Abigail and her boarders, and soon Belle, too. Beets, broccoli, carrots, peppers, collards, and strawberries all outgrew their orderly rows, ready for harvest. They next moved toward a small wooden structure painted barn red and topped with a brown shingle roof.

"This is my storage shed," Abigail said. She yanked open the door and small brown lizards scattered to every corner. Windowless, the shed was dark but sunlight from the open door revealed the space to be tidy. Abigail entered the shed and brushed sand off a counter. Merle ducked his head and stepped in behind Belle.

The shed appeared equipped with items that accommodated common and repeated tasks, filled with everything from produce baskets to a willow fishing creel. There were shovels, trowels, two hatchets, hand tools, rope, and a crock of clothespins. A vase filled with pheasant feathers and arrows shared the space with a Winchester rifle, a ladder, and a wooden stool. Abigail righted a crooked set of mounted deer antlers, then pointed to a small nook at the back of the shed.

"That's a closet I leave empty in case boarders need a bit of extra room for something—fishing tackle or boating gear."

She palmed the perfect bun atop her head and put her other hand on her indiscernible hip. "Now, let's head over to your cottage, Belle."

Your cottage, Belle repeated in her mind. Goose bumps stippled her forearms.

From the shed they walked to a small house painted white with a brown roof. On the front porch, a straw broom leaned against the wall. A watering can with a dented spout sat next to it.

"The Edisons are paying for your room and board here, as promised in the job listing. They don't like anyone but family to stay in the residences when they're up north," Abigail explained. "Norville Decker manages the estate and lives in a caretaker's cottage on their property. Boone lives aboard his boat anchored in the river beside their dock."

"Mina mentioned their need for privacy. Completely understandable," Belle said. She couldn't wait to see inside the cottage, walking up the porch steps before the others.

Merle mouthed, "Thank you," to Abigail.

She nodded and whispered, "Mina welcomed my input."

Inside the cottage, natural light spilled through two windows on opposite walls. One offered a fine view of the Caloosahatchee and was open halfway, allowing fresh air in. A fuzzy bumblebee attempting escape buzzed on each collision with the windowpane.

"That stubborn window is stuck," Abigail pointed out. "It's on Boone's to-do list." She shook her head. "My last renter was a real pill, a handful. Boone couldn't keep up with all her requests for repairs."

Merle walked over and jiggled the frame but nothing budged.

"Does Boone work for you, too, Abigail?" Belle asked.

"When he has time. Decker keeps him busy, but I think Boone enjoys our trade: when he works for me, I cook for him."

"I see," Belle said, her eyes scanning the particulars in the one-room cottage: a bed with a linen coverlet and a goose-down pillow, a dresser, a tin washbowl atop a stool, a water cask that hung on a peg, a rocking chair, and an elegant bedside table with a small drawer on both ends.

"This side drawer has a secret," Abigail said, standing near the drawer closest to the bed. "See how it's locked?" She pulled on the knob, but the drawer remained closed. "If you reach underneath and push up from the bottom, it will open. It's a good drawer for keeping something safe." She explained how a boarder visiting from Boston gave her the clever table. He'd overbought on his travels, and the returning steamboat was at maximum weight. "The best of Baker's furnishings," she said, "are all castoffs from travelers."

Belle was already noting where to put her minimal belongings and what improvements she could make. Curtains would be a nice start.

"It's such a pretty cottage, Abigail. I can move in this afternoon."

"Very good." Abigail drove her hands down into the pockets of her apron. "Squirrel, I hear Captain Metzger's boy threw up one too many times on the mail boat. He may need work on land . . ."

Merle smiled. "Mrs. Metzger is about due in for coffee beans. I'll ask her if he's available."

They walked toward the front gate so Abigail could begin preparations for the midday meal. Belle looked next door for Boone's boat and spotted it bucking on the river's choppy waves.

That afternoon, for the first time in eleven years, Duggan's storage room returned to its original purpose—housing jars of pickled peppers, bolts of butcher paper, and puncheons filled with molasses and kerosene. They'd cleared out Belle's belongings, and now the wide bench on Belle's trike was jam-packed with plants, clothes, fabric scraps, candles, sewing sundries, stacked books, and a shaving mirror. She sat in the middle of the seat with a conch shell in her lap and pedaled slowly. Merle walked alongside, clutching a howling basket with Coquina trapped inside.

At Baker's, they unloaded everything onto the floor of the cottage. The sky began to hint at an angry outburst. A low growl of thunder confirmed the warning.

"You'd better head back home before the rain, Merle." Belle stood with her hands on her hips.

Merle reached into both pants pockets and pulled out something from each one. "I want you to have these." He nodded toward the small table. "Put this skinning knife in that secret drawer."

He then held out the other object.

Belle's arms dropped to her sides. "Don't do that. Keep it with you."

On the dresser, he set down a brush with an ivory handle. "Clara would want it with you, honey. At least for a while. Until you feel settled."

She nodded. "That's very dear of you." She tried to say thank you, but her throat locked up. A happy goodbye was Belle's hope, but her immense gratitude for Merle wouldn't allow it.

Tears filled her eyes and rolled down her cheeks. She covered her face with both hands and cried into them. Merle moved forward, wrapping his arms around her, absorbing the sobs.

"We're just under separate roofs now, honey. Nothing else will change." Palm fronds swished in the swelling wind that gusted through the stuck window. "You're where you should be."

Sniffling and trying to regain control of her speech, Belle whispered, "I . . . I know."

They embraced until she stopped crying. The room had grown dim, the thunder louder and closer.

"You best go now, Merle." She was grateful for a reason to hurry him off.

Merle offered a gentle nod and left the cottage. Large drops of rain pelted the ground. He walked briskly along River Street toward the store. Daggers of lightning took violent stabs at the horizon, so he broke into a run. Within minutes, he scurried into Duggan's and left the door sign turned to "Closed."

•••

Heavy rain pounded the roof and dripped into a bucket on the floor. Merle walked past a kerosene lamp and lit a candle instead. With a heavy sigh, he sat down on a stool behind the counter and poured a glass of Cuban rum. As he toweled off his wet face, thunder rattled the glassware on shelves throughout the store. With a raised glass, he made a toast: "To you, Belley." She was gone from Duggan's, likely for good, and he'd had a hand in it. But now she could spread her wings and let a fresh breeze lift her off the ground. She deserved a chance to glide for a while, to let the view from on high inspire her to thrive, like the fruited groves and billowed sails below.

He tossed back the liquor and thought about his beloved Clara. He pictured her hands, strong enough to yank a life into the world and yet so tender when it came to exploring him. Her memory brought him comfort but anguish, too. He chose more often than not to avoid reliving their time together. But tonight, he needed to be near her. In his mind, he sat beside her and stroked her soft auburn hair as she sewed. Each stitch brought her closer to completing the long white dress she'd wear on their wedding day.

He whispered in her ear, "You're going to be so beautiful," as she worked. He rocked the cradle beside him. "And now we have our sweet little girl who made it into this world because of you." He tried to stay focused on that loving moment, but one staggering image always prevailed: Clara wearing the dress in a casket.

A jagged bolt crackled across the sky, illuminating the store with a white flash.

"I'm so sorry, Clara," he said softly. Tears filled his eyes. "I didn't think I could raise her without you." He folded his hands in prayer. "Please forgive me."

Merle hung his large, heavy head. He could never forgive himself for what happened to Belle after the Carsons agreed to take her.

Chapter 6

My throne, Belle thought. She leaned her head back against the rocking chair's wide wooden slats. Never before had she experienced such a surplus of contentment. She'd eaten a hearty lunch at Baker's and was now surveying the tidied cottage from her soothing perch. A soft breeze visited through the open window and nudged a striped curtain. The previous five days had passed like a parade of colorful boats, each one more enchanting than the last.

Moving into the space had taken scant time—hours instead of days—which wasn't her preference. She'd wanted to indulge her desire to clean and organize and personalize *her* space that *she* had garnered. But there simply wasn't enough square footage or piles of belongings to drag out the process.

The dresser easily housed her minimal clothing. She'd filled one of the drawers with books and outdated gardening periodicals from Baileys' Nursery. On top, she set the conch shell, a keepsake Merle had received in trade for an alligator skull from a customer passing through from Boot Key. Next to the large pink shell, she placed a vase filled with a vibrant mix of flowers from Abigail's garden. There was room, too, for Merle's old shaving stand topped with a mirror. Coquina napped on the bed's linen coverlet, which

Belle had beaten vigorously outside along with the goose-down pillow. A candle stuck with wax to a pie pan sat on the bedside table, along with a pressed-tin match safe. The scene was astounding to Belle, unimaginable in its stark contrast to her bleak childhood with the Carsons, where a floor blanket served as her bed and privacy was limited. Where nothing but distress was hers alone.

For as many years as she lived with Betsy and Nelson Carson, Belle could think of little that she'd learned from either of them. Nelson was often away from home, working or off hunting with Julius. He was never curt or unkind but often swept her aside. "Go help your mother," he'd say. Julius claimed a good bit of Nelson's attention, helping with chores and errands. But Nelson was blind to his son's misdeeds, of which Belle endured the worst. Julius would torment her and demand silence. He claimed that dragonflies—he called them dragon needles—would sew her mouth shut if she told on him. But she never would. How could she possibly say out loud what was happening to her? And surely his word would outweigh hers.

Most of her time was spent with Betsy, who instead of teaching Belle something just told her to do it. "Go collect eggs," she'd say and thrust an empty basket at her. The hens pecked Belle's hands until she discovered that reaching well above their heads and gently lifting them off the nest solved the problem. At mealtime, Betsy would scold Belle if she burned greens or anything cooking in a pot, never explaining that the stove developed hot spots related to where the wood was placed in the firebox. She'd eventually figured that out, and most everything else, on her own. The Carsons fed and housed her, but raising her was clearly not their concern.

Thankfully now, there she sat, happily nestled inside the Baker cottage. Belle rose from the rocking chair and walked to the dresser. She picked up Clara's brush and watched herself in the mirror run its bristles through her long hair. Her reflection revealed a prominent forehead, almond-shaped eyes, and full lips. The square jawline was anchored by a pointy chin, which mismatched the button nose. If Belle looked anything like her natural mother, Clara would have known.

In their first year of living together at Duggan's, Merle told Belle he would cook something special when her birthday rolled around. She thanked him but said she didn't know when she was born, that the Carsons recorded only their son's birth date in the family Bible. Merle explained that he knew she would turn fifteen in March because he was once engaged to Miss Clara Burns, the midwife who delivered her. Belle was eager for details.

He'd described how Clara sailed from Fort Myers to Sanibel Island to assist her mother, a young, unmarried woman named Eva who was working for a castor bean farmer on the barrier island. Merle explained that, sadly, her mother died during delivery, but that Clara told him she was very brave and did all she could to bring her daughter into the world.

"Your mother gave everything she had . . . her last breath . . . to mother you" was the way he'd worded it.

Merle said Clara endured a stormy sail back to Fort Myers with baby Belle swaddled and held tightly in her arms. She was named after the resilient schooner *Maybelle* that safely transported them back home. Merle said he didn't have any additional details, only that an arrangement was made between the Carsons and the town pastor to adopt her. When Belle asked Merle if he married Clara, he said no, that she'd died from a rattlesnake bite just a week after returning to Fort Myers. The conversation had revealed a common bond in each of their losses: Clara.

Thank you, Belle thought, and squeezed the handle of the special brush. Clara once held it in her hand, perhaps the same hand that held Eva's as she gave birth to Belle.

• • •

In 1862, Eva Logan lived in a dusty southwest Florida town bustling with an endless stream of frisky cattlemen. The noisy cattle pens in the deepwater port town of Punta Rassa were busier than the bordellos, but not by much. Both were teeming with sweaty, agitated animals waiting for their turn: the cows to board a southbound schooner to Havana, the cow hunters to mount a prostitute. Tall, short, beefy, thin—the men all smelled of Cuban rum, swamp, and urgency. For weeks, they'd cracked their leather whips and slept in austere cow camps, herding the thousands of scrawny cattle that wandered the dense scrub woodlands. They slept under the stars and dreamed of a woman's voice whispering, "I've been waiting for you," in their sunburned ears.

The parlor girls were certainly waiting for the men's gold doubloons, Eva included. The gritty deeds disgusted her, but shiny money on the dresser paid her way. Had her parents known what she'd resorted to, they would have been devastated. But they couldn't know.

Just weeks after the Logan family had moved to Punta Rassa, a raging house fire killed Eva's mother and father. While she was in town, shopping for provisions, the house attached to her father's blacksmith shop became fully engulfed in flames. She'd returned to a horrifying sight—her smoldering house and people sitting on buckets following a failed water brigade. Neighbors speculated on a variety of calamities that may have sparked the blaze, but all that mattered to Eva was that she was eighteen and alone. The people who offered her a place to stay were generous, but they were all strangers. She chose instead to stay at the Sandy Spur, where her mother had worked as a maid. The sympathetic owner agreed to let her clean the hotel in trade for room and board. Soon, though, the rules changed. Men showed up in the rooms she was tidying, expecting to kiss and touch her. When she told the owner, he said, "You're a pretty girl. Pretty makes good money." Still numb from grief and shock, Eva wandered into her new role at the Spur. She let the men take from her so she could take care of herself.

Months passed, and business at the hotel was brisk and unruly. After a year of working on her back, Eva stopped menstruating. She wasn't surprised. Cattlemen couldn't be bothered with the act of withdrawing, and post-coital douching was unreliable. She kept the news private and continued working, vomiting strategically and waiting for her body to betray her with visible proof. Some of the other "pretty girls" told of herbal potions that stopped their pregnancies; others met with a midwife who flushed out "the inconvenience" with an injection of water. Eva was certain she didn't want a child, but she could never abort one. Surely, she could find someone who'd want the baby.

When she was told to leave the hotel—that she was underperforming in bed and overshowing a bit in the belly—nineteen-year-old Eva boarded a mail boat heading southwest to nearby Sanibel Island. The destination had been on her mind ever since she'd met a man, weeks earlier, in front of the Punta Rassa telegraph office.

He'd walked out of the office and flopped down next to her on a bench. Immediately he began talking to her about a telegram he'd just received.

"A man in Louisiana wants my beans," he said, poking at the paper in his hand. "*My* castor beans."

Eva smiled at him. "Congratulations."

He chuckled and offered his hand. "Where are my manners? I'm Arthur Cooper."

She took his callused hand. The man seemed pleasant, with no hint of perversion or deceit. If she'd gained one useful skill at the Spur, it was identifying degenerates.

"Hello, Mr. Cooper. I'm Eva."

He insisted she call him Arthur and began to explain the deal he'd made with the manager of a cottonseed mill interested in extracting oil from his castor beans. Using his hand, he described a bean plant, shrub-like with long-stemmed leaves that spread out like fingers. He said he grew the plants on Sanibel Island, where he lived.

"It must be wonderfully quiet on the island," Eva said. "It's so . . . smothering here."

Arthur smiled. "There's just plants, my workers, and me out there." He held up the telegram. "But now I'm going to need a lot more help."

It was that brief interaction that prompted Eva to board the mail boat *Spitfire* the very next day. She left Punta Rassa behind, en route to Sanibel.

When she found him on the sparsely settled island, Arthur looked both puzzled and pleased.

"Eva?"

He'd remembered her name, and she got right to the point, explaining her "situation" and inquiring about work in trade for food and shelter.

"And you should know, in time, I'll need your help finding a family to take my baby." She shrugged. "I don't have anyone else to ask."

Arthur wiped his brow and stabbed the point of a shovel into the ground.

"I welcome the help. You can stay in that small palmetto shack." He nodded toward a structure set apart from a group of larger shacks. "We can discuss the other thing later."

Arthur kept her busy, fed, and safe through the months that followed. She toiled beside a handful of other farmhands setting seeds, watering, harvesting—whatever was necessary. She worked hard, infinitely grateful to escape the bustle and hustle of Punta Rassa. The move allowed her to lay in bed every night, alone, listening to the soothing waves of the Gulf.

When Eva appeared quite far along in her pregnancy, Arthur insisted she stop work in the fields. Instead, she helped with bookwork inside the house, a sparse wooden structure with three rooms. One afternoon, as Eva worked a pencil with one hand and rubbed her protruding stomach with the other, Arthur sat down at the desk across from her.

"Eva. The baby. Tell me your plans . . . what you want."

Her eyes instantly welled up with tears. She'd been crying most nights during the past month, terrified of how much she'd fallen in love with the bastard baby, a workplace accident. The powerful bond had crept up on her. Or perhaps she'd labeled thoughts about cuddling and protecting her baby daydreams, a way to pass the time as she worked. But the day she sobbed at the sight of a robin's egg smashed on the ground was the day she had to be honest with herself. She wanted to be a mother.

"I can't do it," she said, tears rolling down her cheeks and onto the calculations in the account book.

Arthur folded his hands on the desk. "Can't keep the baby, or can't give the baby away?"

"I want to keep my baby, Arthur." She sniffled and sighed with her eyes closed. "I'll figure it all out."

Before he could answer, Eva's body tensed. "Ohhh . . ." She grabbed the sides of her stomach and dropped her chin to her chest. "Arthur, what's happening?"

"Let's get you to the bedroom," Arthur said, and helped her shuffle to the bed. "Everything's going to be fine, Eva."

When the *Spitfire* arrived at the island that day, Arthur explained what was needed. Two hours later, the boat returned with help for Eva on board.

•••

When midwife Clara Burns entered the house, Arthur answered her questions quietly and led her to the bedroom where Eva was moaning, her hair drenched in sweat.

"I'll need hot water and towels." She nodded at Arthur and shut the door behind her.

"Eva, I'm Clara. We're going to help each other, all right? Tell me what you can about the pain." Clara pulled off the bedcovers. Blood stained the sheet under Eva's bottom.

"My back." Eva's voice was weak. "It's broken." She rolled her wet head back and forth on the pillow, her eyes shut. Tears ran down her cheeks, mixing with beads of sweat.

Please let me live, Eva thought.

Clara quickly searched for clues outside and inside of Eva's body. A female farmhand knocked on the door and opened it upon Clara's reply, "Come in." She placed a bucket of hot water and a mound of towels near the bed and left. Over the next two hours, Eva's moans became screams of agony. Bloody cloths lay in a pile on the floor. The baby's head and shoulders had appeared, but Eva had stopped pushing, exhausted.

"Take a deep breath, dear." Clara held a cloth doused with ether near Eva's mouth and gently wiped back strands of hair stuck to her forehead.

Eva breathed in the sweet-smelling air and begged again.

Please, God, let me live. Let me take care of my baby.

•••

Belle finished brushing her hair and decided to start her final cottage project: transforming the stark porch into a stage for a showy cast of plants. Abigail had given her permission to dig up some of the snapdragons, blanket flowers, and marigolds that were planted along the border of the vegetable garden to attract pollinators. Her blooms, though, would need only please passersby.

She left the cottage to search for pots in the storage shed. As she walked, she noticed a man on the Edison property bathing a gray mule. Even from across the yard, she could see the skinny animal's backbone. The worker was turned away from her, offering Belle a chance to examine him from head to toe: thick, curly blond hair, broad shoulders under a white linen shirt, long legs in faded dungarees, boots. She stopped to observe the bath. What a gentle touch he was using on the aged mule, whose eyes appeared shut or nearly so. *That must be Boone.* He dropped a damp rag into a bucket and picked up a brush from the ground. Belle ran her fingers through her freshly brushed hair and watched him work through the mule's wiry tail, clumped with snags that he untangled with patient strokes. Whenever she'd noticed Boone on Front Street, he was always alone, frequently making a stop at Dawson's Cabinets or the lumber mill. Soon, Belle would meet him and work near him. As she began to imagine how their first meeting might go, a voice began yammering in her head: *No man will ever want you.* Belle closed her eyes. It spoke again, both whispering and hissing. *Never. No man will ever want you.* She gave her hair a slight yank, as if to punish the voice. Belle despised the sound of it and hated that the words were probably right. Why *would* a man want her? No one chooses the bruised apple or the fork with bent tines.

Dismissing any further thoughts about Boone, she walked to the storage shed and entered, leaving the door ajar for light. It was quiet inside but for the hammering of a woodpecker somewhere nearby. As she rummaged around for pots, Coquina wandered in, alerting Belle with half a *meow.* Her coat was laced with cobwebs.

"Hello there, Queen."

Belle stroked the sticky webs off the cat, whom she sometimes called Queen Coquina because of the crown-like M on the tabby's forehead. The cat padded into the small closet in the back of the shed while Belle looked for pots. There were plenty. When she'd located four suitable containers, she called out.

"Coquina." No cat appeared. She needed to leave and shut the shed door. "Coquina?"

The response was a weak cry from the dim closet. Belle entered and saw cat eyes looking at her from a high shelf.

"Get down." The cat blinked but didn't move.

Sensing a long standoff, she stepped on a three-legged foot-stool and then onto a flat-top trunk. From there, she attempted to grab her pet, but before she could, the agile cat launched herself off the shelf, onto the trunk, and down to the ground.

Belle shook her head. "I would have helped you, cat." As she turned to step off the trunk, she noticed an object pushed to the back of the shelf, turned on its side. Its oddness caught her eye. Long, spiraled wires appeared to have been partially yanked out of a tin container. Curious, she pulled it toward her. She eyed all sides of it, but even with a closer look the item was unidentifiable.

The black contraption, about the size and shape of a square coffee canister, featured a brass crank handle that jutted out from its right side. Lidless, the box was crammed full of snarled copper wires, some spilling out over the sides. She checked the bottom for clues—a brand or date—but there was nothing. She even smelled it. At Duggan's, she was exposed to a wide variety of wares, but nothing that remotely resembled this. She couldn't even hazard a guess about its function.

"How do you work?" she asked the odd container.

Abigail had mentioned the closet was used to store fishing or boating gear; this didn't look related to either. The dark shed was not ideal for further examination, so she tucked the canister under her arm and got down from the trunk. She placed the object inside a small stack of pots and left the shed. Coquina was outside next to a coconut palm, so she shut the door.

On her way back to the cottage, she checked for Boone. He'd finished washing the mule and was leading it up the driveway, per-haps to the livery stable. She recognized his gait, long strides with a limp. His right boot dug into the sand more deeply than his left, compensating for the bum leg. Living with an injury—permanent or temporary—was not uncommon for townsfolk. Belle often saw Duggan's customers with missing fingers, broken limbs, burns, and a variety of random scars. Life in the region required dealing with horses, cattle, fire, saws, axes, guns, alligators—an array of potential risks that could ravage a body. Still, she wondered what specifically had happened to Boone.

Once on her porch, she left the pots behind and took the black gadget inside. Planting flowers could wait. A proper inspection of her find was in order. Settled into the rocker, Belle ran a cloth over the box, which was covered in a thick layer of dust. How long had it sat undetected on the shelf? When was the last time it was activated, if ever, and by whom? If she turned the handle, what would happen? Maybe nothing, maybe something breathtaking. She imagined the eruption of a glowing arch, a rainbow that would wash the cottage walls in a kaleidoscope of color.

As she continued to wipe down the box, the *bong-bong* of a ship's bell rang out from across the yard. In just the short time Belle had lived in the cottage, she'd grown to anticipate the deep, rich tone. It not only signaled a meal, but also that strangers were about to gather under the same roof for food and fellowship. Belle chose to sit in the kitchen, where she could watch Abigail cook and listen to boarders chat in the dining room.

She got up from the rocker. As much as she wanted to continue examining the device, she didn't want to miss a meal. Should she ask Abigail about her puzzling find? Show her? Would a boarder from up north recognize it? She opened a dresser drawer and hid the box under a nightdress. For now, she would stay quiet and keep a secret. Why not? Her other secret caused her shame, but this one intrigued her.

When she entered Baker's, the dining room was buzzing with chatter and laughter. As usual, the aromas floating up from steaming pots and skillets were heavenly—buttery fish and spicy greens.

"May I help with anything?" Belle asked.

She was getting used to talking to Abigail's bun. The cook was always facing the stove, jostling heavy skillets and peeking under lids, fully engaged in the chaos of coordinating a hot meal.

"No, dear," she replied. "I'll dish up the boarders, and you just help yourself when you're ready." The oven let loose a yeasty belch as Abigail pulled out a tray of golden biscuits.

Belle stayed out of the way until all of the loaded plates disappeared into the dining room. She prepared one for herself and took a seat at the kitchen table. Abigail soon reappeared and plopped into a chair across from her.

"Hear that? Not a peep. Sign of a good meal." She smiled at Belle, who chewed and nodded in agreement. "Irwin caught a slew of redfish this morning in the river. *And* he cleaned them for me. Bless that man."

A wide range of clientele rolled through Baker's. Naturalists like Irwin and Collette visited to enjoy the region's exotic plants and animals. Northern physicians often sent patients like George to warmer climes to recover or even relocate. Others arrived to explore investments in citrus groves, while through-travelers simply needed a place to stay as they awaited steamers bound for Key West or Tampa. In recent years, wealthy sportsmen came to battle tarpon in the waters off southwest Florida, heralded in a national magazine article as "the premier place to catch, by rod and reel, abundant silver monsters guaranteed to test an angler's resolve." Comings and goings kept Baker's busy and Abigail in a constant state of exhaustion.

Belle put down her fork. "I saw a man next door with blond hair washing a mule. Boone, I suppose."

Abigail stifled a yawn. "Boone and Byron . . . in that order."

Belle grinned. She resumed eating and waited for more information.

"Mr. Edison's caretaker doesn't like Byron, so Boone tries to at least keep that poor mule presentable. Norville Decker doesn't like anything that complicates his budget, and Byron eats more than he works." Abigail lowered her voice to avoid offending any of her boarders. "Decker's a crusty grump of a Yankee who looks down his nose at the 'crackers' who've lived here a lot longer than he has."

Belle raised her eyebrows and ran a napkin across her lips. "So, Boone works for Mr. Decker?"

"Works *with* Decker. They both work for Mr. Edison, who tells Decker what he wants done, who tells Boone, who gets it done."

Belle recalled the town's excitement when Edison purchased the thirteen-acre riverfront property known as the Summerlin tract for a reported $3,000. The *Press* proclaimed, "EDISON IS COMING!" and ran frequent articles updating progress on land clearing, wharf construction, and the assembly of two residences and a laboratory. When the inventor moved into his self-dubbed Seminole Lodge, he'd already improved both the stock ticker and the telegraph, created the first phonograph, and most astonishing of all, had developed the first electric light bulb and commercial electric power station. Belle had caught glimpses of the visiting genius during his first winter in Fort Myers. Twice she spotted him chatting with Oscar Powell, the town's telegraph operator, outside the Western Union office, which made sense since the *Press* reported that Mr. Edison was a "brass pounder" himself during and after the Civil War. Belle noted that he was always well dressed but a bit frumpy: hair combed but with his fingers, crooked ribbon tie, dusty shoes. She liked that—a man with his mind on bettering the world, not his appearance.

"Have you and Boone met yet?" Abigail asked.

Belle shook her head no.

"Would you like me to introduce you two tomorrow?"

"Oh my, no," Belle replied immediately. "He must be very busy."

Abigail chuckled. "Even a busy man makes time for a beautiful woman."

Deflecting the compliment, Belle teased, "If that's the case, I'm sure Merle would love you to invite him for dinner."

Belle had secretly hoped for years that the old friends would become a couple. Their friendship seemed a kiss away from evolving into romance. Merle always lit up when she entered the store. "My gal, Abigail!" he'd call out as a greeting. She never stopped by without bringing oatmeal cookies baked his way—with walnuts— and teasing him about a tear in his dungarees or a crooked row of spices.

She studied Abigail's face, round with soft skin exposed more often to kitchen steam than sun. Her eyes were the color of a light-blue marble and were rarely still, always observing what problem needed solving. Now that Merle lived alone at Duggan's, Belle's desire to pair up the two friends was even stronger.

Both palms on the table, Abigail raised her bulk up and out of the chair. "Squirrel knows he has an open invitation for dinner. I just think he gets tired of losing to me at cards after the meal."

Belle smiled and hoped Merle would come by soon. He'd lost Clara more than two decades ago. Surely, a man with such a loving heart was overdue for a companion he could treasure and gather into the folds of his daily life.

Declining dessert, Belle thanked Abigail and walked out-side. She moved toward the river, wide and wondrous. The Caloosahatchee was, for as long as she could remember, a place where townspeople gathered. They strolled along the public wharf and watched the river move its water southwest to San Carlos Bay. Belle preferred to experience the river by herself, along its bank. During daylight, boats of all shapes and sizes plied the water along with floating flocks of ducks, geese, and swans. Massive live oaks and slanted cabbage palms overhung the river. From shore, anglers fished for mullet, catfish, and snapper. If Belle was lucky, they'd leave behind an interesting lure: a spinner adorned with a skirt of hair from a squirrel's tail or—better yet—a rare, lifelike, luminous minnow with baked-on paint, shiny glass eyes, and multiple treble hooks dangling from head to tail.

At night, the river made its presence known with noises—the light splash of a gator slipping into the water, the lapping of soft waves created by a mail boat making up lost time, croaking frogs hunting for crabs sheltering in the marsh grasses. When the sky was clear and full of stars, the river might play with a bright, boastful moon. It used the light to decorate itself, aglow with a shimmering current. The enchanting image nudged Belle back toward the cottage to revisit the box. Maybe she could make it glimmer like the river or bring it to life.

Inside, she sat on the bed and examined the machine's brass handle, its shine indicating little or no use. What if flames shot out of the box when it started? She set it on top of the dresser. Standing with the box at arm's length, she slowly but consistently cranked the handle, squinting her eyes in preparation for . . . something. She cranked and waited, but nothing emanated from the box—no heat, light, smell, or sound. She upped the speed of her circular motion, vigorously turning the handle. She kept at it for several minutes with no developments other than a tired arm. The second before she decided to give up, a tiny spark rocketed forth from the ball of wires. She jumped backward and released the handle.

"Oh!" she exclaimed. "What did you do?!"

Never before had she seen such a thing, nor caused such a thing. Stupefied but concerned the momentum she'd built would be lost, Belle moved again to the machine and resumed churning the handle at a fast rate. Within a minute, an orange spark launched to eye level trailed by two and then three more spitting sparks. She forced herself to continue operating the handle, even as the box began to generate heat. A burning smell hit Belle's nostrils, but she stayed the course, too intrigued to quit now. Round and round she spun the handle, a steady fountain of teeny sparks rising from the belly of the box.

Then, a remarkable development: the vibrating machine emitted a faint but undecipherable sound. A voice? Was someone talking? How strange! She released the handle and collapsed into the rocking chair as if she'd taken a punch to the chest. What was this box? Belle stared at the mystery machine and watched it slowly calm, absorbing the small constellation of sparks it had generated. Why in heaven's name was something so intriguing hidden away on a shelf in the shed?

Chapter 7

Boone had ridden horses his entire life, but in 1885 it was the South Florida Railroad's #8 that carried him across the miles, for the worst reasons. The *chuff-chuff* of steam thrusting the locomotive forward sounded to him like the massive machinery's heartbeat, steady and strong. Passengers around him slept, chatted, or watched the passing view out the window. Flocks of wetland birds led to still ponds, then scrubby prairie land as churning wheels rolled across steel rails. The bench where he sat may as well have been a pew, the coach car a rickety rolling church. If his prayers were answered, God would toss him into the engine's firebox.

He'd gathered just enough money to cover the fare from Kissimmee to Trabue and for several meals at eating houses along the route. The last thing he did before leaving the house was add biscuits, salt beef, and apples to his sack of clothes. He had no appetite but knew his body would need food, even if his soul was dead. His parents had been awake when he left but offered no send-off. Why would they? He was now invisible to them.

Staying home in Kissimmee was not an option. That was the only thought he knew to be true; all others were suspect. His thinking brain had vanished, scared off by angst and guilt. When it became clear he needed to uproot his life, he'd boarded the #8, the words of a young cow hunter ringing in his head. He remembered the teenager, gangly and loud. During a long cattle drive, the teen had made a prediction to him and the other men.

"Trabue is my next move," he'd said. "Charlotte Harbor is deep, and there's no question it will become the new boomtown for shipping cattle."

Now, here he was, rolling toward Trabue. He pulled the rail pass from his pocket and examined the year printed in red in the lower left-hand corner. He was a twenty-three-year-old man running away from home like a boy who'd been scolded. If *only* he'd been yelled at by his parents, even beaten to a pulp by his father. Instead, there was a sickening quiet that hung in the house, rotting its timbers. He had to leave before everything collapsed.

The train slowed as a steam whistle screeched, announcing the stop—this time, a sawmill. The air smelled of coal and cut wood. He stayed in his seat, his calf throbbing under its bandage, the only part of him in the process of healing. From his seat next to the window, he watched workers in tattered clothes dart around a flat freight car unloading lumber bound for sawyers and their whirling blades. People moving on, off, and around the train made efficient trips, seeking out food, loading mail, checking the connecting rods on resting wheels. Only the clouds seemed lazy, sheer white smears across the blueness. When a well-dressed man walked down the aisle toward him, Boone shut his eyes, pretending to sleep.

He pictured Daniel. He could have been looking at himself. They shared the same mop of sandy-blond curls and blue eyes. Their frames, though, were different; Daniel's was more commanding in height and bulk. At twenty-six, he was an exceptional cowboy. The only thing Daniel did better than move cows was serve as a loyal, protective older brother. Their father had taught them the basics of riding horses and working cattle, but doing both alongside Daniel for years across endless miles of thick underbrush had inspired Boone to improve. He grew to crack his whip among

the loudest in the crew. The curs executed his commands flawlessly, wagging their tails upon return from herding a stray cow.
Endless hours of blasting tin cans sharpened his aim. But he and
Daniel were different in ways a brother could never practice his
way into. Daniel was somehow able to shed the rawness of life, like
a palm tree dropping a dried husk to the ground. To him, discom-
fort and loss were natural, something to be learned from and then
forgotten. Boone, on the other hand, struggled with the inevitable
hardships of the trail. Shooting a coyote stayed with him for days.
He named all the calves in his mind—Fiona, Buttermilk, Gem—and
wished he hadn't when one died. At night, he secretly scratched
poems in a notebook.

Always younger, never the best
A weaker heart beats in my chest

Some brothers would end up in a ball of flying fists and sand
after working and living side by side for weeks at a time. Not them.
Scorching sun, torrential rains, run-ins with rustlers on the fence-
less prairies—he and Daniel shared everything, peacefully. They
did battle over the mosquito nets in the makeshift cow camps,
but everyone did. Any sniping was far outweighed by ribbing and
laughter.

"My brother here has a way with the ladies," Daniel would
joke. "He starts talking and they go away."

Boone would laugh right along with his brother. Daniel knew
attracting women wasn't a problem for either of them.

Dear God. How was it possible that Daniel was gone?

When the train lunged to a slow start, he opened his eyes. The
man next to him was eating a greasy drumstick, a napkin wrapped
around its bony handle.

"Did you have yourself a proper nap?"

The man was looking at him, chewing. He was well man-
nered—mouth closed as he worked the meat, conscious of where
grease might smear or splash. The smell of the food did nothing

to spark Boone's hunger. The jerking of the train gathering speed made him a bit queasy.

"Just resting."

The man nodded and gestured with his head toward a newspaper on the bench next to him.

"I picked up a Leesburg paper. Have a look if you'd like."

"Thanks."

Within minutes, the steadier pace of the train allowed him to consider light reading. His stomach was more settled, and he was tired of remembering Daniel. Before he could reach for the paper, the man offered a suggestion.

"Interesting project under way down south . . . for Mr. Edison. The article's on page two." He smiled and wiped his hands with more napkins. "I'm an attorney, not a heavy lifter, so I don't mind pointing out the job to you."

In his torn dungarees, faded boots, and sweat-stained straw hat, Boone knew he was easily pinned as a "heavy lifter." And one in need of work. It couldn't hurt to read about the project.

The several paragraphs read more like a job listing than an article. Laborers were needed to clear land and build structures on Gulf Coast property purchased by Thomas Edison. Boone was familiar with the famous inventor's name, but not the town where Edison planned to create Seminole Lodge and a laboratory. Pay was listed as between $1.50 and $2.75 per day. He looked out the window at the swampy landscape void of hills, a mound now and then. The view was endlessly bleak.

The more he read about the job—"Hard workers will be rewarded with a subtropical clime"—the less he wanted to relive his old life. Trabue would be crawling with cows and memories. He laid the paper on his lap.

"Where is Fort Myers?" he asked the pencil lifter.

"Up the Caloosahatchee River from Punta Rassa. I do work for several northern land developers interested in the citrus industry there." He winked. "It's good enough for Mr. Edison and he's pretty smart, right?"

Boone offered a weak grin but slumped in the seat. He didn't deserve anything good. He turned away from the man and looked out into the sameness. His leg throbbed. He'd been fooling himself to think he could ever work cows again, in Trabue or anywhere.

As the attorney began to lightly snore beside him, the journey ahead got longer. He'd take a chance and a steamer to the town called Fort Myers.

•••

Decker sat with Boone as he had for years now, both tasked with keeping Edison's winter estate up and running while their boss was away generating power and headlines around the world. The men were inside the caretaker's cottage, sitting across from one another at a small kitchen table, its wooden top riddled with water rings. Decker was droning on, reading from a long letter and stroking a spray of hair atop his head, the skin around it barren.

"I will send you about one thousand yards of common print cloth, which you can place around the more tender shoots when a freeze approaches," Decker read. "This cloth will prevent radiation almost entirely if you run it through boiled linseed oil and hang it out until dry. I will also ship a barrel of boiled oil."

Boone had his chair tipped back against the wall, arms crossed. Smoke rose from a fat cigar resting in an ashtray on the table. Decker continued reading the latest correspondence from Edison.

"We propose to have our grounds the best manured in Florida. Therefore, you may order for the river grounds six tons of oil cake, two tons of guano, and for the garden four tons of oil cake, two tons of phosphates, four tons of guano. Providing the guano should not cost more than fifty dollars per ton."

"The best manured, eh?" Boone said. "Keep talking, Decker, and we'll be there before we know it."

"Stop your yapping, boy." Decker said and continued. "We want a strawberry patch across the road about twenty by one hundred of the best early bearing strawberries. Also about twenty-five currant bushes and a bed of red and black raspberries, mixed; a bed about twenty by one hundred will do for both. Please plant the following." Decker drew in a deep breath. "Four castor beans, five olives, five jicama apples, five eggfruits, ten mangoes, ten alligator pears, two Spanish gooseberries." He took another breath. "Four pawpaw trees, six pomegranates, two mulberry natives, two custard apples, two grapefruit trees, four Japanese plums, two apricot trees, two persimmons, two tamarinds, and two mulberry trees."

Boone groaned. "This should be fun." He pushed his laced fingers forward, cracking several knuckles.

Edison had ordered a massive refresh of the landscaping and the creation of a large garden, as if new plants would propagate hope for a return trip to Fort Myers. Much was keeping him trapped in the Northeast. His rival, electrical innovator Edward Weston, recently opened a new private laboratory in New Jersey touted as "the most complete in the world." Competitive and fiercely protective of his status as the world's foremost inventor, Edison ordered the immediate construction of a sprawling new laboratory complex. There he could simultaneously work on as many as twenty projects with the assistance of eighty men, dwarfing Weston's staff. The Edison Phonograph Company was also newly formed and required his expertise in garnering international marketing rights. Also, Mina was pregnant with their first child together. The vacation house in southwest Florida sat empty for many and momentous reasons.

"Looks like some bad news for you, son." Decker tapped the letter and continued reading. "We'll need a banana bed about twenty feet square. You can purchase the plants, but I noticed many banana bushes on an island in the narrows of the river." He looked at Boone over the top of his spectacles. "We're not buying anything you can go dig up."

Boone rerolled a sleeve. "I'm well aware that the budget is more important than my back."

When Edison first purchased the property, he'd sent instructions to search for and haul in black freshwater muck from ponds around town. Boone recalled that Edison suggested using a wheelbarrow and boards to wheel the muck onto a flat-bottomed barge for transport to the property. Edison wrote that he hoped the muck would keep all the manure in place and "prevent it going clear through to China." His final line read, "Procure plenty of it. I want to carry everything to excess down there."

Excess, indeed. Boone had walked hunched over for a week.

"Nuts?!" Decker slapped his palm on his forehead. "He wants us to propagate slips from soft-shell almonds, Brazil nuts, filberts, and English walnuts. Does he think we're ten men?"

"Relax. Take a drag on your stogie." Boone pushed the ashtray toward him.

Decker's lanky fingers retrieved the cigar. He sucked in tobacco and released a large cloud of smoke, as if it might make the letter disappear—*poof.*

"What else does he write?"

Decker smoked again, then continued. "Clear four acres across the road for a truck garden and put a board fence around it thusly."

Decker turned the letter so Boone could see a sketch of a post fence with three slats. Boone made the "got it" sign with his fingers.

"Use some of the space here to experiment with different fertilizers." Decker grunted and shook the paper in the air. "As if I'm a studied experimenter!"

Boone reached for the letter and sighed. "Give me that before you pass out."

He snatched it and began to read aloud. "I understand the man who has charge of the place next to the old house will allow the truck garden for thirty-five dollars per acre. The propagating beds can be placed over there."

As Decker laid his forehead on the table, Boone asked in a singsong tone, "Don't you want to hear about the beehives?"

Decker spoke into the tabletop. "Let's talk about the visitor instead."

Seminole Lodge hadn't housed guests since Edison's father, Samuel, and son, Dash, visited several months after he and Mina honeymooned in Fort Myers several years ago. Dash was the nickname for Edison's youngest son with his first wife. Because he called his daughter Dot—a reference to his work with Morse code—Thomas Jr. was lovingly known as Dash. The ten-year-old had traveled with his grandfather, who came to check on the property.

When Dash first arrived, he walked the yard each day, hands folded behind his back, in full dress—polished wing tips, black knee socks and knickers, pressed white shirt, and a boater hat with a wide black ribbon circling its crown. He nodded at Boone but didn't speak. His eyes looked sad, angled downward at the edges, but Boone couldn't imagine a reason why. What could he want for? His grandfather had no air of privilege. Samuel worked a hoe easily, wore dungarees and a cotton shirt, and looked directly at everyone with gleaming blue eyes. His full white beard connected easily to a snowy shock of thick hair that dominated his head. Oddly, his eyebrows and mustache remained brown, trapped in younger years.

"I am a master of smoking, drinking, and gambling," he told Boone one afternoon, ending the admission with a deep chuckle.

He shared other personal details—that he was eighty-two and had, over the course of his life, split shingles for roofs, tailored, and managed a tavern.

"I've used my hands more than my brain," he said, smiling. "The complete opposite of my son."

He was clearly a proud father, describing his buttons busting at the ingenuity of "Al," whose inventions were transforming daily life. He explained that he'd supervised the building of the Menlo Park laboratory but "understood nothing inside of it."

Samuel and Dash appeared close, joking with each other and sharing long conversations on the porch. Boone wondered if Dash saw Samuel more than he did his busy father, who no doubt spent countless hours and days away from the family. Halfway through the stay, Dash shed his shoes and socks and unbuttoned his collar. He passed many of their final days at the Lodge kneeling in the yard, digging shallow holes and filling them with river water.

"So, Mr. Wood is visiting to make good on his promise?" Boone asked.

"Yes." Decker scribbled on a piece of paper. "Should the boss come, he'll be set to reel in a tarpon with gear selected exclusively by the famous W. H. Wood."

"How long is he in for?"

"Just a day. He's boating here and back from Schultz's hotel in Punta Rassa. Only family stays at the Lodge."

Boone traced a water ring with his fingertip. "Wood really gave boss the bug last year, didn't he?"

"Well, he caught a tarpon and boss didn't." Decker rolled his cigar on the edge of the ashtray. "If anything brings Edison back this year, it will be those giant silverfish."

Chapter 8

They were seeing each other up close for the first time. Boone had certainly noticed Belle riding around town on her unique trike, but now he was only a few feet away from her.

"This window is stubborn," he said, setting an ineffective chisel on the sill.

He turned from the problem window to size up Belle more fully. She was sitting in a rocker with a wide board set across the chair's arms, a makeshift desk for her sketchbook and a stack of worn gardening magazines. Her petite frame was unexpected. Atop her fast-moving trike she appeared tall and powerful.

"I hope you're having better luck with your work than I am with mine," he said.

"Slow going," she said softly.

"Do you mind if I see what you've got so far?" He waited to move toward her.

She pulled an issue of *The Gardener's Monthly and Horticulturist* toward her sketchbook to cover it.

"I'd rather you didn't." She rolled the pencil back and forth in her fingers. "I mean, at least not yet. My garden designs are quite rough right now."

Boone nodded and returned to working on the window. He'd have a chance to engage with her more in the days and weeks ahead.

They worked in silence for several minutes. Belle talked first.

"Have you spoken often to Mrs. Edison?"

Boone jiggled the window, which loosened a bit. "Just a few times. The Edisons have only visited twice since I've worked there." He turned toward her. "Once Mina asked me to repair a rathole. Another time she complimented me on my brushwork." He nodded toward the estates. "The yellow and white paint on the houses? Her idea. Apparently, it's a popular combination on homes in Orange."

"Orange?" Belle repeated.

"West Orange, New Jersey . . . where they live."

"Oh, of course," Belle said.

"Decker was clear from the start that I keep my distance from the family." Boone removed his straw hat. He pulled up several strands of his curly blond hair to create the quail-like tuft atop Decker's head. He shook a bent finger at Belle. "'Remember, boy, Mr. Edison can't hear and Mrs. Edison doesn't want to hear anything you have to say.'"

Belle raised her eyebrows. "I'll try to stay out of his way."

With a slam, the jammed window suddenly released. They both jumped and then laughed.

Boone replaced his hat and faced the window. "Success!" He made sure it operated smoothly and gathered his tools. When he noticed several teeth of a broken hair comb on the sill, he shook his head and tucked them in his pocket. *Elena*, he thought. The woman who last stayed in the cottage had lured him inside with constant requests for repairs. Nothing about her was subtle, from her heavy makeup to the black nightdress left out on the bed. She was beautiful and most likely used to getting what she wanted, but he wasn't interested and told her as much. Still, Elena persisted until the day she left. He nearly gave in but reminded himself that he didn't deserve to indulge in women, liquor, or anything else. Not after what he did in Kissimmee.

He turned around to face Belle.

"I suppose I'm done unless anything else needs tweaking."

"That should do," Belle said. "If you have a moment, though, I'd love to know what it was like to build for the Edisons. Abigail mentioned that you worked with the original crew."

Boone set his tools back down on the windowsill. All the work on the other side of the fence could wait.

"Exciting, I suppose. The amount of quality materials shipped in was impressive."

Belle gestured toward the stool. "If you have time, would you mind telling me what sort of things you did and saw?"

He dragged the stool to him, sat, and began to describe his experience during the month of November 1885.

Under the supervision of Mr. Edison's "agent" sent down from New York, he worked alongside three carpenters and four other laborers. He cleared palmettos and other wild scrub from the expansive property and helped build temporary quarters for himself and the other workers. Minor repairs were made to an existing one-room cottage.

"That's where Decker lives now," Boone explained.

In December, he worked with master carpenter Mr. Mendez— one of the town's original settlers—driving wooden pilings into the floor of the Caloosahatchee, a foundation for a wharf long enough to reach deep into the river so the coming schooner, heavy with cargo, could arrive with no risk of getting stuck.

"The two houses you see on the Edison property were actually shipped aboard the schooner," Boone said, "but in a lot of pieces."

A Boston architect designed the two homes and a lumber company in Maine precut the materials and built the doors and windows. The entire kit—along with lime and cement, bricks, and coal—was shipped to Punta Rassa and then upriver to Fort Myers.

By January, two more men arrived from Boston and New York to help manage the assembly of the homes—one for the Edisons, the other for his friend Ezra Gilliland. Crews built large fireplaces for each house and a fence around most of the property. Both residences were wired for electricity. The family's extensive personal effects were transported aboard a lighter.

"If it's not too ill-mannered of me to ask," Belle said, "what items did you see coming off the lighter?"

Boone crossed one boot over the other and described the array of fine goods: decorative light fixtures and hundreds of lamps, a pair of sturdy bathtubs and iceboxes, feather pillows and shams, a walnut washstand and cherry bedroom suite, reed couches, imported lace curtains, dinner sets, and paintings.

"They also included musical things for Mina," Boone explained. "They shipped a piano and several nifty mechanical organs that play music that's punched onto rolls of paper."

He continued, describing heavy wooden worktables for the laboratory along with shelving to house the various glass beakers, vials, and countless unidentifiables that played important roles in Edison's experiments. Chemicals were shipped in as well as pulleys, wire, lathes, and other hardware and tools.

"By mid-February," Boone said, "both homes were assembled and the lab was under construction. A landscaper from Pennsylvania was hired to spruce up the property. He planted lime, lemon, and coconut trees. In between the two homes he put a set of century plants. They've since died, unfortunately."

"Did you also put up the pretty windmill?"

"I did. Mr. Edison shipped that in later, though—about two years ago—along with two cisterns and a pump to create an artesian well. He also shipped two dynamos, one for his personal use and one to light up the town. But as you know, that hasn't happened yet."

"Someday soon," Belle said.

Boone explained that by April most of the men were let go, the majority of work finished. Their temporary living quarters were torn down.

"That's when I moved onto my boat. I was kept on to help Decker manage the property, and as you know, the family returned last winter for a visit."

"That's the visit when the newspaper claimed Mr. Edison was wreaking havoc with the fish by running a wire to the bottom of the Caloosahatchee," she said. "He electrocuted the poor things and they rose to the surface."

Boone chuckled and pointed to her straw hat, resting atop the dresser.

"Quicker than using lures, right?"

"Oh my, yes," she said.

"Mr. Edison has two boats here for fishing. Rifles for hunting, too."

"Oh, good. I'd like to think he has all he needs when he visits," Belle said.

"Trust me, if he doesn't, he finds a way to get it. He managed to have sacks of ice and strawberries delivered during his last trip." Boone smiled and stood up from the stool. "Well, I'd better get going."

"Nice to meet you, Boone. Thank you for the repair . . . and the Edison tidbits."

He lingered for a moment. "Would you like to take a ride on my boat sometime?"

Belle stared at him, silent.

"Good day, Belle." Boone touched the brim of his hat and quickly left the cottage. *What did you just do, fool?* He'd stunned them both. *Damn.* He fixed the window but broke his own rule about enjoying the company of a woman.

•••

When the door shut, Belle got up and watched Boone through the repaired window as he limped toward the caretaker's cottage. His offer to take her sailing had paralyzed her. Was he asking her on a date? They'd just met, for goodness' sake.

But what if she had agreed? *I'd love to, Boone,* answering immediately as if she'd been accepting invitations her whole life. She imagined floating along the Caloosahatchee with such a gentle, handsome man. The wind played with her hair, and he held a protective arm around her shoulder as he navigated the river. She laid her head on his warm, firm chest and listened to his soft humming mix with the rustle of the working sails. A feast of fresh blueberries and smoked chicken tucked inside a wicker basket awaited their first stop, perhaps a shady bend where they would lunch and talk.

Oh, just stop. Stop this gibberish.

Belle gathered her garden sketches and left the cottage to clear her head. On a downed palm trunk along the riverbank she sat to continue formulating garden plans—real plans, not pretend.

Days earlier she'd talked with Gus and Grace Bailey about new plants in their nursery—ornamental roses and other showy varietals, trees imported from Cuba and New Orleans that bore exotic fruits like loquats, Japanese persimmons, tangerines, and satsumas. Grace had pointed out a striking plant called a caladium, its large leaves splashed with vibrant colors and intricate patterns.

"A real beaut," Grace had said. "Lights up a shady spot."

She sketched the plant's unique, heart-shaped leaf on a piece of paper. Beside it she wrote: "BOONE?"

Stop wasting time!

She knocked the pencil against her head. What was it about moving onto the Baker property? Her imagination had ignited as never before, sparked by the unexpected discovery in the shed. More seemed possible here; though more of what, she wasn't sure. Often now, her mind's eye would peer through a fanciful lens and delight in the view: tiny mermaids that leapt from the mystery box, gardens that grew shiny glass flowers, and now, a romantic boat ride with Boone. It was as if magic was all around—as deep as tree roots, as high as shooting stars that sailed across the sky. She squinted toward the river. Perhaps far-fetched thoughts weren't a waste of time.

Belle lifted her sore bottom off the palm trunk and walked toward the cottage. Maybe she could coax out whatever magic was crouching inside that nest of copper wires.

•••

Sparks showered the dresser, and the cottage smelled as if matches had been extinguished. Belle's vigorous cranking had caused the box to finally fire up again after several botched tries in recent days.

She leaned closer to the black canister, which was vibrating lightly and emitting sparks at a steady rate. This was promising. As she turned to sit down on the bed for whatever might come next, a voice entered the room, muted at first but amplifying quickly to a perfectly clear tone.

". . . departs in November. Oh, I can hardly wait the eight months!"

Belle froze in midsit, concerned any movement might interfere with whatever was happening. A second female voice responded.

"It's so exciting! The *World* says it will report on her journey every day. Did you read about the contest?"

"A trip to Europe! Can you imagine? We need to submit a time. How long will it take our Nellie Bly to circle the earth?"

Belle eased herself down onto the bed, her eyes never leaving the dresser. She gripped her kneecaps to steady her hands. Who were these women? Where were they? Was the box some sort of telephone? She'd read about telephones, but they were available only in the bustling Northeast.

"They say she'll travel by ships, trains, sampans—whatever those are—even horses and mules. She's so brave! What do you think, BB . . . could you do it?"

"Oh my, no! I got lost the other day just walking to the ferry. Gerald says I shouldn't go out of the house without him. I just hate when I prove him right!"

"Pshaw. That man would keep you in a fishbowl if he could. He'd demand you put on a water show for him until he needed something. Only then would he fish you out."

Giggling. "I know. But he's as sweet as a Huyler's molasses. I just want to eat him up."

"Oh, BB, you're hopeless. You need to come to a club meeting with me."

Belle listened intently but stared at a growing galaxy of sparks hovering over the box. They were changing color from orange to pale green. *Please don't stop working!* She needed more clues as to what, where, who—all of it.

"Well, you'd have to slip me into your purse, Kate. Gerald and my mother would never let me hear the end of it if they knew I spent time at a women's club."

"Which is exactly why you should go! Women are stronger together, BB. It's not as if we gather to plot against men. We exchange ideas about how to better our lives. We talk about books and art." She paused. "And then we set several pairs of men's trousers on fire."

Belle found herself grinning despite her shock.

Laughing. "My funny Kate. You've always been the more independent gal. I like tradition; you like progress."

"I like taking care of myself, just like Nellie. Oh, BB, I hope she makes the trip faster than Phileas T. Fogg."

"On that we agree, my dear."

"Let's get oysters tomorrow and determine a number to submit to the *World*."

"No to the oysters—too unladylike—and yes to guessing her finishing time."

"Oh . . . of course, Mr. Long. BB, Mr. Long needs to use his telephone. I'll call you sometime tomorrow, Prissy."

"All right. So long for now."

Immediately, the circle of floating sparks dropped down into the canister, which stopped vibrating. The cottage was silent but for the din of the feathered flock wandering the yard. It seemed odd, to suddenly be alone again. The room was just filled with three people, wasn't it? She jiggled her fingers inside her ears, the two voices still bouncing around inside. She'd overheard a telephone conversation—somehow, somewhere—many miles north of Fort Myers. The only reference she recognized was to Phileas T. Fogg, the main character in Jules Verne's book, *Around the World in Eighty Days*. One of Fort Myers's original founders brought books with him from Key West, including Verne's acclaimed work, which was read each year to the town's schoolchildren. Belle recalled the gripping plot, filled with nail-biting foibles like a herd of buffaloes blocking a train track and confusion at the international date line. She marveled at the concept of a real woman attempting to beat the imaginary eighty-day record. Or at least that's what it sounded like.

When the box had fully cooled, Belle placed it back in her dresser drawer. She wanted to know more about these friends. Never before had she heard women talk about men or independence, and she certainly hadn't done so. The most intimate conversations she had with women revolved around books. They'd chat over coffee about favorite characters or twists in the story. But, talk of relationships or aspirations? Never.

Belle concealed the box with clothes and gently shut the drawer. Instead of a mere gadget, she now knew that something unique and unexplainable—at least by her—was tucked inside. She walked to the bed and flopped onto it. *Could Kate and BB have heard me if I'd spoken?* The thought never crossed her mind until now. No matter—she'd been too shocked to utter even one word. With another lucky handle crank, she'd get a second chance to find out more about the pair and whether she could—or would—join their intriguing conversation.

Chapter 9

Abigail spoke to Belle over one shoulder as she washed dishes. "I thought you'd like to hear more about the professor's travels before he leaves today."

"If he has time, I'd enjoy that." Belle finished the last bite of her lunch, venison stew.

"Good. I'll ask him to sit in the kitchen with us, while I clean up and you both enjoy some lemon pie."

Belle walked her empty plate over to Abigail. "Delicious, as always."

"I can confirm that." Professor Ricalton stood in the doorway to the kitchen, smiling and clutching the lapels of his three-button sack coat. He was slight with a head that looked like a skull covered by skin only, a thick gray mustache his only hair. He wore a brimless black cap and thin wire spectacles.

"Abigail, your cooking makes it hard for a boarder to board a boat home."

Belle smiled and Abigail waved him into the kitchen. "Do you have time to talk plants with Belle, Professor?"

"Of course," he said, and walked over to her.

She noted his thin neck, untouched by the stand collar of his shirt. A narrow bow tie helped bolster his neckline.

"Abigail told me that you're an avid gardener, Belle."

"Well, I certainly do enjoy the company of plants," she said.

Abigail wiped her wet hands and gestured toward the small kitchen table. "Why don't you two sit down in here, and I'll wrangle dessert."

"A very sound idea," he said, dropping into a chair. "The new boarder I was sitting beside in the dining room went on and on about sponging and plucking slimy black masses from the Gulf floor." He patted his nonexistent belly. "Not so appetizing."

Belle liked Professor Ricalton already. He seemed comfortable and confident with no air of self-importance. She sat down across from him and fidgeted with a tiny spoon in a saltcellar. He looked back at her with his hands folded on the table. Abigail walked over to the table without dessert.

"So, Professor Ricalton is here as a guest of Mr. Edison, who wanted to reward him with a week of sun and relaxation. The professor spent a year traveling on his behalf, conducting scientific research on thousands of plants."

"A fine man, Mr. Edison," the professor said, nodding. "And I've been honored to stay at Baker's, Abigail. You're known throughout town as its finest cook and host, and now I know why."

Abigail said as she turned, "Now *that* will get you an extra-large slice of lemon pie."

Belle smiled at the professor, who grinned and rubbed his palms together as Abigail walked away.

"So, how does this all fit together, Professor? You, Mr. Edison, plants?"

"Well, I suppose I got very lucky, Belle. A great man noticed an average man, and so our partnership began."

James Ricalton explained that Mr. Edison was in need of a seasoned world traveler who he could train to test for levels of carbon in various species of bamboo. The professor certainly qualified as an experienced trekker. A schoolteacher and principal in Maplewood, New Jersey, he spent his summer vacations wandering the world with his beloved photography equipment. He described a covered wheelbarrow-like apparatus he'd built to transport gear during the day and to sleep in at night.

"Through my camera lens, I explored Iceland, the Amazon, and northeastern Russia. I was alone but never felt that way. My constant companion was the utter newness of the surroundings and people I encountered. Always I returned home with photos, mineral specimens, and curios handmade by native folk."

"How exciting," Belle said, "and what fun to share it all with your students."

"Indeed, Belle," he said. "Why see the world if you can't share its wonders? The children are so curious about what exists beyond their little valley."

The professor continued, describing the day a messenger showed up at his school with a letter from Mr. Edison requesting a meeting that day—no reason stated—at his new laboratory in West Orange, six miles north of Maplewood.

"When I arrived, he had a gleam in his eye. He said, 'You like to travel, I believe?' When I confirmed with an 'Indeed,' he explained, 'I want an experienced traveler to ransack all the tropical jungles of the East to find a better fiber for my electric lamp. I expect it to be found in the palm or bamboo family. Would you like that undertaking?'" The professor threw his hands up in the air. "Can you imagine, Belle? As I said, I got lucky."

Belle smiled up at Abigail, who brought two plates of pie topped with fluffy egg-white peaks browned in the oven. The professor's piece was twice the size of hers.

"Thank you . . . for this." Belle gestured back and forth between herself and the professor.

Abigail nodded at her and moved into the dining room to serve dessert.

"I must tell you, Belle, how much I respect Mr. Edison's infinite thoroughness. He'd already discovered that bamboo grown in Japan was a very desirable carbon for his lamp." He held up his pointer finger. "Yet, he believed that somewhere in God's great laboratory superior varieties—even longer burning—might be found."

The professor explained that he received a leave of absence from school and reported to Mr. Edison the following day to learn the details of drawing and carbonizing fibers in the jungles of the Orient. While Edison's workers created a set of suitable tools for his fieldwork, he was directed to do research in the laboratory's library.

"I studied the geography of where I would explore." The professor ran his finger along the table and around his pie plate. "I drew maps of the tributaries and rivers I planned to visit—the Ganges, the Irrawaddy, the Brahmaputra."

Belle wished a map were spread out on the table to help her visualize his journey. "Were you at all afraid, Professor?"

He poked at his pie with a fork. "Yes and no, Belle. Experience is an effective antidote to fear, and I'd already traveled extensively by myself. Honestly, my biggest fear was that I would disappoint Mr. Edison, that I wouldn't find what he needed."

Belle nodded. "I feel the same way about Mina. I don't want to disappoint her with the gardens she's asked me to create."

"All we can do is to give our very best, Belle." He smiled, pushed the narrow bridge of his glasses toward his eyes, and began eating his pie.

She started in on her slice and sorted through the many questions she had for the professor.

"My students gave me a fine bon voyage and I was off, sailing to Ceylon by way of England and the Suez Canal. Ceylon is tropical and rich with a wide variety of bamboo and palm species. I visited every part of the island and tested nearly one hundred species over the course of three and a half months."

"The working conditions," Belle said. "How did you find them?"

"Well, they certainly found me," the professor replied with a chuckle, sweeping a napkin across his mustache. "Insects were abundant and merciless. The most revolting specimen was the land leech. I had at least twenty removed from my body after emerging from the jungle."

Belle winced. "All filled with your blood."

The professor's eyes widened. "None of that unpleasantness mattered, though, because of my eureka find in Ceylon: *Bambusa gigantia*, an enormous bamboo." He held an invisible reed. "It measures twelve inches in diameter, grows one hundred fifty feet high, and tests *the* highest as a carbon. Eureka!"

Belle raised her eyebrows and pronounced aloud, *"Bambusa gigantia."*

The professor continued. From Ceylon, he trekked to India, then on to China. In Japan he tested extensively in a Tokyo museum, which contained a classified collection of every bamboo species in the empire.

"I returned exactly one year later to Maplewood, where my sweet boys and girls welcomed me with cheers and hugs." The professor beamed. "My students were in my thoughts throughout the trip. And of course, my wife, Barbara."

"What an accomplishment," Belle marveled. She added softly, "I can't imagine wandering the world on my own with such an important task at hand."

"Why not?" The professor crossed his arms. "Don't limit your imagination, Belle. It's the first step toward life's greatest adventures."

She nodded slowly. "I can see why you're a beloved teacher."

Abigail walked through the door with an armful of wood. "Pretty interesting story, eh, Belle?"

"Fascinating," she replied. "I don't want it to end."

The professor leaned toward her. "The ending is the best part."

He explained that after his students' welcome home, he reported to Mr. Edison. Because he'd found the inventor to be a man of few words and limitless diligence, he was not surprised by Edison's four-word greeting.

"He extended his hand to me, smiled, and asked, 'Did you get it?'"

Abigail chuckled and moved toward the stove to stoke its firebox.

"When I told him about *Bambusa gigantia*, he informed me that during my absence he'd succeeded in creating an artificial carbon, which promised even better results than bamboo fibers."

Belle furrowed her brow. "But all of your travel and hard work . . ."

The professor tapped his finger on the table. "That's the beauty of Mr. Edison's process, Belle. He has an invincible determination to leave no stone unturned to solve a problem he's identified. While he was spending $100,000 to have men like me scour the earth, he continued to claw for answers in that big brain of his. By the time I'd returned, my solution was outdated by his advanced discovery."

Belle shook her head. "What a fascinating life you live, Professor." She'd never met a world traveler. "What's your next adventure?"

The professor sighed. "I sense that my wanderlust has begun to overpower my love of teaching. I want to become a professional photographer, perhaps document conflicts around the world." With a swift move, he yanked a hunter-case pocket watch from a slit in his suit coat and flipped open the lid. "Oh dear. I've chatted my way into being late for my steamer." He rose and extended his hand. "Such a pleasure speaking with you, Belle."

She gently squeezed his bony hand. "It was my honor, Professor."

Before she could thank him for his insights, the professor scurried off through the dining room toward his room and luggage.

Abigail and Belle were exchanging thoughts about his world travels when he returned to the kitchen, bags in tow.

"Forgive the interruption, ladies. Abigail, I brought this for Mr. Edison, but I'm afraid I don't have time to place it in his laboratory. Can you make sure it reaches a shelf in the lab?"

He handed her a cobalt glass bottle filled with powder.

"Of course." Abigail took the bottle and set it on the table. "Here are some treats for your trip, good sir." She tucked a box of corn pone under his arm. "I've enjoyed having you. Safe travels."

When the professor was gone, Belle bent over for a closer look at the bottle. On a decorative label with four diagonal edges someone had written "*Sanguin Dragonis*" and below it, "Dragons Blood." A wax cork served as a stopper.

"I would think with a name like Dragons Blood, the powder should be red," Belle said, her nose nearly touching the bottle.

"It looks purple because of the blue glass," Abigail explained. "Would you like to take it to the laboratory?" she asked, retying her apron. "I've got a heap of dirty dishes here."

Belle's eyes widened. "Me?" She added quickly, "I mean, yes, I would." First the professor and now this. How grateful she was for such a fascinating day.

Pouring boiling water into a washbasin, Abigail instructed, "There's a key underneath a turtle shell to the left of the lab door. If Decker gives you any guff, tell him you're doing official Edison business per Professor J. Ricalton . . . and Abigail Baker."

Belle nodded. "Thank you very much, Abigail. I'll be quick and careful."

•••

The flat-grooved key required some jiggling but finally moved the spring-loaded pins in the lock on the laboratory door. Belle looked back over her shoulder; there was no sign of anyone. Even with permission to enter the lab, her heart was pounding with the *thump-thump* of anticipation and apprehension. Gently, she pushed open the door and entered the dim structure, filled with enough light from the hazy afternoon to see everything in it. She took a slow, deep breath through her nostrils, inhaling the scent of wood and rubber. Clutching the blue bottle, she closed the door and turned to survey the space.

Her eyes scanned the room, still and cool. Who was the last person in the lab? Nothing but the mundane—stools, tables, pencils—was familiar. The quiet seemed not to be trusted, as if the large metal machines might spring to life at any moment. She spotted a switch on the wall that would most likely activate the rows of lamps above the worktables, a lighting system she knew was perfected by Edison himself. As tempted as she was to illuminate a room without striking a match, Belle left the switch alone. She was not sent to the lab to burn it down.

With a look to the left, she noted a separate room that seemed to be an office. A cot was set up next to a desk stacked neatly with papers and books. An empty coatrack claimed one corner. In the main room, a variety of bulky equipment was grouped together, as if in a machine shop. A telegraph was recognizable, but a massive boiler served an unknown purpose. Somewhere sat the dynamo awaiting Edison's expertise to light the town. Towering stacks of thick books and printed material rose toward the ceiling like big-city buildings. Belle stood motionless, stuck in place, wondering. *What did people talk about in the lab? Did they yell and curse? Or did they whisper amidst the intense concentration?* She considered that perhaps Boone and the other workers took special care in constructing the building, a nursery for the birth of ideas, for breakthroughs, elation, and meaning. She imagined the walls vibrating from a whirlwind of brainpower.

Slowly, she forced herself to move, holding the Dragons Blood with both hands. Her eyes searched the wooden floorboards for popped nails that might trip her. As she walked toward shelving in the back of the lab, she passed by thick wooden tables crowded with cloudy glass beakers, snaked rubber tubing, and extra-large

glass cloches that protected nothing but air. The room was completely silent but for her footsteps. Before she got to the shelves,
Belle spotted several hardbound notebooks resting atop a worktable. A blue jay feather that served as a bookmark poked out from
one of them. She stopped moving. Gently, she set down the bottle
on the table and lay a palm atop the blue jay book.

"Don't do it, Belle," she whispered, remembering Mina's words.
As you might expect, we value our privacy.

Clearly, the notebooks were not hers to explore, and she knew
better than to boldly break the rules. But she considered it. *Maybe
just a peek.* Her curiosity was misbehaving, as if given permission
by the spirit of wonder that hung in the air. She drummed her fingers on the sturdy cover. Then, she lifted it slightly and let it drop,
as if to release a hint as to what lay inside. When she stroked the
blue feather, it felt stiff, not soft, as if it had been keeping watch
over the marked page for quite a while.

I'll be quick, Belle thought. She dragged out a metal stool from
beneath the table and regretted the loud scraping noise it made.
She froze for a moment and glanced at the door. Her eyes shifted to
a woman's felt hat hanging on a peg near the doorframe. She took
a deep breath and brushed off a light layer of dust from the stool
seat. Committed now to invading the lab's privacy, she sat down
and watched her hands shake as she opened the notebook to its
first page.

Her eyes went straight to the date in the upper right-hand corner: March 18, 1886. Underneath the date, the same hand wrote
"TAE." In noticeably different handwriting, the word "Mina"
appeared below. Was the couple working during their honeymoon that year in Fort Myers? She pictured Mina looking over
TAE's shoulder as he recorded a rush of certainties and hunches.
Surely, Mina knew from the start that her extraordinary husband
would never be able to turn off his brain, even during a getaway.
Newspaper articles referred to her as a loving, supportive wife.

Now, Belle had an intimate look into Mina's devotion, a witness to her husband's grand thoughts and theories.

She carefully turned the book's pages, many filled with drawings that resembled light bulbs. Phrases like "200 volts" and "sealed vacuum" were scribbled next to them. All the diagrams and sketches included commentary or questions. Much of the writing was hard to decipher, as if Edison's pencil couldn't keep up with his thoughts. Page corners were peppered with columns of mathematical equations, some crossed through as if sampled, then dismissed.

On March 23, TAE wrote, "also a telephone where every kind of change of material can be made—perhaps 40 or 50 cheap telephones, every one an anomaly of XYZ devices would be better."

"The black box?" Belle said aloud. *Surely not.* Why would an invention—in progress or completed—end up next door hidden away in Abigail's shed? She flipped to the next page. It featured a sketch of a face with a round device labeled "earpiece" clasped to the outside of one ear. She'd read that Mr. Edison was basically deaf. Perhaps he was trying to better his quality of life and the lives of others with the same affliction.

When she arrived at the section marked with the blue jay feather, Belle was startled by what she read: "shock an oyster see if it wont paralyze his shell muscle & make the shell fly open." Clearly, Edison's mind wandered to places never considered by most. The work continued through March 26 and filled at least one hundred pages of the notebook. Mina had signed nearly all of them.

"Oh dear," Belle said when she realized how long she'd been in the lab, immersed in nothing she understood except that the Edisons, in this very lab, were personal and professional partners. She replaced the notebook exactly where she'd found it, atop the others. Scooting off the stool, she picked up the blue bottle and headed toward the back shelves to find room for the Professor's powder, one more potential "Eureka!" in a lab full of them.

Between bottles labeled "benzaldehyde" and "zinc," Belle jiggled the Dragons Blood into a tight space. Her fingers shook as she focused on not knocking anything over.

"There you go," she said, relieved she'd completed the task without incident. As she turned and walked slowly toward the front door, she reviewed the room, certain she would never get this chance again. How was it possible that someone as ordinary as she had breathed the air of such a revered space? What would next be discovered here?

It was time to go. She twisted the doorknob and pulled. Standing in the doorway, she let the fresh air wash over her skin. *She* was standing in Thomas Edison's laboratory. *She* had chatted with a world traveler. *She* had found a talking box. Already her life had been enriched by moving just one mile down the road. At that moment, Belle decided to give an idea she'd been mulling over a try.

Chapter 10

"It's simply a bicycle, Mother. It gets me to work quickly, and I enjoy the ride."

"Tsk-tsk. Reverend Cole says women who straddle bicycles are riding to the devil in bloomers."

Belle was stretched out on the cottage floor, writing on postcards she'd taken from Duggan's. The conversation in the background was unlike any she'd ever heard. A mother and daughter were both talking, but it was debatable whether either was listening to the other.

"Suggesting we're riding to hell is outrageous. Women who ride bicycles and wear bloomers are merely smart about transport and comfort."

"Have you not considered that women of the lower class wear bifurcated garments? *You* were raised better."

"That's the point, Mother. You raised me, and now I'm a twenty-three-year-old woman who can make her own choices."

Belle was thrilled when the box connected for a second time. After a few minutes of listening, she'd tested whether the women talking could hear her. She bonged her match safe against the washbasin, but there was no reaction. The women continued speaking, obviously unable to hear anything on their end. For good measure, Belle said, "Hello?" into the canister, but again, no response. She'd then settled onto the floor with her project.

"Why do you feel the need to join all of these female clubs? City club, bicycle club, literary club."

"Because I can! If you'd spring yourself from that tight corset, Mother, you'd be surprised by how open your mind would become to progress and the possibilities for self-improvement."

"Watch your mouth, Kate."

Belle stopped writing. Kate? She *thought* the younger voice sounded familiar—Kate from the first call! Belle smiled. The box had "found" Kate again, but she was speaking to her mother this time, not her friend.

Silence.

"Why you insist on denigrating my devotion to your father and the moral character of our home is beyond me. You and your women friends talk about not being submissive while you finish suits worn by the very men who pay you by the piece. You're so enlightened that you allow yourself to be overworked in high season, underworked in slack, and underpaid year-round."

"Mother, if you ever listened to me, you'd know that I'm in line for corner maker."

"And whatever will you do with that extra thirty-five cents for forty hours of work?"

"I'll save it. When *this* Kate Hallock marries, she'll use her hand to spend her own money, not hold it out, waiting for her husband to fill it."

Belle sighed lightly and tapped the pencil eraser on the floorboard. She preferred the tone of the first connection, the light banter between Kate and BB. This verbal sparring between mother and daughter was unfamiliar and uncomfortable. Still, Kate's strong-willed case for women supporting themselves and each other was the perfect backdrop for her task at hand: writing out the same note—except for the recipient's name—on seven postcards.

Dear _____,

I hope this note finds you well. I'm considering forming a club to discuss topics that are interesting and important to women. You are one of several women in town I'm inviting. We can discuss a name for the club should we find the gathering worthwhile. If you are interested in participating, please join me Saturday in the schoolhouse at one o'clock. The bell on the Methodist Church is broken, so it will not be sounding a reminder at one.

Thank you for considering my invitation.

Sincerely,

Belle Carson

The thought of creating a club both excited and scared her, but Professor Ricalton's suggestion that "experience is an effective antidote to fear" had inspired her to try. If she was timid about developing more meaningful relationships, perhaps she needed more experience trying. A women's club—like Kate described—could be a good start. But, would women even be interested? What would they talk about? Small groups already existed in town for women to sew or study scripture together. But Belle decided instead to invite women who seemed to have differing interests and daily routines. Ideally, the mix would spark lively conversation and a range of suggestions for the club's purpose. There was a chance not everyone, or no one, would attend, but Belle was determined to move forward with her plan. Postcards would be delivered to Sadie, a mother of five; Amelia, an unmarried business owner; Paulette, a former beauty queen; Alice, considered "off" by some in town; Poppy, a minister's wife; Hazel, Ida's smothered daughter; and of course, Abigail.

"Why don't you come with me, Mother, to my Aggregation meeting next week? You could talk with some of the women and get a feel for the energy of the group."

"I'm sure I have a Preserve Domesticity meeting that night."

"If you joined me, I think it would help you understand how exciting it is to be a young woman right now. Opportunities to have a voice and dreams are gathering steam by the day."

"Such obsession with *your* needs and desires is selfish, Kate. Mothers and ladies should always put themselves second to the needs of their children, husband, and the proper maintenance of the home."

"Ugh. I give up."

"Your tone, Kate."

"I'm ending the call, Mother."

The box immediately shut down. A tiny spark hung suspended for a moment, then vanished.

"I'm very glad you did, Kate," Belle said aloud.

On the floor, she rolled onto her back and looked up at the ceiling. Would she and her mother have bickered? Did Eva love gardening, too? Mothers spending time with their daughters around town often caught Belle's eye. She'd watch a woman rock her baby girl in her arms, making loving little clicking noises down toward the blanket. Or she'd see a mother and her hip-high daughter holding hands, the young girl gazing up at her beloved mama. To Belle, the bond between the two always seemed tender and unbreakable.

"Why did you have to die?" she said softly.

Belle closed her eyes and imagined creating fragrant bouquets with her mother, the two of them laughing, both with their favorite bloom tucked behind an ear.

•••

The freshly painted white schoolhouse served a variety of purposes—educating children, monthly debates about town business, performances by the Fort Myers Theatrical Troupe. What never changed was the presence of a life-size wooden pineapple, chiseled by Mr. Ritter to represent the town seal. It commanded a prominent position in the room no matter what activity was under way.

On this afternoon, the schoolhouse accommodated the first gathering of a potential club with no name. Wooden chairs were configured in a circle, only one of the seven still empty. Abigail would be stopping by, but not sitting with the group.

"We're waiting on Hazel Cravin," Belle said quietly. She glanced again at the door.

To her right was Sadie Tillis, nursing a baby on her large, half-concealed breast. One of two wet nurses in town, Sadie always had a tiny heart beating next to hers. Over the years, Belle often helped her in Duggan's, amazed that the woman could think straight about what she needed while her five children grabbed at her skirt or touched something she'd warned them to leave alone.

"That busted bell has a lot of people running late these days." Poppy Peck smiled and placed her ever-present Bible under her chair. Someone had crocheted a cover for it featuring a white cross on a background of spring flowers. She was married to Mitchell Peck, the longtime pastor of Fort Myers's Methodist Church.

Next to Poppy was Amelia Polk, who owned the town's apothecary. Drugstores and boardinghouses were fair game for women who wanted to own businesses. Like Abigail to Baker's, Amelia was married to Polk's and no one else. Her face was striking, but not in a pleasant way. Everything but her nose read like an upside-down crescent moon. Her eyes and mouth frowned, and her skin was dragged downward by gravity's mean streak. Ironically, Belle found Amelia to be one of the happiest, friendliest people in town.

"It's curious how much we rely on that bell, isn't it?" Paulette York's voice had its own bell-like quality, sonorous and pleasing. You wanted to listen to her for hours and look at her even longer.

"My house is so noisy all the time," Sadie said, "I never even hear that bell." She chuckled and tried to rock a chair with no rails.

"Why are we here?" Alice Bishop blurted out, staring at the stuffed animal she held as if she'd asked *it* the question.

Belle had never heard Alice's voice. She'd often wheeled by the girl, who looked in age about nineteen, but had never spoken to her. Talk around town was that Alice was a bit off—perhaps mentally afflicted—because she wandered the streets talking mostly to cows and other animals that crossed her path. The worst way Belle overheard someone describing Alice was "a dandelion seed head with some of the parasols blown off." Alice often carried furred or feathered stuffed creatures, and the critter she currently cradled featured the body of a rabbit and the head of a roseate spoonbill. Her father owned the town's taxidermy shop and often practiced "botched" taxidermy. Belle could only imagine what it was like to live around the smell of soured salt, gamy guts, and the relentless buzz of a thousand feeding flies. That would be enough to make anyone seem "a bit off."

"A good question, Alice. I'd like to wait for Hazel, though," Belle said. "Let's give her another minute or two."

The door opened as if on Belle's cue, but it was Abigail who entered, not Hazel.

"Afternoon, ladies. Refreshments have arrived." Abigail walked to the center of the chairs and slowly turned in a circle, holding a tray of assorted sandwiches.

"I see mine," Alice said, and took what appeared to be roast beef between a biscuit from the pile.

Abigail greeted each of the women as she spun.

"Sadie, I'll bet you could use a nap, too," she said, eyeing the drowsy baby.

"Howdy do, Amelia?"

When she got to Belle, she handed her a sandwich layered with smoked turkey. "Your favorite, my dear."

Once Abigail stepped to the side and set the tray on a table, Belle addressed the group. "Abigail kindly agreed to provide snacks for this meeting, and if we decide to have more, for those as well."

The ladies lightly clapped, aside from Alice, who got up for a second sandwich.

Abigail had left the door to the schoolhouse open, allowing Ida to charge through it, followed by Hazel holding out her postcard like a ticket. Abigail looked at Belle, who lightly shook her head.

"To what do we owe the pleasure, Cravins?" Abigail asked, moving forward and placing her hands on Belle's shoulders.

"We received a postcard from Belle inviting us to this meeting," Ida said, sizing up the room. "We're late because no one will take it upon themselves to fix that broken bell."

Poppy smiled. "Lord knows, Ida, it's not for lack of desire. Seems our townsfolk would rather spend money to improve our sandy streets than fix our bell."

Abigail chimed in. "We know how hard you pushed for shelled surfaces, Ida. Remember the last town meeting?"

Hazel looked down at the floor, her perfect blonde curls dangling. A stiff red bow sat atop her head, as if she were a child, not a twenty-four-year-old woman.

Belle was certain she'd addressed the postcard to Hazel only. "I . . . um . . . don't have enough chairs. I was only expecting Hazel."

As Ida moved to drag another chair into the circle, Amelia piped up.

"I'm normally a more-the-merrier gal, Ida, but as Belle said, she invited Hazel."

Ida crossed her arms. She looked in disdain at Alice and then into the glass eyes of the stuffed spoonbill. "Well, it appears you're including everyone and every . . . thing . . . in your little group."

Abigail wrapped a sandwich in a napkin and moved toward Ida. "Please enjoy this treat on your way out, Ida. We'll take good care of Hazel." She put her hand on the doorframe and held out the sandwich.

Ida pinched her eyes nearly shut and twisted swiftly away from the group, her long skirt swishing. Without a single goodbye, she pushed away Abigail's offering and left. Abigail quickly shut the door behind her.

Hazel remained standing in place.

"Please join us, Hazel," said Paulette. She swept her hand across the seat next to her, as if to clear it and the room of anything unpleasant. Hazel sat and pointed to her name only written on the postcard.

"Of course," Paulette said softly.

"Ladies, I've left the snacks on the table and will pick them up whenever you finish," Abigail announced. "As I told Belle, I'm just not good being at rest, even for an hour. If you'll have me, I'll be the member who cooks for the club."

"I'll make you a member of my *family* if you cook for my brood," Sadie joked.

Everyone chuckled. Gratitude ushered Abigail out and all eyes turned to Belle.

She cleared her throat. "So. I, um. I'm curious about thoughts you may have." She shifted in her seat. "I have an idea about why we should gather, but I'd like to know what all of you think." She sat for a moment and hoped someone would speak. No one did. The baby burped, which made everyone laugh.

"Finally!" Sadie said. "My patter was getting sore."

Paulette spoke next. "Well, my sister in Chicago is in a women's club. She's mailed me minutes from their meetings. They talk about projects that could beautify the city or help children in need." She smiled, her white teeth perfectly aligned. "I never thought I'd have the chance to be a part of something similar. But that may not be what you have in mind, Belle."

"That could certainly work here, Paulette," Belle said, jotting down notes.

"Why did you include me?" Alice asked. She was dressed, as always, in men's trousers, a blouse, and alligator boots, perhaps handmade by her father. She kept her hair short. Belle had seen her exit the barbershop more than once.

Hazel perked up, as if wondering why she, too, received a postcard.

"Well, I suppose because you seem to have quite a connection with our town's four-leggeds." Belle tilted her head slightly. "I sense that you're kind. I'd like to get to know you better."

Alice just shrugged.

When Sadie saw Belle's eyes move to her, she said, "I don't care why you invited me, Belle. I'm just glad to be out of that damn house!"

The ladies laughed, and Poppy held up her hand to the heavens. "Amen!" she said. She and her husband had raised four children.

"Seems to me," Belle explained, "that the wisdom of a wife and mother could be of value to us."

Paulette said, "And, I'd be curious to know what both Sadie and Poppy think about the women in my sister's club who say that wanting more out of life does *not* make an inferior mother."

Poppy laid open her palms. "More of what? While you're raising your children and tending to your home—and serving the Lord—you can't imagine finding the energy for anything more."

Sadie nodded. "More comes *after* the children." She shook her head. "But, who am I kidding? With five little ones, my more is never coming."

Belle smiled and turned to Amelia. "Instead of having a family, you chose to start your own business, Amelia."

"I know. What was I thinking?" Amelia said, knocking her knuckles on her head.

The women laughed.

"I do love it," Amelia said. "My drugstore is like my child, I suppose." She paused. "I sure do wish the bottles could grow up and help with my chores, though."

Sadie chuckled and spoke to the baby. "Rest up while you can, little one." She looked up. "This one's mother is upset that she's dry, that she can't feed her baby." She shrugged. "I suggested she worry less and sleep more. She's got a long road of mothering ahead."

"When *does* it stop?" Hazel asked, her voice a surprise in the room. "The mothering . . ."

All heads turned toward Hazel. She was wearing a green silk dress with a yellow sash and white socks that led to black shoes, shiny, with a strap. Belle was certain her mother gave Hazel the once-over before they left the house. In younger years, Belle often saw Ida marching down the street with Hazel in tow. One particular day, she'd heard Ida's loudly delivered instructions to her daughter.

"Hold tight to your doll, Hazel," Ida had said in front of the Abbotts' house, the yard dotted with Seminoles. "It appears the Abbotts have attracted savages. *Again.*" Hazel hugged her toy to her chest and parroted her mother's tone. *"Again."*

Having grown up with parents who paid her little attention, Belle couldn't imagine Hazel's day-to-day life with a mother who seemed to consider it her duty to raise a person in her exact image.

"What are you talking about?" Alice said.

Hazel crossed her arms and sighed. "It doesn't matter."

"Of course it does, dear," Sadie said. "We're all familiar with Ida's . . . way."

Hazel stared into her lap. "I shouldn't have said it."

Poppy offered, "We can and should listen without judgment, Hazel." She held up a finger. "'Judge not, and ye shall not be judged.'"

"Maybe next time," Hazel said. "We'll see."

Next time. Belle sat up straighter. There would be a next time? Her idea for a club may have taken hold. Her heart raced with excitement.

"To be heard is a gift, isn't it?" Belle said. "My hope for the club is that we can share ideas and speak freely." She saw that several of the women were nodding.

Poppy sat to Belle's left, rubbing a kneecap. The years had been kind to her, a woman in her early sixties whose only signs of aging were weak knees, perhaps the result of frequent praying on hard wooden rails.

"Poppy, I was a member of the church growing up," Belle said, "but as you've surely noticed, I haven't attended for years."

For Belle, church was every time she set foot in nature, not a building. To watch a monarch butterfly draw nectar from a pink milkweed blossom with its thread-thin proboscis was proof enough for her that a gentle and artistic creator existed.

"It has been a while, hasn't it," Poppy said, smiling. She folded her hands in her lap, as if sending up a prayer for her.

Belle continued, "We know your faith is strong." She paused. "I could use some guidance and perhaps we all could. For me, forgiveness comes to mind."

Amelia nodded. "That's a tough nut."

Poppy offered a warm smile. "'For if ye forgive men their trespasses, your heavenly Father will also forgive you,'" she recited. "The Bible is filled with verses about forgiveness. For eons, people have wrestled with letting go of anger and pain. There's much to discuss."

Belle turned toward Paulette. Tall and curvaceous, the twenty-seven-year-old wore her fiery red hair long with fashionable bangs. She'd been crowned Miss Tampa years earlier and last year received stellar reviews for her lead role in the local troupe's stage rendition of *Lady Audley's Secret.* Her multiple engagements followed by disengagements were fodder for much speculation about why she wasn't yet married. Trying to argue that it was no one's business was futile in a town as small as Fort Myers.

"Paulette, you seem very comfortable in front of a crowd." Belle placed her palm on her chest and shook her head. "Even with all eyes on you . . ."

Recrossing her long legs, Paulette smiled. "I've been blessed to share what I love to do." She paused. "Honestly, though, I would like to contribute *off* the stage, too." She pointed to the wooden pineapple atop the teacher's desk. "I'm expected to do only that—stand tall and wear a crown."

Belle nodded. "Noted. If you'd like, we can discuss more ideas on how we might contribute . . . as a club."

"Anything but tackle the cow plop problem," Amelia joked.

Alice giggled. "They are good at it, aren't they?"

"Will others be allowed to join the club?" Hazel swept a palm over her skirt, straightening a fold.

"Well, I'm not sure," Belle said. "Maybe we can decide together."

Hazel raised her hand with a bent elbow. "I would vote to leave the group as it is."

All the women—but one—agreed.

Alice made her odd stuffed animal hop, then fly. "It's easy to close off a group once you're in it, isn't it."

The room stayed silent until Amelia offered, "Well, why don't we keep the option open to other women, but never for Ida?"

Alice said, "Agreed."

Hazel pulled on a curl. "Thank you."

Sadie rebundled the cooing baby in its blanket. "I've enjoyed this but I need to go, ladies. Virgil may be hog-tied to the kitchen table. Our little cherubs are also hoodlums." She stood and bounced the bundle. "Belle, thank you for inviting me. Let me know if there's another meeting. I'll be there."

"Thank you, Sadie," Belle said. She then addressed the remaining women. "So, are we in agreement that a second meeting should happen?"

A yes resounded from all.

Belle popped up off her seat, thrilled her idea was well received. "All right, ladies. I'll drop off postcards with details about next time." She scanned her notes. "We'll talk more about our club's purpose, oh . . . and we'll need a name."

As the women stood and headed for the door, Alice suggested, "How about the Circle Club?" She pointed to the empty chairs.

The women agreed, and with that, Belle had introduced a big-city movement to her small, sun-kissed town.

•••

Boone had replaced a small section of lumber that wood roaches had devoured on the Edison home. He was coating it for a second time with yellow paint. The late-afternoon breeze was light and dry—good conditions for brushwork. He smiled when he spotted Belle walking toward him at a brisk pace from across the yard. She began to skip on her final steps toward him. He hadn't yet seen her so carefree.

"Hello, Boone."

"Hello there, Belle." He put down the brush and stood to properly greet her.

"I'd like to take you up on your offer to go for a sail."

Boone smiled. Several surprises, all at once. He silently cursed the day's weather—perfect for painting, horrible for sailing. "A sail sounds wonderful, Belle." He put a finger in the air. "But I'm afraid we'd have to use oars today." He paused. "No wind."

"Oh yes. Of course," she said. "Of course we need more wind." She spun in a circle, holding her dress out on both sides. "Does this help?" She giggled as she continued to spin, her long hair extended like the mane of a horse at full run.

Boone half hoped she'd take a dizzy fall so he could catch her. They laughed together until she stopped.

"When the wind finds its spirit again, we'll sail," Boone said. He grabbed her elbow to steady her as she stumbled slightly. Her skin was soft and warm.

"All right, then," she said. "We'll wait for the wind."

As he watched her walk away toward Baker's, Boone's resolve to deny his desire lessened.

•••

At Duggan's, Merle was dragging heavy bushel baskets from the porch into the store, each *thump* on the threshold the sound of closing time. Whiskey was waiting on the counter next to his evening cigar, potato wedges sizzled in a skillet. When the produce was safely tucked in for the night, he began sweeping the day's dust and debris off the porch slats and stairs. Eager to relax after a busy day, he dismissed the oddity of a small pile of winged insects on the top step. With a flick of the broom, he launched the stack of dead dragonflies onto the ground.

•••

River Street was dark and deserted but for two drunk men fake fighting and laughing between throaty grunts. Each had a whiskey bottle clutched in his armpit. The awkward grappling led them off the street and onto someone's property, where a garden had been freshly fertilized. When one man gave the other a hard shove, he tumbled backward onto a slat of an unfinished fence, his bulk snapping the board in half.

"Oww," groaned the downed man. "Ass."

The other stumbled over to him. "You're the jackass." He poured whiskey down onto the man's shoes. Attempting to step over the low fence, he clipped his boot and fell forward to the ground with a thud.

A clumsy roll brought the other man right next to his friend. He whistled toward the starless sky. "You stink, Frank."

Frank belched and rolled onto his back. "This whole town stinks."

"Well, Franky," said the other man, "you play your cowboy games, and I'll settle some . . . business." He paused to sip whiskey, which dribbled down his stubbled chin. "Then, we'll go back to Tampa, where it smells like cigars, not cow shit." He grabbed at the ground, gathering a fistful of muck. He launched the smelly clump onto Frank.

"Damn you." Frank sunk both hands into the moist ground.

In the early morning darkness, the men engaged in a muck war. Before sunrise, the reeking pair staggered back to the Palms Hotel.

Chapter 11

The following afternoon, in a rowdy crowd of horsemen, Boone stood close to Belle. Cowboys beside them were shoving each other in jest, one falling into Boone, who shoved him back into the scrum. Belle was glad to have him by her side. Blevins Park was full of out-of-towners, mostly scruffy men in spurred boots and similar states of drunkenness.

Nearby, the Fort Myers Band was playing a march, but Merle and Abigail danced as if a spirited waltz were under way.

"Spin, my gal!"

Merle twirled Abigail, stout but agile as she rotated effortlessly below his raised arm. Belle watched, imagining their dance ending with a passionate kiss. Merle would dip Abigail halfway to the ground and pull the pin from her bun, creating a waterfall of wavy hair. Their lips would meet until the music stopped. Boone's voice ended Belle's make-believe scene.

"I think they're about to start," he said, pointing toward some commotion at the far end of the park.

The four had met up to watch the annual Knights of the Scrub Tournament. Cow hunters from all over the region traveled to Fort Myers to compete in the unique tournament that tested a rider's coordination and strength. A contestant would storm across the park, carrying a "lance," a long piece of lumber donated by Ritter's Mill. The goal was to race at top speed and knock coconuts off tree stumps placed around the park. The lumber was heavy, and most riders failed to clear all ten stumps. Excessive drinking made the event even more outlandish. Last year, the newspaper reported that intoxicated cowmen lowered an unconscious contestant into a freshly dug grave in the cemetery.

"We welcome to the start line: the Knight of the Spittoon." *Press* editor Stephen Fitzgerald's hands were cupped around his mouth as he shouted across the park. He served every year as tournament announcer and took great pride in dreaming up silly names for each "knight."

While Merle and Abigail stayed near the band to help with a booth offering hand pies and coffee, Boone and Belle found a shady spot under a wild cinnamon tree with a good view of the riders, the first under way. She spotted Augie sitting next to Mr. Fitzgerald and also noted her replacement at Duggan's, ten-year-old Henry Metzger, who proudly donned his father's captain's cap, too big and tilted to the starboard side of his head. As the first rider crossed the finish line, the town's saloon owner walked by with a tray full of free whiskey shots.

"I'll pass," Boone said.

"That ride's not going to be good enough," Belle noted after counting six downed coconuts. Last year's winner had cleared eight stumps.

"Our next contestant," boomed the announcer, "is the Knight of the Pickled Beet!"

Amused by the nickname, Belle looked up at Boone and grinned. All around them, people clapped and let loose high-pitched whistles. Belle applauded, too. The rider removed his straw hat and circled it in the air, around and around, pumping up the crowd.

Suddenly, Belle stopped clapping. The noise around her began to fade. She shielded her eyes from the sun and squinted at the rider. Could it be? She hadn't seen him in eleven years, but . . .

Frank.

With the hat removed, she now recognized the rider as Frank Dolland, a childhood friend of Julius's. She despised them both. As youngsters they would point out how obvious it was to everyone that she was adopted: her brunette hair to Julius's flaxen, her wiry body to his bulk. Frank made up stories about how her mother died—wild tales that ranged from Seminole squaws roasting her on a spit to teams of alligators feasting on her from head to toe. Frank had relocated to Tampa not long after Julius moved there more than a decade ago. She hadn't seen either of them since nor ever heard word they were back in town.

As Frank thundered across the park atop a stocky pinto, Belle scanned the cheering crowd. Her line of sight was obstructed by people jumping up and down or waving palm fronds in the air. Familiar faces mixed with those of strangers, all focused on the knight firing off coconuts like hairy cannonballs. Belle crossed her arms, no longer relaxed or enjoying the event.

Frank raced across the finish line and threw his lance to the ground, apparently frustrated at his low coconut count. A man in a suit approached the rider, his back toward Belle, and handed Frank a shot of whiskey. They bumped fists. Belle's stomach flipped. *Oh dear God.* She'd witnessed that move countless times. She shrunk down slightly and began to shake.

"Are you all right, Belle?" Boone lightly placed his palm on the small of her back.

Belle flinched at his touch. She sidestepped away from him and continued to shield herself from the rider's view. Then, she leaned in and wrung her hands. Gradually, from behind a thick cloud of white cigar smoke, the face she hoped to never see again emerged, as Julius turned around to grab Frank another shot.

"I need to leave," Belle said, her mouth dry. "I don't feel well."

She turned and darted through the crowd. Somehow Belle's rubbery legs were powering her forward. Maybe she was floating, rising quickly so the Past couldn't grab her ankle and yank her down to the floor of a musty shack. She exploded out of the throng and onto the street, slowing to a brisk walk in the direction of her cottage.

"Belle!"

She closed her eyes at the sound of Boone's voice. *Please go away,* she thought.

He caught up to her, breathing hard. "What's wrong? Do you need help?"

She shook her head. "I just need to lie down. Thank you."

"Should I come by and check on you in a while?"

You're too late, Belle thought. "Please don't. I just need to rest." She thanked him again and scurried along, eventually reaching the cottage where she shut both windows and barred the door.

She flopped down in the corner farthest from the door and welcomed Coquina into her lap. The cat was warm and purred with a soothing rumble. She tried to blink it away, but the wretched image of Julius—his eyes half-shut, his jaw hanging open—wouldn't disappear. In the quiet of the cottage she heard him panting and whispering.

You're a hideous, stupid, smelly orphan. No one else will ever want to do this to you. You're lucky I'm willing.

Her stomach lurched, churning with a jolt of acid.

"I hate you," she growled.

Hideous, stupid, smelly orphan. Why had she thought for a moment that Boone could ever one day care for her? Memories of Julius's yellow teeth and fat fingers flashed through her mind.

Belle slammed both fists on the floor, launching the cat from her lap. If she hurried, she could put a few more miles between Julius and her young self.

The beaches of Sanibel were quiet but for the waves and seabirds vying for fish and the loudest call. The crescent-shaped barrier island was twelve miles long, dotted with twenty-one homes, population ninety. Settlers had requested for years that the United States government construct a lighthouse on Point Ybel, the eastern tip of the island and the entrance to San Carlos Bay. They hoped, through light, to draw passersby and trade to Sanibel. Finally, Congress allocated funds to construct one, a pyramid-shaped iron skeleton tower with an interior spiral staircase. The lighthouse was crowned at ninety-eight feet by a lantern room featuring a kerosene lamp that produced a fixed white light, interrupted every two minutes by a robust flash.

Belle had caught the one o'clock mail boat to Sanibel and was walking barefoot along the beach near the lighthouse. Her boots hung around her neck, tied together by their laces. The breeze was cool, the sun welcome. She'd left her straw hat at home and instead tied a strip of fabric around her forehead. Her hair was loose but kept in check by the headband.

At that very moment, Julius was somewhere in Blevins Park. Seeing him was so unexpected that she hoped maybe it hadn't really been him. But she knew it was. In an instant, she'd recognized his close-set eyes, crooked nose, and crossed front teeth. That ugly face—she'd tried to erase it and everything about him from her thoughts, but still, images of him remained crouched in the dark corners of her mind. She sighed and looked down the beach, no end in sight. Somewhere off in the distance, her young self was heading toward her, trailed by bad memories.

Walking slowly, Belle began to revisit the terrifying trips to an abandoned fish shack near a creek that ran along the western edge of Fort Myers. Julius would tell her it was time to fetch sawdust from the lumber mill or to check on a bridle under repair at the harness and shoe shop, the ever-helpful son. Always, though, he took her first to the shack. In the summer it smelled like moss and mud. In the winter, fish. Her mouth twisted in disgust as both scents came back to her.

On the first trip, Julius told her that it was her job in the family to do this, and if she didn't, she would have no family, no food, and nowhere to sleep. With each repulsive visit, the shack experiences became more involved. Julius would shove her to her knees and threaten her, warning about a panther that would attack her if she told anyone about the shack. He claimed the yellow cats could smell tattletales and were always hunting for them. By nine, she learned to displace herself during the trips. She'd imagine lying down in a field of blooming wildflowers, weeds like her that had discovered their beauty. Then, the truth would return with the sound of his grunts.

She stopped for a moment in front of two wooden keeper houses built atop iron pilings. *Where were my keepers?* A gust of ocean breeze fluttered the ties of her headband. All alone, she'd endured the physical and mental torments inflicted by Julius. Of course, looking back, he was manipulating her with his threats, but one in particular had stuck with her through the years. Quietly, she spoke.

"No man will ever want you."

Admittedly, part of her believed that. She wanted so badly to completely dismiss the idea, to finally fight it off for good like she had Julius. Closing her eyes, she thought back to that stormy night. Fourteen years old, she was asleep on the floor of the Carsons' living room. Heavy rain hammering the roof had kept her awake, but she'd finally fallen asleep. Then, suddenly, a sweaty palm covered her mouth.

Belle winced and opened her eyes. Peeping sandpipers zipped and zagged across the sand in front of her.

Her heart pounded as she remembered details of the seconds that changed her life. Julius hadn't attacked in several years and had rarely ever done so in the house. But that night, he'd kneeled beside her and covered her mouth, his face inches above hers. She stared up at him, shocked and incensed that he'd expected to take from her yet again. As he grabbed at her nightdress, she sunk her finger-nails into one of his cheeks and slammed her fist into the other. He reeled backward but with a swift move smashed his arm across her face, launching her onto the hearth. She scrambled for a fire poker and swung it as hard as she could, landing a blow on his ribs as he lunged toward her. He cried out in pain as she dashed out the front door into driving rain and darkness. As fast as she could, she ran through the storm in the direction of Duggan's.

Belle dug her toes into the sand. She *had* beaten back Julius once and for all, with the merciful help of Merle. Now, she and Julius were adults and he couldn't hurt her. The sight of him had unnerved her, but as she thought back on the strength she'd found as a girl, it was clearly time for her, as a grown woman, to break free from the ugly words of a disturbed boy. She looked out across the Gulf, cupped her hands around her mouth, and yelled.

"You're wrong! You are wrooooong!" She screamed until her lungs ran out of air, her throat raw. "You are nooobody!"

Coughing, Belle flopped down onto the beach. Slowly, she dropped her body back onto the soft sand and stretched her arms out to her sides. The cool surf licked at her hand. She rolled her head sideways to watch as a small heron stepped near her. Its head jerked at odd angles, trying to swallow a green anole wriggling in its beak, the battle nearly over.

"I'm somebody," she whispered. "I'm somebody . . ." She kept saying it, grabbing handfuls of beach on either side of her. Small, shiny coquina clams burrowed back down into the wet sand she'd disturbed.

When the tears began, Belle realized why she came to Sanibel, who she came to be near. She imagined her mother's body buried directly below where she lay right then.

"Are you here somewhere, Mama?" she said quietly. "I'm right here."

Belle wrapped her sandy arms around herself and hugged her ribs. Slowly, she curled up into a ball, lying sideways, facing the turquoise sea. Tears rolled down her cheeks, dripping onto the sand to join an outgoing wave.

•••

After the Knights' tournament, Julius and Frank strutted around Billy's Saloon, boasting about their "major role" in Tampa's booming cigar industry. Julius pulled gold doubloons from both pockets of his striped, spike-tailed coat and bought shots for locals and strangers alike. Both smoked several cigars, dipping the tips in whiskey before puffing each to life.

Irwin and Collette sat at the bar, discussing the highlights of their visit to Fort Myers and offering toasts.

"To the sunset-pink flamingos," Irwin said.

"Just extraordinary," Collette agreed. "To Abigail's heavenly biscuits."

Irwin nodded. "And to all the fine people we've met at Baker's."

"Oh, so true, dear. George and his sweet son, Professor Ricalton, and that lovely Belle Carson. I told her what a wonderful job she's done, decorating the porch of her little cottage in the backyard."

Standing behind the couple, Julius threw back the last of his drink. He stumbled toward the door while Frank continued drinking on the opposite side of the saloon.

Chapter 12

The evening was eye-catching, the sky a moody mix of pink and purple fighting for dominance. Belle watched the battle from her bed. Slipping both arms under the covers, she listened to the soothing coos of mourning doves. The breeze smelled of pine straw and honeysuckle. She yawned, exhausted. Seeing that face had rattled her deeply. She'd hoped to never again be anywhere near Julius once he'd left town at twenty-two. Still, as draining as it was to see him, the jolt had made her rethink the notion that he could limit her, stop her from exploring the many opportunities unfolding before her. She was a capable woman now, not a powerless little girl. When the sky finally turned black, Belle closed her eyes and fell into a deep sleep for hours.

Then, an explosion. The cottage door came crashing open. The board that braced it shut split in half, spitting shards of cypress across the floor. Coquina flew off the bed to the half-open window and sprang out into the night.

Terrified, Belle sat up in bed and froze, her hands clutching the covers. The silhouette of a large man was framed in the open door. He stumbled toward her, his hat crooked, an empty bottle of whiskey dangling from two fingers. It dropped to the floor with a thud as the man fell forward onto Belle.

The blow from his heavy body knocked the wind out of her. She gasped for air just before the man clamped his large palm over her mouth. A scream was trapped in her windpipe as she drew in oxygen through her nostrils. The man's bulk immobilized Belle's legs but not her arms. She beat and slapped the intruder's ears and head, managing only to knock off his hat. He seemed oblivious to the blows. With his free hand, the man began to grab at Belle's nightclothes. When his fingers found skin, he began to moan.

That's when she smelled it. With one whiff, Belle's level of fear tripled. The potent scent of alcohol was overpowered by the unmistakable and unforgettable sour-mash-and-rotting-onions odor of Julius. Adrenaline surged through her body. She grabbed his hair and lifted up his head, punching his face with as much force as she could muster in her pinned position. He glared at her with bloodshot eyes. With a clumsy sweeping motion, he drew back his arm and smashed Belle across the face.

When she regained consciousness, Julius was still on top of her, snoring deeply. Her head throbbed. As quickly as her aching body would allow, she extended her right arm toward the bedside table. With shaking fingers she reached underneath the drawer, pushed up from the bottom, and pulled it open. Whatever was forming this plan, she stayed out of its way. Rage, fear, revenge— *get on with it.*

Mumbling something, Julius drooled on her shoulder. Belle kept her body still while her fingers frantically searched for the skinning knife, her nails scratching the bottom of the drawer. When she finally located the knife, she plucked it out by its blade. Carefully, she worked her fingers toward the wooden handle, then gripped it tightly. She inhaled and, with one swift jab, drove the knife into her attacker's greasy, beefy neck.

Julius groaned loudly and stiffened. Three more times she thrust the knife into his neck, twisting the handle on the last blow.

His dense body finally went limp. With no idea whether he was dead or unconscious, she pried herself out from under him.

Dazed and drained, Belle stood in the cottage, shaking uncontrollably. She forced herself to move. Feeling her way around the dresser, she located the pie pan with a candle stuck to it. It took her three tries to light a match, but with trembling fingers she touched it to the wick. The light revealed that her chest was covered in blood, her hair moist with it. Terrified, Belle tried to make a plan. The conch shell on the dresser caught her eye, so she grabbed it and hurried out the door, holding the candle, too.

When the fence between the Baker and Edison properties ended at the riverbank, she slipped around it and headed toward the long wharf. Halfway along it, Belle set down the candle and blew into the conch shell toward Boone's boat. She assumed he kept guns on board and didn't want to startle him. Out of breath, she waited several seconds before firing off another blast on the shell.

When Boone appeared on the boat's upper deck, she hurried down the dock and looked up at him.

"It's Belle," she said, shivering. "I need your help."

•••

"Of course," Boone said. "Where?"

She pointed toward the cottage.

"Wait right there. I need to grab my revolver from the boat."

When he returned, the pair walked briskly back to the cottage. With his Colt .45 drawn, Boone entered through the busted door, Belle staying close to his side. A large man lying motionless on the bed was the obvious source of blood on the floor and on Belle. His hat and a bottle lay on the floor. Boone walked to the bed and, with his free hand, touched the intact side of the man's neck.

After several seconds, he looked over at Belle. "He's dead."

She collapsed to the floor and wept into her hands. Boone went to her and sat down. He laid aside the gun and draped his arm around her shaking shoulders. She leaned her head against his chest and sobbed. They sat side by side until she quieted.

Boone asked softly, "Belle, does this man need to disappear?"

She vigorously nodded yes.

He stood and helped her up from the floor. "I'm going to wrap him up in these bedsheets and drag him to the river."

She nodded again and turned to face the wall while Boone cleaned up the mess.

"Belle, I need you to give me your gown. I'm going to turn around. Let me know when you're dressed again."

He heard the dresser drawer open. In less than a minute, Belle said softly, "Done." He turned and took the soiled gown from her, adding it to the rolled linens.

Belle plugged her ears as Boone dragged the body across the floor and out the door into the moonless night.

As he pulled the heavy load, it dug a deep trough in the sand, slowing his journey toward the river. Once there, he dropped the end of the long roll with a *thunk*. He took a quick break, breathing hard, hands on his hips. Who was this rat? Would Abigail need to know what had happened? He knelt down and began to push on the roll. Nothing else mattered right now. The heels of his boots dug into the sand as he strained to move the man toward his watery grave. Once momentum cooperated, the roll easily spun down the bank and into the water. The splash was brief and minimal. He exhaled, relieved the evidence would now be concealed. Boone watched the wrapped body sink. The black moon stayed hidden as the river quietly swallowed up the last of the secret he now shared with Belle.

•••

When Boone returned, Belle was sweeping up debris on the floor. She hadn't washed her face or hair. A bloody knife lay on the bedside table.

"Stay here for a few minutes, Belle. I'll be right back with tools to fix the door."

She squeezed the broom handle. "Can I come with you?"

"Of course," Boone said. He chided himself for suggesting she stay by herself any longer.

Aboard the boat, Belle sat on deck while Boone gathered what he needed below. He returned with a sack of tools, a cloth, and a towel jammed into a bucket.

"Let's get your hair washed."

He helped her lie down on the deck and lean her head over the side of the boat. Her long hair dangled close to the still water. Boone scooped the bucket into the river and gently poured water over her hair, running his fingers through the ends to clear the blood. He repeated the process several times. Using a damp cloth, he lightly washed her face, careful to avoid touching the swollen area. He gave her the towel to wrap up her hair.

They slowly and silently walked back to the cottage by candlelight. Once inside, Boone began to repair the half-hinged door as quietly as possible, even though the cottage was quite far from the boardinghouse. He made fast work of it.

"The lock bar is in good shape now; it's very secure." He knew the fix was too little, too late but wanted to comfort Belle.

She was on all fours, washing blood from the floor. He walked over, knelt down, and took the rag from her.

"Let me do that."

As Boone scrubbed the wooden boards and cleaned the knife, Belle sat cross-legged on the floor and rested her head in her hands. He covered the bare mattress with two extra blankets, the pillow with a fabric remnant. Once he closed the window, he sat down across from her.

"Do you want me to stay with you until morning, Belle?"

"Please," she said, and removed the towel from her head. Wet hair spilled down around her shoulders. He watched her run her fingers through it and create a thick side braid. She touched her throbbing cheek.

"He hurt me for so long."

Boone tensed. "Belle, you don't need to tell me *anything*."

"I just killed a man, Boone."

"A man who broke into your cottage and, from what I see, brutally attacked you."

"Yes, he did. But that's not the only reason I killed him."

Boone stayed silent.

"That man is Julius Carson. I grew up with his family because my mother died when I was born. For much of my childhood he did . . . unspeakable things to me." Her hands drew together and linked fingers. "His depravity found me convenient." She looked away. "He just kept getting away with it."

He watched her eyes, looking beyond him. He hated where she must be and drew her back quietly. "Not anymore, Belle."

Neither talked until she continued with her story.

"I finally got away from him when I was fourteen. Merle took me in. Julius moved away, and I never saw him again . . . until the tournament."

Boone blanched, stunned and disgusted by the real reason she'd left the park so abruptly. She wasn't sick; she was terrified. Had he known who Julius was and what he'd done to Belle, he would have beaten him to within an inch of his life and dragged him to Sheriff Clark. Boone clenched his jaw. The man he'd rolled into the river deserved more than a knife to the neck.

"I'm very sorry, Belle." He shuddered at the thought of her horror when she realized who had smashed his way into the cottage.

She rubbed her neck and sat quietly for a minute. In a soft voice, she said, "I've always wanted to kill him, Boone. I've done it in my head a hundred times in a hundred different ways."

He scooted closer to her and took her hands. "Yes. He deserved it. He was overdue for it." He waited until she looked into his eyes. "You're very brave, Belle."

She squeezed his hands and looked down. "I'm glad he's dead. God help me for saying it, but it's the truth."

"No one will ever know." He reached up and placed his palm on her unharmed cheek. "It never happened."

She leaned into his touch. "I don't want to burden you with this secret."

He offered the slightest grin. "I've got some of my own. What's one more?"

She sighed. "But nothing could be worse than what I've done."

He sat back and chewed on his lower lip. "I shot a man when I lived in Kissimmee. He died."

She tilted her head. "And no one found out?"

"Only my parents." He tapped the floor with a finger. "I left home after it happened and found work here."

"Well, your secret's safe with me." She rubbed her eyes with both hands.

"Would you like to rest, Belle?" He wasn't sure if the bed was an option she could stomach.

"I guess I'll try."

He stood and gingerly helped her up. She walked to the bed and sat on it.

"What about you?"

Boone pointed at the rocking chair. "My boat rocks me to sleep every night. This will do just fine."

She swung her legs up onto the bed and lay back. "Thank you, Boone."

"I'll be right here."

He blew out the candles and settled into the chair.

Chapter 13

The broad, deep puddles in the yard the next morning surprised Belle. She must have slept through a heavy rainstorm. Boone's presence last night, three feet away, had allowed her to consider sleep. She'd expected to get none at all, her mind and body vaporized. How could she, as a vapor, fall asleep? But she did. Thankfully, a new day came all the faster for it.

Through the cottage window she could see Abigail's youngest current boarder, Jamison. Several days ago, when she asked him in the kitchen how old he was, he stuck out his right palm, all fingers up. Now he was playing with a red wooden sailboat in a large puddle beside the vegetable garden. She'd noticed the toy boat in the shed and wondered if Boone built it for Abigail's youngest guests. How sweet Jamison looked with his bedhead hair and bungled buttons on his shirt, a welcome sight for her tormented mind churning through the horror of last night. She hoped her brain would cycle through it all, somehow. All she wanted right then was to be out of the cottage, moving through the first day of her life without a monster in it.

Righting a blown-over porch plant, Belle headed down the steps to say hello to the sailor. He was barefoot with his pants rolled up, calf-deep in what must have seemed to him like a proper lake. She waved as she approached and readjusted the head scarf she wore to conceal her swollen, bruised cheek. Her straw hat helped keep the scarf in place. She'd left her boots in the cottage so she could wade with the boy, which she did, lifting her skirt just high enough to avoid soaking its hem.

"Ahoy, Jamison," she said.

He smiled and moved the boat across the water, clutching the top section of the boat's mast.

"Ahoy, Miss Belle." He looked up at her and rubbed one sleepy eye with his free hand.

"You're a good sailor, little man. I like how careful you are . . . making sure your boat stays upright."

The boy squatted and blew hard into the sail. His bottom dipped into the water.

"Oops," he said, standing up and touching his soggy backside.

"That happens," Belle said. "Sailors and their boats get wet during adventures."

Jamison grinned and resumed powering his trusty vessel, making it lurch in pretend choppy waters.

Suddenly, an unpleasant memory interrupted the innocence—another time, a different place. *Move through,* she thought, and saw herself at Jamison's age.

There she sat, clutching the coarse hair of a mule's mane. The day was brisk, and the Carsons were participating in a sugarcane grind with several other families. Julius, knowing she was timid around large animals, had plopped her atop a mule. The animal was hitched to a long wooden pole and walking in endless circles, powering the cane press extracting juice to be boiled into syrup. She gripped the mule's mane with both hands, her eyes pinched shut. She was certain the creature would break free from the pole and race off into the woods with her on its back. She'd fall off and be attacked by ravenous vultures, their black heads banging against each other in the fierce battle for her flesh.

"Look how my boat can tip over and still float, Miss Belle."

Jamison's face was beaming as he discovered the toy's new trick.

She smiled, grateful to be pulled back to his sailing puddle.

"Now isn't that a clever boat," she said. "It's always good to be able to rely on something, isn't it?"

Jamison nodded and poked at the boat, testing its resolve.

When George walked from Baker's toward them, Belle said her goodbyes.

"Have fun, Captain." She saluted. The young boy saluted back, then waved to his father.

She left open the possibility of more flashes back to the past. There was no telling what to expect on this day, washed clean with rain.

•••

The river had done its job, moving its water, keeping its secrets. Boone walked along the muddy riverbank, searching for any potential threats to the body that lay below. No one was fishing nearby; gators sunned on thick logs, but some slipped into the water. All good signs.

Last night seemed impossible. The eerie moan of the conch shell sounded again in his mind. The rank smell of whiskey and sweat filled his nose. Never before had he learned so much about someone in such a lightning flash of a moment. He hadn't known anything about Belle and—*snap*—in an instant, she'd revealed to him both immense courage and intense fear. Then, in the flickering light of a candle, she'd shared her darkest secret with him. He shuddered again at the foulness of Julius.

Before he left the cottage this morning, he'd sat on the bed's edge and talked softly to Belle.

"How are you feeling?" he said, searching her eyes for pain.

"It's over, right?" Her tone was flat.

He took her hand, warm from rest. "Yes. It's finished, Belle."

They spoke for several more minutes and decided he would sleep in the rocking chair for however long it took Belle and the cottage to reclaim the peace that was so violently abducted.

Boone turned from the river and headed toward the Edison property. Belle would be on his mind as he swept the porches in preparation for Mr. Wood's visit to Seminole Lodge.

Chapter 14

The *Press* editor greeted his interviewee with an angler's hello.

"How are they bitin', Mr. Wood?"

Stephen Fitzgerald shook William Wood's hand and sat down with him on the porch of the Edison home.

"They're biting like it's January," William said, a pile of fishing rods next to his feet. "Still hooked two yesterday, though," he added, and smiled.

Belle glanced at the men from her neighboring position near the guesthouse steps. She was preparing the soil for the first set of gardens. Earlier, she'd filled a pushcart with compost from Abigail's well-aged pile, a rich mix of sawdust, coffee grounds, eggshells, horse manure, and chicken feathers. With a shovel, she moved the pungent fertilizer from the cart to the turned, sandy soil. She was surprised to see both men arrive on the property but kept working, much of her face concealed by her scarf and straw hat. When the editor said, "Mr. Wood," Belle connected the man with the heap of fishing tackle.

Last year, the newspaper covered Wood's brief visit with Edison, describing him as a New York architect one year shy of thirty. A successful building designer, W. H. Wood was invited to Seminole Lodge for a different set of skills, ones he exhibited on the water, not on land. In 1885, Wood was declared the first angler to catch a tarpon using a rod and reel. Previously, the feisty fish were taken only and infrequently with a hand line or harpoon. When *Forest and Stream* magazine reported Wood's feat in the waters off southwest Florida, the country and world took notice. The *London Observer* wrote, "Sportsmen may yet go to Florida for the tarpon, as they now go to the Arctic zone for the reindeer, walrus, and musk-ox." Wood, like Edison, had given the world a reason to notice southwest Florida.

Stephen grabbed a pencil from behind his ear. "What brings you to the Lodge, Mr. Wood?"

William laughed lightly and smoothed each sleeve of his cream-colored suit. "I suppose I'm baiting the hook. I told Al that if he visited this season, I'd outfit him with first-class equipment, flawlessly rigged. I want to give him every opportunity to outsmart and overpower a tarpon this time."

"We here in Fort Myers certainly hope he takes that bait, Mr. Wood," Stephen said. He eyed the pile. "So, just a day trip to drop off the gear?"

"Yes. I'll head back down to Punta Rassa later in the day," William said, and reached down for a rod. He laid it across his lap.

Turning to a blank page in his notebook, Stephen said, "Please explain what you've selected for our neighbor."

"First of all, I chose what works for me. Last May, I used this exact setup to catch a six-foot, five-inch hundred and forty pounder; a five-foot bamboo rod and a Silver King reel." He ran his hand along the line. "Of course, a durable fifteen-thread line and a number ten O'Shaughnessy hook rigged onto a three-foot link chain."

"Bait?" Stephen asked, scribbling.

"I used mullet, but I'll be suggesting live crabs and pinfish as well to Al."

"So, now we know the tools required," Stephen said, and leaned forward. "But, Mr. Wood, what of a man's heart? What is the state of the heart when a monstrous fish agrees to do battle?"

Belle stopped turning soil and gently laid the shovel on the ground. She kneeled and fiddled in the soil with her hands, hoping to hear William's answer clearly. Anything to push aside the terror of last night was welcome, and she was grateful to be within earshot of yet another accomplished world figure.

Leaning over, William placed the pole on the floor. He crossed his arms, closed his eyes, and began. "When you feel the bait lift up from the sandy bottom, you stop breathing. You steady your feet. Is it a shark or a tarpon?" His chest and arms rose and fell with a deep breath. "You force yourself to breathe, calming your body for either foe. Then, when you feel the line going out . . . and out . . . you let it run. The fish thinks it's free." His eyes popped open, and he whipped back an imaginary rod with both hands. "Now spring that hook into the fish with a yank!"

Stephen jumped in his seat, making them both laugh.

"*Pow!*" William's palm cut up through the air. "It's a Silver King! Up he leaps, unmistakable in his armor of hammered silver. Flashing in the sun and jackknifing midair, he tries to shake the hook, the rattling of those deep-red gills his battle cry."

Stephen kept writing and, with his head down, asked, "And then the tug-of-war begins?"

"Precisely!" William said, and looked toward the sky. "Don't fail me, rod and reel!"

Belle stared at William, captivated by his story.

"An hour passes and your arms and lungs beg for rest, but if you crave the title of tarpon slayer, you must persist." Holding the imaginary rod again, William worked the reel and jerked the pole. "Keep reeling him in closer. Grant him no gulps of air, no second wind." With a swoop of his arm, he gaffed the imaginary fish. "Using no less than a five-inch-diameter gaff, grab your prize. Another King dethroned!" He exhaled and smiled.

Stephen finished writing, underlining several words. "A tale well told, Mr. Wood. My readers will appreciate such a rousing how-to." He scratched his scalp with the pencil tip. "What do you say to those who describe you as a skilled but particularly lucky angler?"

Without hesitation, William responded, "I say hogwash. Luck is earned, Stephen. I studied my opponent before I ever engaged him. And when I did, *his* luck ran out."

"Ah, a good lesson for us all," Stephen said. He closed the notebook and reached over to William for a handshake. "Mr. Wood, I'll be sure to get you a clipping of our interview."

William stood. "I hope you can hand it to me when I'm here fishing with Al."

"Our hope, too," Stephen said.

Beyond the porch, Belle noticed Boone and Decker walking down the stairs of the caretaker's cottage. They must have been watching out the window, waiting for the interview to end. Should she need to, she'd tell Decker and anyone else who noticed her swollen cheek that a mason jar in the storage room fell from a shelf and hit her in the face. As the men approached the Edison home, Boone glanced at her but continued up the porch with Decker.

"Get what you need, Stephen?" Decker motioned for Boone to gather up the fishing poles.

"That and more, Norville." Stephen walked down the porch steps toward the driveway to leave.

"Mr. Wood, we'll make sure all this tackle is in easy reach for Mr. Edison." Decker put his hands on his narrow hips. "Can't promise the same for the tarpon."

William smiled. "Well, that's fishin', right, gentlemen?" He stretched his tall frame. "Sounds good about now."

Chapter 15

Boone barely heard the whistle over the racket of his handsaw gnawing through a downed tree limb. When he turned around, he saw William Wood on his sailboat close to shore, clutching his fishing rod with both hands. The boat, its sails tied down, was leaning slightly to the port side. Gentle waves born of the Caloosahatchee's incoming tide licked at its hull. Wood was not smiling, and when Boone reached him in a rowboat, he learned why.

"It's a body," William said, his face ashen. He nodded toward the water.

Boone winced and maneuvered closer to the sailboat. Before he could make anything out in the water, his mind began racing about what to reveal or conceal.

"It's been . . . compromised," William said, "so prepare yourself." He pulled back on the pole, straining as the catch rose closer to the surface.

Boone squeezed the oar handles. Several inches under the water, he saw the striped suit of the ogre he'd dragged out of the cottage. As the body partially broke the surface, he could see that it was missing most of its face and both arms. "Oh my God," he said. He swallowed and looked at William. He'd met Mr. Wood twice now and found him a polite, unpretentious man. His passion seemed reserved for fishing, not promoting himself or his friendship with Mr. Edison. In the next few split seconds, Boone hoped that he was making the right decision as he opened his mouth to speak.

"Mr. Wood, I know who this is and I know why he was at the bottom of the river. You know nothing about me, I realize that, but I'm asking you to believe me." He paused to reposition the boat as it strayed in the current. "What's on your hook is an animal, not a person. He's where he belongs and needs to stay there until every inch of him ends up in the belly of a beast, like him." He shook his head. "That's simply the truth."

William sat for a moment, squinting at Boone. "I *don't* know you." He paused and reworked his grip on the pole. "But I do know there are evil men who walk the earth." He let the body drop down several inches. "This beast . . . would most believe he deserved to die for whatever it is he did?"

"Yes, and they'd all agree that he didn't suffer enough in the end," Boone said. "Twisted, evil, disgusting." He shook his head. "Mr. Wood, I promise you, that body is in the river for a very good reason."

The men stared at each other.

"All right, then," William said. "What do we do now?"

Boone exhaled his immense relief. "If you're willing, I'll anchor my boat and join you to unfurl the sails. There should be enough of a breeze to work our way to the deepest channel in the river."

William nodded. "Climb aboard."

•••

In the late afternoon, Belle had taken a brief nap in the cottage. She'd then resumed moving compost from Baker's to the Edison gardens. As she returned from Abigail's yard with her final load, she saw William Wood standing near her work area. Earlier in the day, she'd noticed him pacing on the Edison's porch, aggressively smoking a cigar. Eventually, he'd settled into a chair. Now, she rolled toward him.

"Hello, there," he said. "I'm William Wood."

"Hello, Mr. Wood," she said, still gripping the handles of the pushcart.

"Call me William," he said, and smiled. "May I get your name?"

"It's Belle." She dropped the cart to shake William's outstretched hand, first wiping hers on the front of her dress. She nodded toward the turned soil. "I'm creating gardens for Mina."

William pocketed both hands. "She does love her flowers, that one."

Over William's shoulder, Belle saw Boone approaching.

"I must say that's a fine hat, Belle. I noticed it from the porch and hoped I might get a closer look at your collection."

"So you two have met?" Boone said as he joined them.

William turned toward Boone. "We have. I just told Belle I'd like a look at her lures."

Belle said, "Of course." She slowly removed her straw hat, making sure her scarf stayed in place.

Holding the hat in both hands, William spun it slowly, examining each lure. "Well, this one's a beauty," he said, jiggling a spoon lure. "A Hibbard. Where did you find it?"

When he looked up at Belle for the answer, he tilted his head slightly and leaned in toward her. "Your cheek," he said, wincing.

Belle looked at Boone, who moved to her side and slowly reached toward her scarf. She pulled away.

"Boone . . ."

"Don't worry," he said softly. Gently, he pulled back her scarf to reveal her swollen cheek. "That beast did this," he said, looking at William. "And that's the least of what he put her through . . . when she was a young girl."

William grimaced. "All right, then. You needn't worry about me."

"Boone?" Belle couldn't imagine why Boone had revealed their secret.

"Everything is all right," he said. "I promise."

William returned Belle's hat. "Miss Belle, I want to give you something." He reached into his pocket and pulled out a translucent circle the size of a silver dollar. "I carry these with me as good reminders." He held up the thin disc with two fingers. "A single tarpon scale. Simple, right? But when you wrap hundreds of these around a living thing, it becomes much more complicated." He handed it to Belle.

She took it. "I'm afraid I don't understand."

"Life is simple. It's human behavior that complicates everything. As I see it, we humans have to save ourselves from each other, as best we can."

"Save each other how?" Belle said, pulling her scarf back into place.

"Well, I can only speak for myself," William said, "but I've found that compassion and forgiveness are a good start." He shook his head. "Life would be so simple if we all just behaved, wouldn't it?" With a small nod, he said, "You take good care, Belle."

William turned and walked away toward the caretaker's cottage. Boone looked at Belle. She was staring down at the milky scale that filled her palm.

He touched her shoulder. "Belle, we need to get our story straight."

Chapter 16

Parker's grapefruit grove was vast and quiet, a place where Belle wouldn't be disturbed. Her thoughts were doing enough of that, banging against her brain and bouncing off each other.

Along the river, in front of the mill.

Boone had talked her through a story that would infer that Julius drowned: He was last seen drunk and stumbling around near the water in front of Ritter's Mill. The mill was located on the opposite end of the river from where Belle's bedsheets, that once held Julius's body, might remain. The plan was for Belle to speak privately with Augie about the "tip." She'd assured Boone that Augie could be trusted to pass along the "witness accounts" to the *Press* editor without mentioning her name. When Boone told her that William had hooked the body, she'd dry-heaved, spitting acid and shaking uncontrollably. Boone had tried to comfort her, but his hands on her made it worse.

"I need to walk for a while," she'd said, and headed for the grove.

Now, she sat on the ground in the shade, still shaking. Her stomach was in knots, the back of her neck sweaty. Maybe immense shock had been choking off her disgust and anger and fear, but an hour earlier, all of it began to break free. How had her life changed so suddenly and violently? Just when her fresh start seemed like it was taking hold, she was forced to defend it and herself with deadly blows. What if the knife hadn't been in the drawer? She hugged her body, shivering as she recalled blindly searching for it.

Twice now she'd run from Julius, this time to Boone. Why hadn't she gone to Abigail? Maybe she didn't want to break her heart. Belle could explain to Boone why she killed Julius because he barely knew her. The story of her past would certainly disturb him but not devastate him like it would Abigail or Merle. None of that had occurred to her until now. She'd just instinctively run to Boone for help.

Leaning over, she picked up a grapefruit from the ground and chucked it, agitated. Every time she'd imagined Julius dying, *she* was the one who killed him—with her bare hands, with a shovel, tied to a chair as their house burned. But now that she'd actually taken his life, she was a nervous, jumbled wreck. Julius was finally dead, but the absolute relief she'd anticipated as a child was now muddled with other emotions.

Why me?

She pounded her fists on her knees. Why did *she* have to be the one to kill him? He deserved it, but why couldn't someone else have rid this world of him before he came crashing back into hers? She'd never forget the sound of the knife blade puncturing his skin, the feel of her fist ramming against his neck with each stab.

"Oh my God," she said aloud.

Would she end up in hell, *with* Julius, because she killed him? She looked around at the fallen fruit beside her. There she was, a sinner who'd taken another person's life. Maybe her punishment would be that Julius would continue to haunt her from the grave. She could never escape him.

"*Ugh* . . . stop this, Belle!" she yelled, and knocked her palms against her head. "Just stop."

She stood and wandered through the rows of trees. *Try not to worry. He's finally gone.* This was her chance to look forward, not back. Julius lay deep in the river and only she, Boone, and William Wood knew it. Her shot at a meaningful future depended on the secret they shared remaining just that.

Belle left the grove and headed straight for the cemetery.

Chapter 17

Betsy Carson lightly ran her fingers across the top of a small sand-stone grave marker. The Fort Myers cemetery was still but for the rustle of squirrels scampering through dried debris. She sat down in front of a cabbage palm with a lanky fern growing in its criss-crossed boots. The tree's trunk offered a fine backrest as she stared at where she and Nelson had buried Benjamin. In that peaceful spot, she hoped one day that the mystery of his death would be solved. Right there, she'd fold her hands, drop her head, and say, "Thank you, God. I see now."

Well before Nelson died, he'd stopped coming here with her. Daily obligations—like shadows on a waning moon—eventually obscured the past and its torments. Staying away for him became routine. She sometimes wondered, *Will that day ever come for me?* "Absolutely not," her anguish would answer. It was stubborn and refused to be diminished by the decades that had passed since the incident, bullying her to that very spot most Sundays. She'd grown used to her solo trips, even embraced the solitude. Alone, she could attempt to pry grief from the hands of guilt. Or was it the other way around? Was Benjamin taken from her or did she hand him over? The cemetery seemed a place where answers might just float up from the mouths of those who lay below. So what if her boy hadn't yet learned to talk? She would listen anyway, just in case.

"I'm here, Son."

She leaned her head back and closed her eyes, thinking. Yet again, she began to relive the moment when Benjamin crawled into the cool creek.

There was some drinking that afternoon. Not much. She'd poured whiskey into a glass, but only enough to douse the small fires that would inevitably flare up in the smoldering ruins of her mind. No one else was at home, as usual—just her and the baby. Julius was at school while Nelson worked. When she'd initially recounted the details of that day to Nelson, he'd gently corrected her.

"Julius was home," he'd said, explaining that the seven-year-old had misbehaved at school.

But that's not how she recalled the day. She remembered sitting in the yard, alone but for the baby and the truth. Her husband would soon leave her, and she couldn't blame him. No man deserved a wife who woke up every morning irritated. The worst days always led her to the kitchen knives. She'd pull out the drawer and stare at their long blades.

Choose the longest handle. Hold it tight.

The madness told her to stab Nelson and kill the children, too. Imagining the violent scene both soothed and terrified her.

The wild brain began again after Benjamin's birth and lingered for months. It paralyzed her ability to properly mother him or anybody. In what seemed a house full of too many people, she wished she were anywhere else. The baby cried too much; her family ate too much. She stayed famished to balance out the gluttony. Nelson seemed blind to their dismal existence, playing and laughing with Julius. She despised the way he ignored the misery they'd created together.

On the afternoon of the incident, Benjamin was scooting around the yard on his bottom, using a hand behind and a foot in front to propel himself. He'd discovered the move earlier than his brother and was faster at it. At least that's what Nelson told her. She hadn't noticed, absent of any urge to bond with the scooting, suckling, screaming baby.

Every now and then she'd look up from her darning to see where Benjamin was, but mostly she worked the needle and sipped whiskey. Her empty stomach welcomed the warm burn; she knew it would lead to a numbness that made the day tolerable. Her eyelids were heavy, but she could certainly see the sock and its hole disappearing with each stitch. When she pricked her finger, the jolt made her look up from the task. Benjamin was sitting in the sand—facing away from her—where the yard sloped down to the creek that ran along their property. Recent rain had boosted its volume, but still, its depth could be measured in inches. She noted that the skin on the back of the baby's head was growing red from the steadfast sun.

Next came the part that made Betsy think of that afternoon as "the day in question." She rubbed her closed eyes. *Did I see him move toward the creek? Did I let him do it or did I simply not see him heading for the bank? Did I fall asleep?* There was an image in her mind of Benjamin disappearing over the edge, but she was uncertain if it was an actual memory or her mind conjuring it up. Either way, Benjamin drowned in the creek that afternoon.

The sight of his body, face down in the water, had looked odd to Betsy. *Why was there a baby lying in the creek?* Strands of blond hair waved in the weak current like seaweed. She picked the body up and flipped it over to see the face, which was blue and belonged to Benjamin. She remembered nothing after that, which didn't matter. Her son was dead.

Nelson didn't blame her, at least not out loud. She'd dumped what remained of the whiskey into the sand and never made it part of the "what happened" sequence she relayed to him, the neighbors, and the sheriff. "It was simply a horrific accident," they all said, and added how sorry they were that it happened. At the time, she wasn't sure whether she was sorry it had happened. She cried but had already been crying when Benjamin was alive. In the end, she was deemed a victim, not a villain, and with no punishment came no redemption. Shame eventually slithered in to fill the gap between the two.

A year later, Nelson sat her down at the kitchen table. He explained that he'd spoken with Pastor Peck and that a baby was available for adoption.

"I'm convinced it's what you need to get better, Betsy," he said. She remembered thinking how absurd it was that he thought she could. Her brain had burned after she gave birth to Julius, too, and Nelson should have known. She'd told him as much, but he insisted "the smoke" would clear. It never did, some days even thickening to fog. Why would Nelson think another child would do anything but push her further into the haze?

The newborn arrived with the name Maybelle and an impossible mission: to cure her new mother. *Go away,* she'd thought when the tiny brown eyes locked with hers. Here was yet another innocent heart, an unwelcome reminder that her own was stone-cold. She felt nothing when Nelson placed the baby girl in her arms; it was as if he'd handed her a sack of cornmeal.

When year after year went by and their daughter didn't make her "get better," Nelson distanced himself from her and the children. He worked more and cared less about his makeshift family, the one with a mother who didn't act like one. Then, perhaps the fire in her brain spread to Nelson's. He gave Belle away and sent Julius to Tampa.

"Find work," he'd told him. "Don't come back until I send word, if I ever do."

When Nelson died the next year, she thought it perhaps best. Nelson was with Benjamin, Julius was gone, and she could finally be alone with her confusion about why God ever put people in her life to look after.

A light breeze dropped in on the cemetery, fluttering the ivy that clung to Nelson's gravestone. Betsy rubbed her temples and considered lying down. Instead, she stopped thinking about anything and fell asleep.

•••

"Betsy?" Belle stood adjacent to her, certain that Betsy must have heard her footsteps as she approached the cemetery.

Betsy opened her eyes, blinking repeatedly. She looked at Belle and raised her eyebrows. "Never thought I'd see you here."

Belle crossed her arms and sighed. She hadn't talked to Betsy in eleven years, and the first thing out of the other woman's mouth was a lie. Betsy *had* seen her there. When Belle was about five years old, Betsy took her to the cemetery nearly every Sunday after church. Spending time among the gravestones scared Belle, especially since Betsy didn't talk during a visit. She'd just sit and stare at the headstone marked "Benjamin." Once, when Belle asked who Benjamin was, she'd waved her off, as if she'd interrupted a conversation Betsy were having with a ghost. It was Julius who told her that Benjamin was his baby brother, and that he'd drowned him in the creek—another lie to scare her into silence.

"I'm only here because there's talk," Belle said.

Betsy ran a bent finger across her cheek, sweeping aside a strand of hair. "There's always talk."

That voice—still indifferent. Belle hadn't heard it since she'd moved in with Merle. In the year that followed, she'd catch glimpses of Betsy, on the porch of Cravin & Company or walking somewhere in the rain without an umbrella. But after Nelson died, Belle rarely saw her. Sometimes she'd overhear a snippet about her: "Betsy's yard could use some cleanup," or "Betsy fainted in church." Betsy was of no interest to Belle. But today, to protect her secret, she'd sought her out.

"I need you to listen carefully," Belle said. "I've heard that your son was seen stumbling around the river down by Ritter's Mill, extremely drunk."

"My son? Here?" She yawned. "I haven't seen the boy since Nelson sent him away."

"Are you listening, Betsy?" Belle surveyed her: coarse gray hair, swollen knuckles, dress with a torn pocket. She was thin, as always. "People say he was tripping all over himself."

Betsy slowly turned toward Belle. "Is Julius dead?"

Belle said nothing. She examined Betsy's face, plain with smooth skin. The eyes appeared neither sad nor wise, the lips thin and straight. Nothing about the features appeared pained or burdened. How was that possible? Betsy had buried a baby, a husband, and surely, somewhere in her soul, a dark secret about her son. Still, her face hadn't aged. Maybe her insides looked like a tree trunk infested with termites.

"He was very drunk and stumbling around the riverbank," Belle repeated. "Make sure to tell that to Frank and anyone else who may ask."

Betsy folded her knobby hands in her lap and looked toward the grave markers. "Maybe I'll put up a stone for him."

"What?" Belle walked over and stood in front of Betsy. "Dammit! Don't you do *anything* more for him." Her heart was pounding. "Not one more thing."

Tapping together the toes of her worn boots, Betsy said, "You're probably right. That boy has gotten away with enough."

Belle jammed her hands on her hips. "Did you know? Are you now telling me you knew . . . what he did?"

Somewhere in the cemetery a bird trilled. "I'm not sure." Betsy sighed. "Nelson said Julius was there, at home, that day."

Belle glared at Betsy. "What day?"

She looked up at Belle. "The day our baby died. Did you know we lost a baby?" She added softly, "Julius was there that day . . . maybe."

Belle's arms dropped to her sides. She clenched her fists and stomped her foot in the sand. "What *you* lost, Betsy? Do you know what *I* lost? You do know, don't you?" She threw up her hands. "I was a child! Would you have protected me if I was actually *your* daughter?"

Betsy's chin dropped toward her chest. "I don't know anything for sure."

It was all she could do not to kick sand in Betsy's face. She squinted, pressing her fingertips into her throbbing forehead. *Stop now, Belle.* What needed to be said was, and more.

She spun away from Betsy and headed out of the cemetery, shouting over her shoulder, "Your son was extremely drunk and stumbling around the river down by the mill. Remember *that*!"

Chapter 18

Chest-deep in the Caloosahatchee, two men circled slowly as if opposite ends of a weather vane. They poked around in the water with long bamboo poles. Nearby, a half dozen more people waded in a shallow strip of the river that fronted Ritter's Mill. Several boaters floated close by, some curious, one to transport a body if found. The search was organized following the release of a *Press* article reporting eyewitness accounts of a missing man's last-known whereabouts. Citing anonymous sources, the story indicated that former town resident Julius Carson was seen intoxicated and stumbling along the river in front of Ritter's sawmill.

•••

Pulling back a frayed curtain ever so slightly, Betsy watched Sheriff Clark walk through her yard, kicking aside dead branches as he approached the porch. She moved away from the window and waited for him to knock.

"Yes?" Betsy peeked out from behind the partially opened door.

"Afternoon, Betsy. I just need a minute."

"I don't have coffee on."

"Doesn't matter. I already had mine."

The door creaked as she pulled it open. The sheriff entered the house and stood in front of Betsy in the dim hallway.

"So, Julius and Frank Dolland have apparently been in town for a few days. Frank says Julius is missing." The sheriff reached for a notebook in his back pocket and flipped it open. "He says that Julius never returned to their room at the Palms."

"Frank Dolland," Betsy murmured. "He was such a noisy boy."

Somewhere in the house, a clock marked the hour with a deep *bong*.

"Frank claims Julius would not have returned to Tampa without him. So, I'm doing some checking. Have you seen or talked to Julius, Betsy?"

"My son? I haven't spoken to him in more than ten years." She squinted at the sheriff. "What about you? Have you seen him since he left?"

"No, I haven't, Betsy."

Several days before Julius left town, Nelson had beaten him severely with a leather strap. Even with her hands over her ears Betsy could hear the yelling and snapping.

"I warned you a long time ago that if I ever caught you doing that nonsense again—"

Snap.

"—that I'd beat you nearly to death."

Snap. Snap.

Betsy had never seen Nelson so angry. What "nonsense"? The beating continued as she'd left the house, overwhelmed by Nelson's eruption. A year later, when her husband killed himself, she was shocked, along with the entire town. Even the sheriff had said to her, "I'm not convinced Nelson took his own life, Betsy, but I have no evidence to the contrary." She'd come home to find his body on the kitchen floor, his face blown off by his hunting rifle lying next to him. Why would he end his life? Nothing had seemed different about him, at least from what she could discern through her fog. When word spread that Nelson was dead, food baskets and vases of flowers covered their porch. But in the days that followed, some neighbors seemed to shun her, crossing the street to avoid her, as if Nelson's blood and brains were sprayed across her dress. She'd accepted their snubs. Maybe she *was* to blame.

Turning a page in the notebook, the sheriff said, "Frank was last seen at Billy's. Witnesses say he was so inebriated that he required assistance back to the Palms. The Gibbses confirmed that he and Julius were sharing a room at the hotel." He cleared his throat. "Frank says they'd been drinking all day and then more at Billy's. He says he doesn't recall seeing Julius leave the saloon, but, as you may have seen in the *Press*, witnesses supposedly saw him stumbling around down by the river."

"So you think he drowned?" Betsy stared at the sheriff.

"Well, we're checking, Betsy." He paused. "I know you've already been through that once. I certainly hope not."

Betsy looked down and picked at a fingernail.

"Frank came by."

The sheriff took a pencil from his breast pocket. "And?"

"I told him what I told you." She rubbed a bony finger across her chin, scratching it.

"That you haven't seen Julius?"

"That, and about the stumbling . . . near the mill."

"Did someone tell you they saw Julius there?"

"No. I just heard talk." She looked toward the door. "Is that all?"

Sheriff Clark closed his notebook. "That's all, Betsy. I'll keep you informed about the investigation."

"No need to," she said.

The sheriff tilted his head. "Are you sure?"

"I'm not sure about anything, Frederick."

She motioned for him to let himself out.

Chapter 19

Directly between guava and grapefruit groves, the branches of a large red maple stretched far beyond the tree's thick trunk. During the day, the quiet space below was popular with picnickers, and at night with lovers who kissed on the aptly named Sparking Seat, a wooden bench under the maple's cozy canopy of leaves.

This afternoon, the Circle Club had claimed the relaxing spot before anyone else. The women sat on blankets arranged in the round. Belle had already explained her bruised cheek, and Poppy was wrapping up a brief opening prayer.

"In God's name we pray," she said, and made the sign of the cross.

Shaken by the attack days earlier, Belle had considered calling off the meeting. But she pressed on, William's words nudging her. *Love and compassion can save us from ourselves.* She needed some saving. Her nerves were twitchy and, worst of all, the fear that Julius would somehow grab her from the grave or haunt her forever lingered, stubborn and absurd. Still, she was determined to keep moving forward. For too long, her past had defined her future, and she'd allowed it.

"I thought we'd start the meeting with Paulette," Belle said. "Would you like to share any ideas about projects we might take up as a club?" She passed around a plate of deviled goose eggs that Abigail had dropped off earlier along with a bowl of boiled peanuts.

"I'd be happy to," said Paulette, sitting up even straighter. "I feel strongly that there's a place in our school for several Indian children. We have plenty of books, and I'm sure if there aren't enough desks, our Seminole or Miccosukee youngsters won't mind sitting on the floor."

Poppy nodded. "That's a fine idea, Paulette. Our town doesn't have much money, but what it does have is big-hearted folk. I'm sure several families would take in students for the school session."

"Some will whine about it," Sadie said, cupping a deviled egg. "We know that."

"Probably my mother," Hazel said, and sighed. "She's oblivious to need. Her days just line up like lovely sunsets—predictable and guaranteed."

The other women stayed quiet, giving Hazel room to talk. When she didn't add more, Paulette offered, "If you'd like to share anything with us about your mother, we're happy to listen."

"Absolutely," Amelia added, crocheting without looking down at her handiwork.

"Well," Hazel said, "your father should probably stuff me, Alice." She pointed to a red fox preserved in the running position set next to Alice's blanket.

"Huh?" Alice said.

"If I was stuffed, my mother could carry me around, forever fixed in the position of her choice, with perfect hair and perfect clothes. Perfect, like her."

Belle said, "Hazel, your mother is *not* perfect." She added, "I mean, no one is."

Poppy opened her Bible. "Ecclesiastes 7:20: 'For there is not a just man upon earth, that doeth good, and sinneth not.'" She paused. "There are plenty more passages . . ."

As Poppy flipped pages in search of scripture, Belle thought back to a spring day several years ago.

Still working at Duggan's, she'd ridden over to the Palms Hotel one afternoon to trim a Calusa grapevine she'd noticed growing up the side of the building. She knew where the Gibbses kept the ladder; always leaning up against the rear wall of the hotel. She rocked it back and forth on its two feet until it stood where she could safely prune the vine. As she climbed the rungs, she glanced into one of the second-story windows as she passed by. It looked to be a maintenance closet, filled with extra linens and brooms. She then froze on the ladder. Inside the closet, she saw a cow hunter with his head tipped back, eyes shut, hat resting on a wash table. At his waistline, a puzzling sight: a long plume darting up and down. When Belle slowly climbed up one more rung, she saw Ida Cravin on her knees, performing like a hard-driving oil rig dressed in petticoats and a fancy hat. The cow hunter looked over at Belle, winked, and then returned to his role as Ida's fall from grace. The grapevine could wait. Belle climbed back down the ladder, aghast but not all that surprised. Ida was probably kneeling on her Bible as she sent the cow hunter to heaven and back.

"Seems to me, Hazel, you're beyond old enough now to stand up to your mother," Amelia said. "What would you like to say to her?"

Hazel shook her head. "Nothing. She doesn't listen." She reached up and untied the white ribbon securing her ponytail. "What I'd like to do is make a mess of the checkers in the parlor room. I'd like to let the poor parrot out of its cage for a spin." She fiddled with the long ribbon. "I'd very much like to ask my father why he lets my mother boss him around."

Sadie said gently, "Your father's just trying to keep the peace, darlin', just like you."

"Well then, that's the problem," Hazel said. She shook her fingers vigorously through her loosened hair. "There's so much peace in our house, it feels like a cemetery, like everyone but my mother has been laid to rest."

Amelia stopped crocheting and set aside her hook and yarn. "Why don't you do some work for me at the drugstore, Hazel, get out of the house? I've never understood why you don't work at Cravin & Company."

"Oh, heavens no." Hazel shook her finger. "'No daughter of Ida's is going to work like some sort of low-class . . .'" She glanced at Belle. "Her words not mine, Belle. She believes a man won't marry a woman who shows interest in anything outside the home."

"Then why did she let you interview for the gardening job at the Edisons'?" Belle asked, irritated.

"She *made* me, Belle. My mother is desperate to become friends with Mina. She clips every newspaper article about her and organizes them by date."

Alice rolled her eyes. "They're just people."

"People with money and status," Hazel explained. "My mother is embarrassed to be a full-time resident of what she calls an 'underdeveloped cow town.'"

"The cows are the best thing about our town," Alice said. "Ever hear *them* whine or say mean things?" She combed her short hair to the side with her fingers. "Nope."

"In my opinion," Paulette said, "Ida should be careful what she wishes for. My sister in Chicago writes to me about neighborhoods choked with people working twelve-hour days in harsh conditions and sleeping in cramped tenement buildings. The factories hire women and children for lower wages than men, and the work is monotonous and dangerous." She centered a silver locket on her chest. "No, we don't have the railroad or ice or a fire department. But progress doesn't guarantee a good life."

"What does?" Belle asked. "What does guarantee a good life?"

Paulette pointed both palms outward, toward the women. "*This* is one spoke on the wheel . . . realizing we need others to create a meaningful life." She shrugged. "We also need love, which, as you all know, has been an ongoing search for me."

"Oh, bless your heart, Paulette," Poppy said. "Even when you find love, marriage is hardly uninterrupted pleasure."

Sadie laughed. "You got that right, Poppy. Don't search *too* hard, Paulette."

The women all laughed.

As the meeting continued, Belle sent a silent *thank you* to Kate. Without her, she'd never have opened her heart and mind to these interesting, entertaining, honest women; these people who might save her and she them.

Sadie was talking when Belle's mind rejoined the gathering.

"Now pass me those peanuts, Alice. That fox is spying them with his lopsided eyes."

• • •

After the meeting, as the other women walked off, Poppy lingered.

"Belle, would you like to take a moment to talk?" She gestured toward their blankets on the ground.

"Um, was there something we didn't cover at the meeting?" Belle had never before talked privately with Poppy.

"Probably not," Poppy said, "but why don't we relax for another minute."

The two sat down across from each other, Belle caught off guard by the pairing.

"At our first meeting, Belle, you mentioned a bit of an inner battle with forgiveness. Since it didn't come up today, I thought perhaps you needed a smaller audience to share your thoughts." She paused. "Our congregants often ask for guidance regarding forgiveness, and as you know, I've had some experience with that in my own life."

Belle chewed on her bottom lip. *Oh, Lord.* Was Poppy going to explain how she forgave her husband? Last year, Poppy had discovered Pastor Peck and Darla Johansen kissing in the bell tower of the church. She and a neighbor had climbed up to polish the bell and happened upon the pair. Word was that after Poppy moved out and spent a month with her mother—and the Bible—she agreed to return home to her repentant husband. Townspeople rallied behind the couple, but not before gorging on rumors up to their Adam's apples. *Darla was getting back at her sister, who Mitchell had chosen over her as church pianist. Poppy had flirted one too many times with the choir director.* And on and on. Ultimately, if Poppy could forgive Mitchell, so could they. Darla moved away.

"As I said at the last meeting, Belle, humans have always hurt each other, been hurt themselves, and struggled with the heavy burdens that come with having relationships."

Belle braced herself, certain the next thing Poppy was going to say was her husband's name, or Darla's.

"That's why the Bible is filled with verses about forgiveness. One of my favorites is 'But if ye do not forgive, neither will your Father which is in heaven forgive your trespasses.'"

"That *is* a notable one," Belle said, hoping to lead her toward another verse and away from the scandal. "Do you have any other favorites?"

Poppy picked up the Bible and quickly found the page she needed. "Here it is. 'Let all bitterness, and wrath, and anger, and clamor, and evil speaking, be put away from you, with all malice: And ye be kind one to another, tenderhearted, forgiving one another, even as God for Christ's sake hath forgiven you.'"

Belle added nothing and brushed a fly off her forearm.

"Dear, is there something you'd like to talk about . . . specifically? Maybe I can help."

Belle lightly cleared her throat. "Well . . . I . . ." She took a moment to consider her struggle with forgiveness. Does evil deserve absolution? And what of those who aid evil with their blind eye?

"I don't know." Belle shrugged. "I suppose I have trouble doling out forgiveness to people who've hurt me."

"I understand. Most of us do, Belle." Poppy closed the Bible and set it aside. "Perhaps consider that we forgive others not because they deserve it, but because *you* deserve some peace. It allows you to move forward, beyond the hurt feelings."

Belle smoothed the sides of her blanket. "The peace part sounds good."

Poppy smiled. "You should give yourself some credit, Belle. Look at the loving relationship you have with Merle. You forgave *him.*"

Belle heard the words, but they made no sense. She sat up straighter. "What?" Her chest tightened. She didn't like the way Poppy's face was changing, from pleasant to pale.

"Oh. I . . . I assumed you two talked about it years ago."

"Talked about *what*, Poppy?" Belle wanted to run off, into the fruit groves. No more secrets. *Please no.*

Poppy's hands shook as she reached for the Bible. She placed it in her lap as if to anchor herself for the coming storm she'd just brewed.

"I'm afraid I've spoken out of turn."

"Tell me what you're talking about." Belle stared at her, motionless.

Poppy let out a puff of breath. "Oh dear. All right."

She began to tell a story Belle had never heard before—at least, not this version. The story started with what unfolded after Belle's mother, Eva, died giving birth.

When Clara returned from delivering Belle on Sanibel Island, she went straight to Constance Donner, a wet nurse in town. Baby Maybelle was in distress following the devastating delivery and stormy sail back to Fort Myers. When Clara was sure the baby was comfortable and feeding, she went to Merle, whom she would marry the following month.

"Merle said Clara was exhausted and distraught having just watched Eva die, but would not lie down before she told him how much she felt called to keep you, Belle, and that she hoped together they would raise you."

It was as if Belle's body had turned to stone; her limbs were frozen and heavy.

"Why do you know this, Poppy?" Her tone was flat.

"I promise I'll get there," Poppy said softly.

Merle loved Clara and instantly agreed to her beautiful plan. Soon they'd be husband and wife, and parents to little Belle. But then everything changed. One week later, Clara sustained a fatal rattlesnake bite to her ankle while gathering kindling along the river.

Poppy shook her head. "I'd never seen a man so devastated. When Merle showed up on our doorstep, it took me a moment to recognize him. No big smile, just sunken eyes and slumped shoulders. He was holding both sides of the doorframe simply to stay upright."

She explained that Merle sobbed through much of the time they spent with him. He was grieving Clara's loss and now agonizing over a decision about the baby that would cause him even more pain. They prayed for him and with him, and after nearly two hours, Mitchell helped Merle up and walked with him back to Duggan's. A plan had been made.

"Belle, Merle just didn't feel he could raise a baby on his own. He loved you the minute he laid eyes on you, but when Clara suddenly died, he was struggling even to breathe. The decision he made was for you, for your chance at life with a family, not a broken man."

Belle was scrunching her face as if weathering a rainstorm. Poppy's words seemed to pelt her, a relentless barrage of new truths. She realized right then that the very few details she knew about her infancy—facts Merle had shared with her—were stunningly incomplete.

"He told me," Belle said, pointing her finger at Poppy, "that *your* husband asked the Carsons to adopt me."

"And that's somewhat correct, Belle. They'd lost a baby boy, and Nelson was concerned about Betsy's well-being. She was acting out of sorts, neglecting their other son. A month before you were born, Nelson had asked Mitchell to let him know if an orphaned baby was made known to the church, that the family would take it in." Poppy placed her palms together. "The way it all unfolded, Belle, it seemed like God's plan."

Belle stood up and grabbed her blanket, snapping sand off it. She looked down at Poppy and then at the Bible in her lap.

"I'll *never* forgive a God who made that plan. And neither should you."

She walked off, unsure of where she was headed.

Chapter 20

Merle cleared his throat and held open the *Press* with both hands. Surrounded by colorful seed packets, Henry Metzger sat nearby on the floor. From his seat behind the counter, Merle began to read aloud from an article titled "EDISON HAS LEARNED TO EAT."

"A few years ago, when wholly absorbed with his electrical experiments, Mr. Edison could hardly be induced to eat enough to keep himself going, as he could not spend the time for it, though often hungry. The only way he could be made to take proper nourishment was by leaving tempting edibles all over his laboratory and his house, on his worktable, beside his machinery, in his hat, on his shelves."

Merle peered over the top of the paper. "What do you think about that, Henry?"

Without looking up, the boy said, "I never forget to eat. I guess I'm not that smart."

Merle laughed. "Well, you're smart enough to alphabetize those seed packs. I never thought to do that for our customers."

The sound of boots pounding on the porch steps was followed by the store's screen door opening. Belle was halfway to the counter by the time the door slammed shut.

"Oh." She stopped moving when she saw the boy on the floor. "Hello, Henry."

"Hello, Miss Belle." He grinned and held up a packet of cucumber seeds that featured a man's head atop a pickle body.

She squatted down to see it up close.

"I love that one," she said, "and the tomato man, too."

She stood up and looked at Merle.

"Do you think Henry could run an errand? I need to talk to you."

Merle put down the paper and popped open the cash register. "Sure, honey." He fished out several coins from opposite ends of the drawer. "Please go to the cannery, son. Buy five cans of guavas and four orange marmalades. Grab a basket off the porch." The boy took the money. "Millie keeps a jar of lemon drops on her desk."

Henry leapt over the seed packets and out the door.

Merle walked out from around the counter but didn't move toward Belle. "Is something wrong?"

She crossed her arms. "Why did you lie to me?"

He took a moment, confused. "I don't understand."

"Why didn't you tell me the whole story . . . about you and Clara . . . and me."

He stared back at her, stunned by her question. *How could she know?*

"What story?"

"Poppy told me, Merle . . . by accident. She thought I already knew."

"Belle, I . . ." He paused, searching for words to explain. "I didn't lie to you. I just left out that part of the story."

"But, why would you do that? It's my story, too."

"Belle," he said, moving toward her until she put her palm up.

"Please. Just tell me why," she said.

Merle looked down, running the back of his hands over his beard for a few moments. When he raised his head, Belle was still looking at him. *That dear, sweet face.*

"I don't know. Maybe I thought you'd be angry with me, or even worse, think less of me." He shook his head. "When Clara died, I collapsed inside. I could barely function, the grief was so deep. And then there was you, brand-new to this world. My heart wanted to keep you, but it was so broken that I couldn't be sure what was best . . . for you." He blew out a prolonged puff of air. "The Pecks helped me through a very difficult time, Belle. We agreed in the end that you should be raised by a family, as every child should. The Carsons were willing, and it all seemed for the best." He wrung his hands. "And then, so many years later, you show up at my door, terrified and injured. When I found out Julius had hurt you, I was devastated . . . and angry at myself. When you came to live with me—when I got you back—I wanted to protect you from any more pain. How could I tell my . . . ?" His throat locked up for a moment. "How could I tell my beautiful Belle that I was the reason she got beaten up?"

Belle stood, squinting at him. He watched her expression slowly soften as she took a few moments to work through all he'd said.

"No, Merle. What happened to me was not your fault."

He exhaled loudly. "Well, honey, thank you for saying that. But when I saw you that night, I told myself it was." He added quietly, "The sight of you, shaking and bleeding. How could you be the same curious little girl who'd wander into the store, eager to learn . . . about anything." He walked over to her. "I am so sorry, Belle."

She took his hand. "You couldn't possibly have known, Merle. No one could."

Lightly squeezing her hand, he said, "Thank you." He grimaced and asked softly, "Had he hurt you before that night?" He'd always wondered but was too afraid of the answer.

Shaking her head, Belle said, "No. That was the worst of it."

He pulled her to him and wrapped her in his arms. As he felt her hug him back, relief washed over him. She was all right. They were all right.

When they parted, Merle saw a tear rolling down Belle's cheek. "Let's sit down."

He led her to a stool at the counter and walked behind it. She sat and reached into her pocket as he poured two glasses of water. Squeezing a bit of orange juice into hers, he said, "Just the way you like it."

Belle nodded and dabbed her eyes. Merle gestured toward a letter C embroidered on a corner of her handkerchief.

"I know this is making my dear Clara happy. She'd want us to remain close . . . no matter what." Through the years, Merle had rarely talked about Clara with Belle, or anyone, but at that moment it seemed like the three of them were together. "Clara loved you dearly, Belle. 'My tiny fighter,' she called you." He smiled, picturing Clara holding Belle in the air, singing to her or kissing her wiggling baby toes. "Clara was the first person to see you enter the world."

Tracing the stitches of the pink C with her finger, Belle said, "My mother . . . Eva . . . she didn't make it long enough to see me?"

"No, honey, I'm afraid not. Clara didn't share many details with me—she was so torn up about losing Eva—but she did say the ether offered your mother relief . . . from everything . . . before she passed."

Belle took a sip of water. "Have you told me all you know about my mother?"

Merle blinked and thought. "Yes. Unfortunately, Clara had very little time to talk with the bean farmer. By the time she arrived, Eva was in bad shape. She was small-boned like you, and childbirth for any woman is dangerous. Clara told me she'd lost other mothers, and babies, too." He leaned over and rested his crossed arms on the counter. "I wish I knew more."

"Well, what I do know is that I wouldn't be here if it weren't for Clara," Belle said. She sat quietly for a moment or two. "How did you meet Clara . . . if you don't mind my asking."

He chuckled. "I don't mind." He pointed at Belle's handkerchief. "I've given you things that were special to Clara but haven't talked very much about her."

"I certainly don't want to make you sad."

"No, I want you to know more about her." He smiled. "Actually, a stamp brought us together. Clara came into the store one day when I was still running the post office out of Duggan's. She was holding an envelope and asked to buy a stamp, but I didn't hear her. I was too busy surveying this beautiful woman before me." He shrugged. "She just looked perfectly designed—hair swept to the back, warm smile, skin the color of her pearl earrings." He grinned. "The poor thing had to shake her coin purse to get my attention. She kindly asked me a second time for a stamp. So I sold it to her and asked her to go for a stroll with me sometime."

"Merle!" Belle said. "You didn't waste any time, did you?"

"I sure didn't," he said, smiling. "Honestly, I surprised myself. When I lost my wife in Georgia, I never thought I could love again, then in walked Clara. As I got to know more about her, she revealed herself as much more than just beautiful. That woman was so smart and passionate about her work. She loved babies dearly." He added softly, "Clara couldn't get pregnant—something to do with falling ill with yellow fever as a child—but she did everything she could to bring any and every baby into this world."

Belle folded her hands on the counter. "I know how much you still love Clara, Merle. I love her, too, and I never even met her. But you lost her decades ago. Surely, it's time for another love in your life." She tapped one thumb against the other. "What about Abigail? You two are so good together . . ."

Merle opened his mouth to respond just as Henry came bounding into the store with a jam-packed basket and a mouthful of lemon drops.

"Look who's back!" Merle said. He winked at Belle but didn't answer her question, one he'd often asked himself over the years.

Chapter 21

Weeks after the attack, Belle's face was healed, her nerves calm. When the *Press* reported that the search for Julius had been called off, she was convinced his body would never be found. Thankfully, her anxiety had lessened, stripped of its oppressiveness like an autumn breeze. This afternoon, she was enjoying the growing sense of relief with Boone by her side.

The two were working together in the Edisons' driveway, unloading plants she'd bought at Baileys' for the gardens. Byron's collared neck hung low as he tried to sleep off the fifteen-minute return trip that any other mule would've completed in five. As Boone removed a pot of caladiums from a flatbed cart, Belle admired their heart-shaped leaves and thought, *Those are for you, Boone.* She stuck her nose into a pale-pink bloom and let out a long, "Mmmmm." Gus Bailey had recommended a Souvenir de la Malmaison rose to please Mina. The ornamental was a prolific bloomer and would grow no taller than three feet. Belle would give it an extra dose of Abigail's fertile compost.

"These are heavenly for any nectar lover," Belle said, waving her hands over a group of flowering plants already being visited by petite blue butterflies. From atop the cart she handed Boone orange-and-yellow lantana, oxeye daisies, and fuchsia pentas. For Mina's vases she'd chosen plants that would provide hearty, long-lasting blooms when cut—tickseed, purple salvia, and her requested black-eyed Susans.

"You're practically floating back and forth across that cart," Boone said, smiling. "Happy?"

"Very," she said, and indeed she was. Flowers and all plants had always served as family, the ones she could rely on and delight in.

She next handed Boone a plant that was now unavailable at the nursery. She'd bought every last one. It featured vibrant pink blooms on long stalks that shot up from grasslike foliage. "This is my very favorite find," she said. Each flower had six pointed leaves and a lime-green center. Bright-yellow stamen burst forth from the middle of the blooms.

Taking the pot, Boone said, "Pretty. What are they?"

"They're called pink rain lilies." Her fingers caressed a petal. "Gus told me they explode with blooms after heavy rainstorms." She said softly, "I just love that."

Boone reached a hand up to Belle. She took it. "They're strong and beautiful." He laced his fingers through hers. "Like you."

When the cart was nearly empty, Boone put his hands on his hips. "How about that sail? The wind is perfect."

She ran a sleeve across her sweaty forehead. "That sounds wonderful."

They finished placing the plants in a shady spot and went their separate ways for just a few minutes: Boone to the livery with Byron, Belle to Baker's to pack a lunch.

• • •

As Belle walked up the dock, Boone untied the *Judith* from a piling that extended up through the dock's planks.

"We're ready to ride," he said, helping Belle aboard.

Heading out, Boone kept the boat close to the edge of the river where the water was smooth. Belle was impressed by how easily he made the wind serve him. She tipped her head back and let the breeze dry her moist neck, imagining her completed gardens: tall red firespike rising above orange and yellow marigolds; Cheddar pinks and wild petunias forming a border; fragrant freesia attracting bees and hummingbirds.

"Here it is," Boone announced, interrupting Belle's colorful musings.

The trip was brief, just twenty minutes up the Caloosahatchee to a quiet niche where Boone said he liked to think and nap. Thick-trunked cypress and oak trees overhung the water, providing wide patches of shade. Soft splashes revealed juvenile fish jumping in the shoreline mangroves. Atop a trunk jutting up from the water, a lanky anhinga dried its outstretched wings. The bird kept losing its balance, its wet wings heavy, lopsided curtains.

While Boone tied off the anchor line, Belle yawned. Her mind and body were already relaxing, afloat in the sheltered, peaceful setting. When he finished securing the boat, Boone sat down across from Belle on the deck.

"Do you still use this?" She touched the handle of a coiled cow whip. It looked like a braided-leather snake ready to strike.

He shook his head no. "The *Judith* is named after my favorite cow horse, a pretty little Marsh Tacky." He removed his hat and tousled his hair. "Everything else about my cracker cowboy days I've left behind."

Belle ran her fingers along the bumpy leather. She was used to seeing the whips wound and tied to the saddles of working cowboys in town. Loose leather at the end of the whip created a loud crack that drove stray cattle back into the herd.

"Well, let's see if you still have it," Belle said as she pushed the whip toward him and smiled.

He shook his head but grabbed the whip and stood with a grunt. The breeze flirted with his curls, shifting his hair her way.

He drew in a deep breath and tightly gripped the whip's handle. In a smooth, swift motion, he snapped his wrist and arm. The twelve-foot leather rope snaked through the air, breaking its silence at the tip, exploding with the sound of a pistol shot. A flock of startled ducks took off from the water, chattering through liftoff.

Belle shielded her eyes from the sun and smiled up at him. "Well, now. If I were a cow, I'd do whatever you told me."

Shifting his grip on the handle, Boone snapped the whip again. A group of pelicans rose from the water in slow motion, their long wings feathered lungs, gulping for air.

"That's enough," he proclaimed. "I've caused enough of a ruckus." He smiled and sat back down to recoil the whip. As he did, Belle set out lunch on a tablecloth—roasted chicken and skillet cornbread slathered in orange blossom honey.

"Those are fresh out of Abigail's oven." Belle pointed to dessert wrapped in a towel.

When Boone peeled back two flaps, he closed his eyes. "Mmm. Her ginger cookies."

As they ate, Belle peppered Boone with questions about his friendship with Abigail, building up to the one she was most interested in asking.

"Do you think Abigail and Merle could be more than friends?"

He raised his eyebrows. "Would you like that?"

She clutched the bottom of her braids, her fists resting on each petite breast. "I like them together. They've known each other for a long time, they make each other laugh, and they look out for each other."

Boone broke a cookie in half. "Is that what you think love looks like?"

She shrugged. "I guess it's what I'd like to think it looks like."

He set down the cookie and smiled. "So, if you haven't known someone for a long time, you can't fall in love? I don't believe that."

She didn't know what to believe. "Well . . . then what does love *look* like to you?"

He slowly swiveled his body on the deck so he was facing Belle. As the *Judith* gently rocked, he said, "To me it looks like a beautiful woman with a spirit so strong you can't help but want to be near her." He brushed the back of his hand across her cheek. "It looks like brown eyes that see beauty in all things growing." He lightly placed his palms on Belle's shoulders. "It looks like me taking some of the weight off your small shoulders."

Belle drew in a deep breath. She wanted to believe that Boone could fall in love with her. He'd certainly fallen into her life when she needed someone to trust with a secret.

"May I kiss you, Belle?" Boone cupped his broad palm on her cheek and ran his thumb across her lips.

She answered by closing her eyes. He leaned in and whispered in her ear, "I'm going to kiss you now."

Her arms circled his neck as he gently pressed his lips to hers. Boone then drew away slightly and gazed into her eyes. He said softly, "It looks like this."

They kissed again, and Boone pulled her closer. He parted his lips slightly, and she followed his lead. When she dropped her arms from around his neck and placed her hands on his crossed thighs, he stopped kissing her and ran his hand down one of her braids.

"I want us to go slowly. You're so special, Belle."

She bit her lip. "Did I do something wrong?"

He chuckled. "No. You did everything so right that I need to . . . cool down a bit."

She smiled and took his hand. "All right. Maybe we should lie down on the deck and watch the clouds."

White puffs budded and bloomed above the pair as they lay next to each other, holding hands. As the sun faded behind a cloud, a wave of nausea passed through Belle's body. She swallowed, surprised by the sudden sickly stomach. Was it something she ate? She used her free hand to cover her eyes. After several minutes, the queasiness passed. She tenderly squeezed Boone's hand and decided she was simply not used to the rocking motion of a small boat.

Chapter 22

Merle had invited Abigail to Duggan's for a chat, but she'd declined, saying that if he wanted to visit, it would have to be with a spoon in his hand at Baker's. She needed to gut two pumpkins so the pies she'd promised to boarders would have time to bake before supper.

"Just plop everything on the ground," she now instructed, plunging a large spoon into the pungent, stringy mess.

The two sat along the river with pumpkins in their laps. Abigail had already carved holes in the tops of both.

Merle chuckled. "I don't know if I've ever had a conversation with you eye to eye, Abigail. You're always . . . doing." He gripped his spoon and began scraping.

Without looking up, she said, "The day I slack off is the day Mary Mather takes out an entire page in the *Press* to announce that I did."

Mary Mather owned the other boardinghouse in Fort Myers and ran it as if the entire town worked for her. She and her daughters, Cora and Celia, made it known to locals that all visitors should be directed to the Mather House. Their announcements in the newspaper read:

"SEND US THE SICK AND THE SOON TO
SETTLE—WE'LL SHOWER THEM WITH
SUNSHINE AND HOSPITALITY!"

They "invited" guests to spread the word that the Mathers offered better service and softer beds than the Palms Hotel. Any suggestion that their food was superior to Baker's was ignored by residents. It was common knowledge that Mathers' guests ate in the saloon to avoid the gut-roiling grub turned out by the bossy sisters.

"Oh, phooey," Merle said, his hand at rest inside the pumpkin. "Baker's reputation is untouchable." He softened his tone. "You could take a trip with me . . . let me spoil you for a week . . . and your business wouldn't skip a beat." He resumed the spoon work, pleased he'd gotten the words out.

Abigail ignored his comment and pointed toward the river. "There it is." She put down the pumpkin and spoon. "C'mon." She motioned for Merle to do the same.

He sighed. She wasn't going to make this easy for him.

They stood on the riverbank, looking at a large whiskered snout, its nostrils flared, breaking the surface of the water. A manatee that often fed in the area was up for air. Within seconds, it dropped back down to continue eating wild celery on the river bottom.

"My first sighting this season," she noted.

"Hmm," Merle said. He waited a few beats. "You know something? I'm a bit like that sea cow." He kept his gaze toward the river, as did Abigail. "I'm ready to come up for air after a long stretch of holding my breath."

Abigail crossed her arms and sighed. "Please don't make me do this again, Merle. It was hard enough the first time."

He laughed lightly. "I'll say."

When Belle was seventeen, Merle told Abigail he was interested in spending more time with her, in a romantic way. The topic was risky, but he was tired of reining in his feelings for the woman who'd captured his heart. They'd been good friends for years before Belle ever moved into Duggan's, but in the three years she'd helped him care for the teen, he realized that he not only admired Abigail, he desired her, too.

"I have to stop myself from grabbing your hand whenever we walk somewhere together," he'd confessed.

What he didn't tell her was how often he'd found himself wondering how long she'd lounge in bed with him after they made love. He imagined himself telling her, "Forget about those noisy coops and dirty cups." He'd offer to keep watch over the minutes while she rested in his arms, her unwound bun spilling long locks across his chest.

But back then, she'd immediately shut down his offer. "You're a wonderful man, Merle. The best I know. I simply will not risk losing your friendship to an experiment," she'd said.

And that was that. Awkward weeks led to the eventual return of a solid, caring friendship. He was Squirrel again and she was his gal.

Abigail turned away from the river back toward the chairs but left her pumpkin on the ground once she sat down. Merle joined her and turned his chair to face hers. A wide grin stretched across his face.

"That sea cow thing scared you, didn't it?"

She couldn't help but laugh.

"Oh, all that kind of talk scares me." She held her palms up and shrugged. "If you're a sea cow, I'm a gopher tortoise. I like to crawl around all day and then tuck back into my shell at night. I like my predictable life."

He shook his head and scratched it at the same time.

"I think you can like your life *and* love me."

Abigail waved him off. "I'm just saving you time," she said. "This town is full of women who'd love to stroll hand in hand with the strapping Merle Duggan." She counted off names on her fingers as she spoke. "Harriet Stone, Marge Addison, and Opal Ann Jackson are all interested."

Merle tilted his head to the side. "Why do you say that?"

"I'm not blind, Squirrel. Each of them has deliberately dropped something while shopping in your store, right near you, so you'll come around the counter and give them some extra attention."

He raised his eyebrows. "And you noticed this?"

Abigail rolled her eyes. "How could I miss it? One dropped an entire ham, the other two somehow each lost their grips on a sack of flour."

Merle leaned his head back toward the sky and lightly snapped his suspenders.

"My goodness. The ways of women are mysterious." He looked again at Abigail. "That ham bounced around the floor for quite a while, didn't it?"

They laughed together, Merle using his fist to mimic a ham bouncing across the air.

"Oh, my gal. That's one of the many qualities I love about you. No mystery. You tell it like it is." He rubbed his beard. "I just wish you'd tell me something different when it comes to us." He put his hands on the chair seat, about to raise himself off it. "I suppose I'll leave you be for now."

She picked up her pumpkin and nodded toward his. "I'll finish these." She patted the side of the squash and said quietly, "I'm a pumpkin, Merle. A bit of a mess on the inside." She looked up at him.

He squinted at her, wondering.

"Well, this 'wonderful man' is headed back to work." He stood. "Please let yourself think about it a bit longer this time."

He turned and moved toward the gate, his hand held up in a wave.

Chapter 23

As Belle approached the Abbotts' house, she was relieved to see that the Seminoles who'd traveled in from the Everglades were still awaiting the doctor's return. Several tribe members busied themselves in the sandy yard, re-thatching their temporary chickee huts with palmetto fans. Others collected eggs from the Abbotts' chicken coops, a gesture of gratitude in advance of the doctor's care. The Seminole women wore colorful skirts, capes, and weighty strings of pea-sized glass beads, light and dark blue, red the most prominent. The striking beads hid their necks within a thick stack that started under their chins and graduated down to their shoulders. At small trading posts along Florida's southernmost rivers, including the Caloosahatchee, Indian women traded dressed deerskins and alligator hides for the coveted beads.

Belle typically enjoyed admiring the women's dramatic appearance, but this afternoon she was focused only on what she desperately needed from them. She parked her tricycle and nodded at the Indians who watched her walk up to the house and knock on the door. Dr. Abbott's wife answered after what seemed like ten minutes.

"Well, hello there, Belle."

"Hello, Mrs. Abbott." She looked down. "Hi, Lulu." The little girl ran off, leaving her smiling mother in the doorway.

"It's nice to see you. We've missed you riding by."

Belle forced a smile. "I've moved from Duggan's to Baker's, and I'm afraid I've been busy with some gardening work for the Edisons." She gestured toward a clump in the yard that was more graveyard than garden. "But I'd be happy to give yours a freshening up if you'd like."

"Oh heavens, no. Thank you, but I'll just neglect it again. You focus on the Edisons'. Are they returning this winter?"

Belle nodded. "They hope to." She drew her palms together as if in prayer. "I know you're very busy, Mrs. Abbott. I came to ask you a favor." She lowered her voice. "Abigail has a young boarder visiting from Virginia with her family. I overheard her telling a fellow traveler that she's pregnant . . . and terrified."

"Poor dear," Mrs. Abbott offered.

"I didn't mean to eavesdrop. They were in the dining room and didn't know I was in the kitchen. She was crying as she spoke to the other woman. Maybe she felt she could confide in a stranger, I don't know. She's convinced her family will disown her because she's not married."

The sound of giggling children floated through the doorway from inside the house.

Mrs. Abbott shook her head. "I'm sorry, Belle, but Dr. Abbott is working in Key West, and he doesn't do . . . that sort of thing."

"Oh my goodness, no." Belle touched Mrs. Abbott's arm. "Forgive me for not being clear. I'm not here for Dr. Abbott's help. I thought perhaps the Seminole women knew of anything that might help this girl. An herb or . . . something natural."

Belle pulled out a wooden clothespin doll from her pocket and showed it to Mrs. Abbott.

"How clever. Did you make her?" Mrs. Abbott reached out and touched the doll's tiny beaded necklace.

"I did." Belle had gathered together fabric remnants, a wooden clothespin, and paint she found in the shed. She'd dipped the tip of a pine needle into black paint and dotted two eyes on the bulb of the pin. Onto the stout body she sewed a Seminole-inspired red skirt, white blouse, and yellow cape. Tiny glass beads in her sewing stash worked beautifully as a thread-strung necklace.

"I thought perhaps you could help me ask one of the Seminole women for a remedy in exchange for this doll."

Mrs. Abbott put her hands on her hips and sighed. "I know how grueling it is to get a baby from the womb into this world, Belle. And even if this young girl survives the delivery, with no family support she'll face a bleak future."

"Yes," Belle said softly.

"Well, Richard is much better than I at communicating with the Indians, but we can certainly try. Let me get his word notebook and check on the children, then I'll be right out."

Belle crossed her palms over her heart. "Thank you, Mrs. Abbott."

Once alone, Belle leaned her forehead against the doorframe, weakened by relief. She hadn't slept for days, horrified that her fear Julius would haunt her from the grave had actually come true. When her bleeding hadn't come that month, she refused to believe he'd violated her the night of the attack. When she felt sick aboard Boone's boat, she still denied the possibility of a pregnancy. But when both conditions continued for more than a week, she had to take action, before there was any movement inside of her.

Every night since she'd accepted the hideous truth, that Julius had impregnated her, she lay in bed staring into the dark and berating herself for thinking she'd escaped a destiny out of her control. The growing sense of freedom inside her had been real; she'd truly turned a corner. But there was Julius, waiting for her, demanding to shape the rest of her life with yet another despicable secret. And this time, the secret had to remain with her. Merle and Abigail would be at their wits' end with worry whether she chose to carry or miscarry a baby, not to mention having to reveal her history with Julius. Boone? She certainly couldn't tell him. He'd never want to be with a woman whose body once carried such a twisted man's child, even if only its beginnings.

She rubbed her dry, burning eyes. The one emotion that cut through her agony was intense desperation. *I have to stop this.*

When Mrs. Abbott returned, the two walked off the porch and into the yard where children dressed in short calico shirts rolled coconuts back and forth. The Seminole men stopped working and stood erect, balancing large colorful turbans shaped like grindstones atop their heads. They offered a nod or wave, as did two young women, one carrying a baby on her back in a cradleboard. Belle quickly looked away from the baby and noticed an elderly Seminole woman sitting in the shade of a live oak. The tree's bark and her skin bore similar patterns, weathered furrows, deepened and darkened with age. Her gray hair was swept up into a topknot and bangs fringed her forehead.

"Let's speak with her," Belle suggested, gesturing toward the woman.

They walked over and sat down on the ground next to her. The three women smiled at each other.

"Istonko," Mrs. Abbott said.

The old woman returned the hello with a nod.

Belle held up the clothespin doll and offered it. The woman took the doll, inspected it, then smiled, her cheeks forming two craggy mounds. Belle pointed at the doll and then at the woman, hoping she understood it was a gift.

Mrs. Abbott began the exchange without using words. She touched Belle's shoulder and then made a sweeping arc over her stomach to mimic a pregnant belly.

The woman looked at Belle and made the same motion.

Belle played along with the unfolding story. She pointed at her stomach and frowned. She pushed her hands away from her body in an attempt to indicate she didn't want a baby.

Mrs. Abbott leafed through the small notebook and found the Seminole word for *husband*. She shook her head no while she said, *"Acahay."*

The woman nodded slowly.

Mrs. Abbott searched for the word *medicine*. *"Hilliswaw."*

Pretending to draw with her left hand, the woman said, *"Swat-tchah-kah."*

Belle pulled a pencil out of her pocket and handed it to the woman, who gestured toward the notebook. Mrs. Abbott handed it over.

Her gnarled hand moved the pencil lead across a blank sheet of paper. She drew a rough sketch of a stem with long, narrow leaves. Tapping the drawing with the pencil point, she said, *"Eto micco."*

Belle didn't recognize the plant and looked at Mrs. Abbott.

"Hold on," she said. Her husband had alphabetized the words in the book, so she flipped to the *E*s. She scrolled down the page with her finger.

"Eto micco," Mrs. Abbott announced. "There it is."

"What does it mean?" Belle said, trying again to identify the penciled plant.

"Red bay."

"Red bay," Belle repeated.

The old woman cupped her knobby hands and mimicked taking a drink. *"As-si."*

More leafing through the notebook. "Tea," Mrs. Abbott said.

Belle looked at the woman and made the same drinking motion with her hands. She made it three times and then flipped her palms upright and shrugged her shoulders, as if confused.

The woman repeated the motion four times.

Belle nodded. Mrs. Abbott added a simple yes. *"Enca."*

"But do you think she means four times each day?" Belle asked.

Mrs. Abbott located the words for *one* and *day* and made the four sipping motions. *"Ham-kin neth-lah?"*

The woman nodded.

Belle reached out her hand to the Indian, who took it with a light squeeze. When their hands fell apart, Belle was pleased to see that the woman kept hold of the little doll.

Mrs. Abbott and Belle got up and walked to where she'd left her trike.

"Thank you, Mrs. Abbott. The girl departs from Baker's soon. I'll let her know privately about what we've learned."

Mrs. Abbott placed her hand on Belle's shoulder. "We have to help each other, right? Please let me know if you need anything else."

Belle didn't meet her eyes, unsure if Mrs. Abbott suspected the remedy was for her. But the thought left her mind immediately. She focused instead on her next step: taking a life to salvage her own.

Chapter 24

You could call it borrowing, but Belle knew she had stolen a little something from Abigail. Alone in Baker's kitchen, she'd taken at least ten dried bay leaves from a tin canister on the counter. She shoved them into her dress pocket and left.

"Please work," she'd whispered on the way out the door.

Now, several leaves were steeping in hot water inside something she really did borrow—an old teakettle she'd found in a kitchen cupboard. For several days now, she'd drunk tea in the morning and evening, trying desperately to lose the beginnings of the baby inside her. But so far, the only change she noted was a fuller bladder. Maybe the bay leaves weren't the red bay variety. Perhaps the Seminole squaw misunderstood. Belle could barely hide her panic, chatting with boarders and working away while managing the fact that her brain was now a spongy cesspool, soaking up every dark thought that spilled forth.

Life isn't simple, Mr. Wood. Watch me slit my wrists with your tarpon scale. Or, *Does Belle's son look like the Carson boy, or is just me? Tsk-tsk.*

The waiting and wondering was excruciating, and she was burning through *What ifs* like so much kerosene. Sometimes she

just stared at herself in the mirror. *What if the baby already has feet?*
What if Julius knows in hell that you're pregnant? She'd bear down,
as if she could push something out of her. Once again, Julius had
twisted one of life's most intimate experiences into a traumatic
mess. She loved children and wondered over the years if her life
would ever include them. Now, because of him, she was doing
everything in her power to cut short a pregnancy.

"... and, as you know, we're inviting delegates from more than
sixty clubs across the country."

Belle was trying to keep her mind off the miscarriage by listening to Kate on the box. She was also making a to-do list for
the Edison gardens. The plants were tucked into their beds, but
they would require weeding and care based on the whims of the
weather.

"Oh, I'm just so excited to attend the convention, Mrs.
Langley—"

"Please, Kate . . . again, call me Caroline."

"Yes. My apologies—Caroline. It's just that I listen to you
speak, and I've read about why you founded Aggregate. And now
we're talking in person!"

"Well, I wanted to call to congratulate you on winning our contest. Your motto best captures my vision for the coming national
club. After this convention, I hope that the local clubs will become
better organized and recruit more women . . . from all walks of life.
That's why your entry won."

Squealing. "I must tell you, I was at work, thinking about the
contest, and it hit me! There I was, surrounded by women who
look and sound nothing alike. American farm girls working alongside immigrants from Germany, Ireland, and England . . . all bat-
tling our way through the long day. The minute I thought of the
phrase, I wrote it down on my pay envelope: 'Unity in Diversity.' It
just rings so true, doesn't it? We women need to stick together, to
lift each other up." A loud sigh. "Oh, Caroline, I must be wearing
you out with my jabber."

A chuckle. "Not at all, Kate. As you know, I've been at this for twenty years. It's encouraging to hear such enthusiasm from a young member. Frankly, our movement needs new energy. I'm getting tired."

Belle looked over at the box. Caroline was tired. She was tired, too. Stretched out on the bed, lying on her stomach, she let her head drop down to the blanket. When—if ever—would her life allow for a long stretch of happiness? How weary she was of despair. She'd lived with it as a child, and now, just as she was coming into her own as a woman, here it was again. Belle pounded the bed with her palms. A romance with Boone had been unearthing itself like a spring crocus, and despair, in a dead man's boots, had stomped the promise of new love back underground.

She deeply missed Boone. Only when she saw him head toward town or across the street for some sort of digging project would she walk next door to work on the gardens. For his sake, she had to squelch their budding attraction. She was damaged goods—doubly now—and Boone deserved better. He was a good man worthy of a woman who required no repair, of a love that needn't look over its shoulder for the next hardship.

Belle closed her eyes. She pictured his blue eyes and remembered how it felt, his nose brushing across her neck one night by the river. He'd whispered, "You smell like lavender." His lips then explored her shoulder. "You taste like the bees made you." Every thought of him lay gently on her burdened heart. *Damn you, despair.*

". . . forward to it, too. Seek me out at the next meeting so we can say hello in person."

"Oh, I would love that! Thank you, Caroline. Can you tell me what topic we'll be discussing? I mean, if that's not against the rules . . . to tell me before the agenda goes out."

"No, not at all. I'll be leading a discussion on how women are portrayed in art as well as shedding light on some of our most prolific female artists in the city. And I'll share a little surprise with you, Kate, that won't be printed in the agenda. Our club will be sponsoring a scholarship for a promising art student of our choosing."

"How exciting! Caroline, I want you to know how much I enjoy being involved with Aggregate. Your efforts have brought so much hope to young women like me."

"Well, thank you, Kate. I do find myself wondering what sort of things you hope and long for . . ."

Belle was, too. "Yes, tell us, Kate," she said. Maybe Kate's hopes and dreams would have a chance.

"Well . . . um . . . I like to write. I don't have much time to, but I scribble poems and essays in a notebook. I find that writing is freeing. My mind can wander wherever it desires, which is rarely allowed. All day long a bell tells me when to start work, when to eat, when to go home. Clang, clang, clang. So, I suppose I hope for more time and freedom to express myself. That's why the club means so much to me. I'm surrounded by women who dare to long for more. We want to share our voices, support ourselves and each other, and contribute to society beyond just maintaining a home."

Belle mumbled into the bedcover. "Good for you." She envied Kate. Her work sounded suffocating, but her spirit was clearly strong and free. She sat up slowly and reached over to the bedside table for the teacup—her chance at freedom.

"Your words are very meaningful to me, Kate. And I understand your attraction to writing. I also was interested as a young girl. I edited my school newspaper and a publication for my brother's church. I worked hard to create a career as a writer. As you may know, I wrote a regular women's column and now I edit a magazine."

"And you didn't stop working after marrying and having children," Kate added. "You make us young women realize it's possible."

"Even more so for you, Kate, as society continues to progress."

Belle left the bed and walked to the window for a glimpse of open space. The cottage seemed smaller. Perhaps she was just bloated with tea. She swept the curtain to the side and looked out.

"Oh no." Her heart sank.

In the Edisons' yard, Paulette was talking to Boone. The sun was angled perfectly to make her red hair appear a seductive, crackling fire. Her pink dress was fluttering in the breeze. Boone was standing across from the glowing, beckoning Paulette. They were visiting and smiling.

"Don't. Do. This." Her words toppled onto each other like felled trees.

Stop it! She squinted through the windowpane. *What did he just say to make her laugh?*

Weak, Belle dropped to her knees and gripped the windowsill. Of course they were together! She'd pushed Boone away, and now Paulette was charming him. Beautiful, smart Paulette. She knew a decent, handsome man when she saw one.

"Please no." She hated how Boone was gazing into Paulette's green eyes. She'd probably already sung to him with her velvet voice aboard the *Judith*. For certain he was attracted to her womanly hips and ample breasts, round and nestled together like agonizingly perfect cantaloupes.

Belle slapped the sill when she saw Paulette reach over in her graceful way and touch Boone's muscular shoulder. She wanted to bang on the window so hard that the two would stop falling in love. She might just break the glass and cut out this damned baby from her stomach. Overwhelmed, she laid down on the floor, below the open window, a prisoner in her polluted world. *Be quiet!* She wanted the box to shut down, the chatty women to shut up. In fact, she wished everyone everywhere would just stop talking.

•••

Abigail walked toward the shed. She needed extra clothespins for a busy laundry day. As she passed by the cottage, she heard several female voices coming from inside. None sounded like Belle or any of her boarders. She turned and walked toward the cottage window that faced the river. Did Belle have guests? Who were they? She listened for a moment.

"... introduce you at the convention, Kate. That's part of winning the contest."

"Well, my goodness! What an honor. I'll be the proudest gal in New York City that day!"

Abigail listened for another minute. Why wasn't Belle talking? She didn't want to intrude but was curious. Slowly, she approached the window, pushed aside the curtain, and looked in. The room was empty, filled only with the sound of women chatting. Her eyes were immediately drawn to the dresser.

"Huh . . ." She gasped. Could it be? She stuck her head a bit farther into the window and stared.

Yes! There it was, looking nearly the same as she'd last seen it, except now it was churning! Belle must have found her contraption in the shed closet.

But, how in the world did she bring it to life?

Chapter 25

Several days later, a steady morning rain showed no sign of surrender, quenching thirsty gardens and all that drank from the sky. In the predawn darkness, Belle was flat on her back in sandy sludge, defying all the raindrops that were seemingly on a downward mission to blind her. Between forced blinks she stared upward.

Has it happened? Is it over yet?

She lay still, recovering from the gnawing pain of uterine contractions. Two hours ago her body had begun working through a miscarriage, wrenching her insides. When the cramps began, she'd stretched out on the cottage floor, unsure of what would happen next but hoping the pressure on her back and pelvis would end quickly. The air in the cottage seemed to grow thick, laboring her breath. When her head began to spin, Belle assumed she was going to die right along with the baby. She'd stumbled out into the rain, just as she had many years ago to escape Julius. As the sun rose, concealed by gray clouds, she'd collapsed behind a clump of wax myrtles several feet from the riverbank. The soft, wet ground was a relief from the hardwood floor.

Please get out of me.

The sand was cold and the rain was, too. Surely by now, there would be proof. Gingerly, she eased herself up to a sitting position. When she gathered up her sopped dress and looked down, the mess indicated she had miscarried.

"Thank God," she said, and sunk back down onto the soaked ground. Julius was fully gone, no trace of him. The realization overwhelmed her, but no tears came. Instead, Belle began to moan, her throat and chest vibrating, somehow soothing her. She closed her eyes and listened as immense relief moaned its way out of her body.

"Hello? Who's there?"

Belle recognized the voice and became silent. She could hear his nearby footsteps splashing in puddled water. And then he was next to her.

"My God, Belle," Boone said, kneeling down. "Are you all right? What's happened to you?"

She stared up at him but said nothing.

"Belle," Boone said quietly, as he took her hand. "Are you injured?" He lightly brushed back wet hair that was stuck to her cheek.

She closed her eyes, humiliated. Once again, one of her nasty little secrets had brought them together. In a weak voice, she said, "It's best you just stop helping me."

"No," Boone said. He gently drove his hands underneath her body and stood up with her in his arms. She offered no resistance, too weak to do anything but let him take care of her. "Should we go to Abigail?"

"Please no," she said. "I don't want anyone to see me like this."

Boone nodded. "Decker's already in town, and Abigail's probably busy fixing breakfast."

As Boone began walking, Belle quietly moaned.

•••

In the cottage, Belle undressed and put on a nightgown as Boone faced the wall. She got into bed and placed a towel underneath her. When she told him he could turn around, Boone shut the windows and barred the door. Once he'd removed his wet shirt and dried himself off, he sat down next to her on a stool.

"Belle, please tell me what happened," he said softly.

"If I tell you, you'll just try to help me. I don't want your help, Boone. I want you to stay away from me."

"But I don't understand," Boone said. "What have I done? You've been avoiding me, and now this."

She looked away from him. "Nothing. You've done nothing."

He dropped his head and sighed. "Look, the truth is, I *have* done something, Belle. Something very, very bad."

Belle turned back to him. She slowly pulled a hand out from under the covers and placed it on his knee.

"I haven't been fully honest with you. Let me tell you everything . . . and then maybe you'll tell me what happened this morning." He drew in a deep breath and blew it out. "So, I told you I killed a man when I lived in Kissimmee." He ran his fingers through his damp hair and rubbed the back of his neck. "It was my brother, Daniel."

Stunned, Belle whispered, "Oh my God."

"He was three years older, and we were close. We fought from time to time, but over stupid things, like whose horse was faster, who was or wasn't afraid of lightning. But we had each other's back. My father always told us, 'Look out for each other because no one else will. I'm not going to be around forever.'"

Boone stopped talking. Belle thought he might not be able to share the rest, but he continued.

"One afternoon, we snuck a bottle of our father's whiskey into my saddlebag and rode out to a hammock near one of our cow camps. After a few swigs, we decided to compare guns." Boone shook his head. "Stupid, I know. Our rifles were tied to the horses, but we were sitting with our revolvers, across from each other. We both made sure to empty our chambers—we weren't too drunk to forget that."

Boone twisted on the stool and turned away from Belle. He rested his elbows on his kneecaps. He put his head in his hands and spoke to the floor.

"I've been over it a thousand times in my head, and it seems impossible. I know I removed all six bullets. Daniel was bragging about what better care he took of his gun, joking that he was amazed my dirty piece even worked. And so, I pointed it at him . . . and I pulled the trigger."

Belle flinched, almost hearing the blast.

"I shot my brother, Belle. Right in the face." Boone sat silently for a minute. "He had the best smile, and I wiped it off forever."

Belle could almost feel the pain surging through Boone, as she gently rubbed his back.

"He was dead instantly. Blood was everywhere. I went to him and yelled at the top of my lungs. His horse had run off but Judith stayed. I crawled back over to where I'd left the bullets and counted. There were only five. I must have counted wrong, but I swear . . . before I pulled that trigger . . . I counted six." His voice dropped. "There was nothing I could do. Daniel was dead. So I put a bullet in my gun and pointed the barrel at my leg. The bullet tore through my calf muscle. I didn't even feel it."

The limp, Belle thought.

"I was desperate to feel anything other than . . ." Boone stopped talking.

Belle dragged herself up to a sitting position. She wrapped her arms around Boone from the back and hoped that every step, every day, was not an anguishing reminder of the accident.

"I'm so sorry," Belle said with her cheek resting on his bare back.

Boone's voice was barely audible. "My mother was sweeping the porch when I rode up with Daniel's body draped across my horse. I'd wrapped his head with my shirt, but the bleeding was overwhelming." He stopped talking and let the drumming of rain on the roof fill the cottage for a few moments. "I had to leave home after a few weeks. I couldn't stand to see the black circles under my mother's eyes and the anger in my father's. In a way, when Daniel died, my parents went blind. They couldn't see anything beyond his gravestone. They didn't care that I moved away because I could come back. They focused on the one who couldn't."

Belle said softly, "I see you, Boone. I see you." He slowly turned back around to face her. She wiped away his tears with her thumbs, then gently held his cheeks. "Forgive yourself, Boone. It was a horrible mistake."

He hung his head. When he finally looked up, into her eyes, he said, "Please don't push me away, Belle." His hand shook as he placed it on his chest. "Shame was the only thing in my heart . . . until I met you. Now, there's . . . everything." He took both of her hands. "When Daniel died, I told myself I didn't deserve a woman's company and certainly not what I'm feeling toward you. But I can't seem to stop myself. I care for you, Belle."

She slowly shook her head and pulled away. She drew the covers closer. "I'm sorry, but I won't allow it. To be near me is to be near calamity. It keeps coming. I can't break free." With her eyes shut, she said, "You should stay with Paulette."

Boone wiped his cheeks and shifted on the stool. "What are you talking about?"

"I saw you with her. She touched you. Paulette."

He squeezed his temples with a thumb and middle finger. "Paulette?"

"By the river. You two were talking and—"

"Ohhh, right. She came by to ask me if I'd be willing to build extra desks for the schoolhouse. Something about a project to help Seminole children."

Boone took back her hand and lightly kissed the top of it. "My heart wants you, Belle. Only you." He added softly, "Now, please. Tell me what happened today."

She let out a heavy sigh. For him—so he could stop caring about her—she told the truth. "I just lost a baby, Boone. I got pregnant the night Julius attacked me."

Boone's shoulders slumped. He rested his forehead in one hand and shook his head. Belle saw that she'd made her point. He now understood that loving her was not an option.

"You've been through too much, Belle." He looked up at her. "He's done too much."

Her eyes filled with tears. She looked away. "Surely, you're disgusted by me."

He gently turned her chin back toward him.

"Belle, you now know I killed my own brother. Can you care for *me*?"

She squeezed her eyes shut and brushed away a tear.

"You're strong, Belle. Stronger than anyone I know. But please, let me in. Something about you . . . is healing me." He leaned in and kissed her lightly. "I thought that was impossible."

Her body seemed to melt into the bed, suddenly relaxed, maybe for the first time in twenty-five years. A good man sat before her, honest and vulnerable. *Can you care for me?*

She wanted nothing more than to tell Boone yes, that they could care for and even love each other. She in fact already loved him—her Knight of the Two Rescues. But instead, she gave herself a moment, a chance to put some sleep between the ghosts of her past and the guardian angels of her future.

"I'm going to rest for a while," she said. "Will you watch over the world while I sleep?"

Boone nodded. "Always."

Chapter 26

Baker's was never completely quiet. Even when every boarder was out and about, there was still noise. Abigail didn't mind, though, because today—and every day—it was the sound of progress. The cover on a simmering pot was lightly clanging, a new fire in the stove was popping, and she was banging a jar against the counter. She'd promised her "famous" bread-and-butter pickles to George, and he was going to get them. When the lid finally released, she twisted it open and sampled a pickle.

"Mmm. Good batch."

As she buzzed around the kitchen, stacking clean plates and gathering ingredients for lemon fritters, Abigail thought, *Merle's right.* She was always on the move, all the while feeling behind schedule. Cooking kept her from cleaning, which kept her from yard work, and so went her days. Over the years, Merle would tease her about her state of perpetual motion. "Stand still at your own risk, Abigail." And then he'd let his bent arm fall flat, like a tree toppling. She would laugh, knowing he respected her determination to run an esteemed and successful business. He'd certainly told her so and also sang her praises in town. A boarder might tell her, "That Merle over at Duggan's sure seems sweet on you," or "Merle from Duggan's says you outwork everyone in town." And so, Merle knew very well how busy she already was when, eleven years ago, he'd asked for her help with a personal matter.

"The Carsons' daughter Belle is going to live with me now. Can you stop by Duggan's a little more often . . . get to know Belle?"

Abigail remembered being startled at first, shocked that the Carsons would release Belle from their care. She didn't know the family well, only that they were reliable churchgoers. Betsy struck her as quiet or tired, or both, often leaning into the arm of the pew with her eyes closed. That Merle would permanently take in the fourteen-year-old had surprised her, but she'd come to know him as kindhearted and a sound decision-maker, at least when it came to his business. Once Merle relayed the disturbing details of Belle showing up at his door, scared and injured, and with no explanation from the Carsons about what had happened, she'd understood why he wanted to protect her. Word of Belle's new living arrangement had caused a brief stir around town, but whenever Abigail heard gossip about the Carson-Duggan arrangement, she'd say, "I imagine you've shared those thoughts with Merle?" shutting down the conversation.

Before Abigail met Belle at age fourteen, she hadn't had but one or two brief exchanges with her over the years at Duggan's. Once, the little girl offered her raspberries from the handful Merle had just given her. Then, when Belle moved in with Merle, Abigail quickly grew fond of the quiet, curious girl. She stopped into Duggan's as often as she could to visit with her or check on what she might be sewing or drawing. If she had time, she'd walk with Belle to Baileys', the girl swinging her pail of gardening tools, a notebook in her other hand. Ever since she'd begun spending time with Belle, plants were the way to get her to talk the longest and light up with excitement, a passion that blossomed as she grew older. Abigail wasn't surprised when Mina shared Belle's comment to her about "being a plant in another life." Mina seemed pleased by her recommendation, referring to Belle as "just lovely."

As her relationship with Belle grew deeper over time, she and Merle further bonded as friends, supporting Belle in their own unique ways. She admired Merle's steadfast commitment to Belle, determined to guide her as best he could as she matured. He shared with Abigail how grateful he was that Belle could go to her with any "womanly" concerns. When Belle was seventeen, Merle asked if he could talk privately with Abigail. Because of how close she and Merle had become, she wasn't surprised that he'd developed feelings for her.

"I find myself wanting to hold your hand when we walk together," he'd said.

She'd quickly pushed back. As much as she liked the idea of truly becoming "his gal," she wouldn't allow it. Five years earlier when she still lived in Boston, a man had betrayed her and the pain still lingered. But she simply told Merle that she couldn't risk losing their friendship if a relationship failed.

Abigail pulled out a chair from the kitchen table and sat down. She wiped flour off her apron and sighed.

"Oh, Merle," she said quietly.

How she marveled at his open heart. Twice now he'd invited her into his life in a way that could change everything, but still he was willing to take the risk. Both times she was flattered but wary. Rubbing her neck with both hands, she made herself sit a while. Maybe she did owe Merle a longer look at whether their dating was a sound idea, even a wonderful idea. After all, the man in Boston had indeed broken her heart, but not because she'd once loved him.

"One thing at a time," Abigail said softly.

She was already wrestling with another big decision—whether to tell Belle the story behind the black box.

Chapter 27

Norville Decker was hard to miss. If you spotted flailing hands, they were Decker's. If you noticed pacing feet, they were Decker's. Belle could see a man in the distance pounding the sand with his fists and shaking his head.

Decker, she thought.

Returning from a quick visit to Duggan's, she was peddling down River Street when she saw him planted firmly on his hands and knees in a long row of sugarcane. He and Boone had been working on the new garden for weeks, located across the street from the Edison property. The board fence around it was incomplete, just two of the three levels of horizontal slats in place. She'd watched the garden take shape in fits and spurts, Boone and Decker at times working alone, sometimes together, surrounded by mounds of slips and potted plants awaiting their chance at a future. Always the men were making large piles of fertilizer disappear with their rusty spades, the muck spread liberally across all four acres. Maybe no one else noticed the haphazard layout, but she did. Instead of tidy rows there were random patches, as if plants fell out of the sky and rooted themselves wherever they landed. Perhaps those were

Edison's instructions, but she doubted a scientist would prefer such disorder. Then again, chaos was likely a part of experimentation.

Belle pulled her tricycle to the roadside and waved at Decker.

"Hello, Mr. Decker," she said from the trike's bench.

She'd only spoken to him a half dozen times in the course of her stay at Baker's. More often than not he was hidden away in his cottage doing whatever he did, which apparently wasn't eating very much. His clothes appeared as slack sails, with no meat or muscle to fill them. His long, thin neck served as the mast. When the two did have a conversation, it was brief. He'd always end the talk with "I'll take those," as he snatched nursery receipts from her hand.

"Can I help you?" he replied without looking up from a mound of withered strawberry plants.

"Well, actually, I was wondering if I could help *you*." She remained on the trike.

Decker looked up and eyed her, his face skewed sideways. "Help with what?"

She chose her words carefully, Decker's tone clearly defensive. "Well, as a fellow gardener, I know there are always more weeds and work than there are hands." She raised hers in the air and wiggled her fingers. "Mine aren't busy right now."

She hoped Decker would accept her help. Since the miscarriage, a deep sense of relief had washed over her. She had endured—and herself done—a horrible thing, but she was now the grateful owner of her life and future. A renewed energy compelled her to support the people she cared about more than ever, even Decker and especially Boone. Mr. Edison had them both scrambling to keep up with his projects.

Decker unearthed a clump of wilted strawberry stems and leaves, talking again to the ground. "Boss wants twenty by one hundred of these." He sighed. "I'm quite sure he wants them alive, too."

Belle dismounted and invited herself to the edge of the garden.

"Strawberries love cooler weather, but they have to stay warm. You just need to plant them in full sun." She knelt down. "The sugarcane is blocking their light."

Decker sat back on his knees and looked up at the cane. "Ugh." He reached for a book buried in a thick nest of ryegrass.

"I've got so much to do and so many instructions that I can't keep it all straight." He shoved the book toward her. "Mr. E sent a dozen books, but you know what he didn't send? Clocks with more time on them." He sneezed twice. "He calls this a truck garden; I call it the devil's backyard."

Belle grinned and took the book, *The Florida Agriculturist.*

"So, we've solved the strawberry problem. What else are you planting?" She flipped to a random page.

Decker removed his spectacles and rubbed the lenses with a clean patch of his dirty shirt. Belle thought he favored a mouse with them on, now a mole without them. One might call his look distinctive, a staccato of sharp features including piercing brown eyes, their lids devoid of lashes. Whether he wanted it to be or not, the upright tuft of black hair in the middle of his bald head was his signature feature.

Gesturing toward a grouping of seedlings, he said, "I'm supposed to plant something called poor man's dish-rag. *Pff*—could be named after me. I haven't been paid in a year."

Belle pursed her lips. She wanted nothing to do with disparaging words about Mr. Edison. He was her boss, too, and she found Decker's complaining unbecoming. They were all extremely fortunate to work for the renowned family.

"Let's see here," she said, and began to leaf through the book. "Poor man's dish-rag . . ." She soon tapped a page. "Here it is." She read aloud from the guide. "Poor man's dish-rag is also known as bonnet gourd, dishcloth gourd, and vegetable sponge." She hummed lightly as she skimmed the article for pertinent information. "As the plant is tropical, it can stand the full heat of the sun all day without drooping and grow all the better fruit." She looked up and smiled.

Decker's face showed nothing but a slight sunburn on his sunken cheeks.

Belle continued, "The luffa is fully entitled to membership in the cucumber family and is in no sense a gourd, as it has sometimes been called."

"Boss called it a *squash*," Decker spat.

Belle hugged the book to her chest. "Mr. Decker, I'm sure they are all in the same plant family." She abandoned any effort to curb her tone. "Our boss has changed the world for the better, for goodness' sake. We can give him 'squash,' can't we?"

Decker narrowed his eyes until the whites disappeared. "You don't know the stress I'm under . . . because of him."

Belle put down the book, marking the page with a wide blade of grass. She decided that perhaps Decker could use an ear.

"Why don't you tell me about it?" she said. "The stress. You've made it clear you're owed a chunk of money. Fair enough."

Decker stared at her. He sneezed into the crook of his arm and then began to vent.

"If you must know, Mr. Edison and his close friend who owns the guesthouse are at war, something about a business deal with a phonograph contract. Word is that Ezra Gilliland worked a deal behind E's back." He muttered "idiot" toward the ground. "I'll bet the firm of Edison and Gilliland will soon be"—Decker cut the air with a palm—"no more."

Belle said, "Oh dear."

"And 'no more' means *more* work for me. Now I'm doing two sets of books instead of one." He raised and lowered his palms like scales. "Wharf repair: one-third Gilliland, two-thirds Edison. Posts for the main gate: fifty/fifty. And on and on." He groaned. "Why people go into business with friends, I'll never know."

"Well, I'm sure the math is pesky, but it must be devastating for Mr. Edison to lose a dear friend over a business deal," Belle said.

Decker shrugged. "Dangle a big pot of money in front of people, even a cucumber and squash—in the same family—and the relationship ends up in the muck."

Belle was beginning to regret stopping by the garden.

"Perhaps they'll work it out one day," she said, pulling weeds around her. "Good friends are to be treasured."

Decker followed her lead and ripped up clumps of grass. "Good friends don't stab you in the back."

"Agreed, Mr. Decker," she said, happy to hear him say something of merit. "Where is Boone today?"

"Knee-deep in banana bushes on a channel somewhere up the river. Boone likes to dig." He flipped his fingers toward the book. "Anything about creating banana beds in there?"

"I'll check." Leafing through the book, she asked, "Did you hire Boone?"

Decker stopped weeding and gingerly separated a stick of grass from its sheath. He chewed on the end, and said, "Yes, but against my better judgment."

Belle flipped pages and waited for an explanation.

"He showed up with a bandage wrapped around his calf on the outside of his dungarees. I wasn't impressed. What did I need with a gimp? There was an enormous amount of physical labor to be done over several months. I told him to move along."

She looked up, irritated by his use of the word *gimp*. "And?"

"And, he refused to leave. He said something about outworking every man and animal in sight. He grabbed a pick and uprooted cabbage palms until dark. The bandage was soaked with blood, but he just kept tearing out palmettos, like they'd wronged him." Decker shrugged. "No man I'd ever met worked as hard or as long. Even the mules fell asleep before he did. That bum leg? Didn't notice it anymore. I just noticed how much work he got done."

Proud of Boone, Belle said, "I'd say right now that those banana bushes are losing the fight to stay in the ground."

Decker nodded. "I've got to give it to the boy," he said. "He stays focused on the task at hand. Even the gal who lived in the Baker's cottage before you couldn't distract him." He rubbed his palms together to shed the dirt. "She sure tried, though. A real schemer."

Belle pushed up the lid of her straw hat to better see Decker and fully focus on this new information.

"Oh, really. Who was she?"

Decker smiled, revealing a row of tiny square teeth, each violated by cigar smoke.

"Elena Larkspur. That woman would think of any reason to get Boone over to the cottage." He raised his voice to mimic hers. "'Can you kill a spider for me? I think a squirrel is nesting in the roof. Will you fix this stubborn window, Booney?'"

"Booney?" Belle repeated, the word blasting forth from her mouth. She was already annoyed by this Elena.

"Oh, sure. She had lots of nicknames for him: Booney, Boone Boone, Bunny."

Ridiculous! Belle pulled her hat back down, retreating from the nicknames. *She probably broke that stuck window on purpose.*

Decker continued. "She sometimes wore a black silky . . . thing . . . that seemed like it should be worn behind closed doors." He shrugged. "Any man would have gladly done whatever she wanted. But not Boone. And that woman was persistent."

"And attractive?" Belle mumbled from behind her hat.

"Oh my. Elena was head-to-toe beautiful, the kind of woman a man wants *on* his arm, and *in* his arms, and . . ."

"Enough," Belle said, interrupting.

He stroked his tuft. "I don't know how or why, but Boone showed that girl no interest, as if she was just another task to cross through on his chore list." He swatted away a wasp. "About a week before you arrived, she moved out." He shook his head. "Word was she had buckets of money."

Belle let out a long sigh as the truth washed over her. Elena wanted Boone, badly. How many other Elenas had tested him and his promise to swear off love after Daniel died? Boone had chosen her. *My very special Boone.* She knew now more than ever how lucky she was that he'd opened his heart to her.

"Boone is a good man," Belle said softly.

"Boone is a good digger," Decker replied.

Belle removed her hat and eyed Decker. "Boone does *not* like to dig, and you know it."

Decker grinned. "Let's talk about bananas."

Belle reopened the book and began to search for more information. As she scanned the pages, she wondered if there was a chance that Decker was a bit like a banana—tough peel, soft center.

Chapter 28

Abigail was doing two things she never did: sitting still and thinking about her life before Baker's. She found neither pleasurable, but seeing the contraption in the cottage—and listening to it work—drove her to the riverbank to reflect, undisturbed. The last meal of the day had been served, and a full pot of coffee was on the stove for the boarders.

Her girth made sitting cross-legged uncomfortable, so she was lying on her back on a thick blanket that she'd fished out of an armoire reserved for winter gear. Typically, in this position, she fell asleep instantly after a long, strenuous day. But tonight, her eyes were wide open, watching dusk give way to a sky full of eager stars.

I've got it, Papa! I've got it right here! Abigail smiled, thinking about her father's toolbox. He used to let her tote it around whenever he wasn't using it. She was allowed to tinker with whatever tools she wanted. *Just be careful, Abi.* At nine years old, she was building the fastest sleds in the neighborhood and fancy pull-along wagons, some with a roof. Her brothers adored her creations and collected scrap wood to keep their toymaker busy.

And then her father died suddenly. He dropped to the floor with a thud that Abigail could still hear in her mind, as if she were twelve again. Widowed with three children, her mother pulled her and her brothers out of school and—in desperation—secured jobs for them at the town's cotton mill in Springfield, Massachusetts.

The work was deafening and dangerous. Still, Abigail was fascinated by the towering machines—some with sharp metal teeth, others with large rollers or bobbins. Hired as a doffer, she spent her workday removing fully threaded bobbins on spinning frames and replacing them with empty ones.

One day, a woman running a loom was nearly killed by a heavy, steel-tipped shuttle that flew off the machine when a thread broke. A thud was followed by a scream that even the churning machines couldn't drown out. It wasn't the first time a flying shuttle had injured a worker; others had even died. The fatal flaw in the process engaged Abigail's mind. At home, she sketched drawings and built a wooden model of what she deduced would solve the problem. The shop assistant, eager to keep his mill workers working, agreed to try her solution, a small piece of wood screwed into the loom's frame close to the spring where a thread could break. An added wooden bar kept the shuttle from ejecting itself. Her invention worked! It was immediately added to all six hundred looms in the mill and also in factories across New England. She knew nothing of patents at the time, only that she'd used her brain to protect people. The achievement was exhilarating.

Abigail now drew in a deep breath and groaned as she rolled her thick body up to a sitting position. There was no need to share those details with Belle. She left the blanket on the ground and walked toward the cottage. She wanted to see the box up close, and if Belle was interested, share the story of why she'd moved from Boston to Fort Myers.

•••

"I certainly didn't mean to disrespect your privacy when I looked through the cottage window that afternoon, Belle."

Abigail was sitting on the bed in the cottage, across from Belle, who was gripping both arms of the rocker.

"I don't see it that way at all, Abigail. In fact, I disrespected your privacy by taking the box out of your shed. My apologies."

"None necessary, Belle. It's high time I talked about that blasted box." She gestured toward it, dormant on the dresser.

"I'm glad we can talk about it." Belle paused. "Honestly, I'm still a bit in shock."

"Me, too," Abigail said, and smiled. "If you'd like, I can explain." She lightly touched a yellowed roll of paper beside her.

"Yes, please do." Belle would never have guessed that her discovery would lead to Abigail sitting in the cottage discussing an invention of *her* creation. Then again, so much had surprised and challenged her since she'd moved to the Baker property.

"When I was your age, I worked at a plant in Massachusetts that manufactured paper bags."

She explained that all day long she stacked bags made by a machine that formed what she deemed an inferior product. The bag was designed as a narrow sheath, flat like an envelope. The user had to hold the bag upright while awkwardly stuffing items into it.

"Everyone sees me as a workhorse," Abigail said, "but I have a very active brain. For as long as I can remember, I've always been on the lookout for something to create or improve upon. I don't know . . . I suppose it's like your passion for gardening. We all have a golden compass inside of us, one that points us toward our best selves."

"So true," Belle said. *Astonishing.* An altered Abigail was emerging before her like a cicada from its split shell.

"Every day at work, I stared at that bag machine and its process," she said. "I knew there was a better way."

Abigail said she mulled over what could and should be altered on the existing machine. Ultimately, the answer was a device that could fold and glue a bag with a flat bottom. The new rectangular base would allow for the bag to stand on its own when filled with food or wares.

Abigail grabbed the rolled paper and unfurled it on the bed. "I haven't looked at these in so long." Belle got up to help her hold the corners and to examine the images on it.

"My goodness," Belle said. She marveled at the detailed images. "Did you draw these?"

Abigail nodded. "They are quite something, aren't they?"

The paper included two drawings of the same machine. Fig. 1 featured a side view of what she'd labeled "bag machine." Fig. 2 was a drawing looking down on the same device. The side view made more sense to Belle. It appeared that a series of interlacing gear wheels would move several metal arms tasked with folding responsibilities.

"Such intricate work," Belle noted.

Abigail said that from the drawings, she had built a wooden model of her invention. After more than a decade of work experience behind her, she realized the need for a patent to protect her design and the potential earnings the machine would generate.

"I moved to Boston and found factory work. I needed to be there to supervise the manufacture of my prototype in a machine shop." She let loose the paper, which rerolled itself. Belle seated herself back in the rocker.

Abigail sat without speaking or moving. Belle had never seen her look so forlorn.

"What is it, Abigail?" Belle asked softly.

She shook her head. "He stole my design. That bastard stole it."

Belle placed her palm on her chest. "No."

"Yes. When my machine was perfect, I applied for a patent. It was rejected. I couldn't believe it. I *knew* I'd invented a machine that didn't yet exist." Her eyes welled up with tears. "That patent belonged to me."

She explained that an inventor in the Boston machine shop had memorized the basic design of her prototype, built his own, and received the patent first.

"Oh, Abigail. I'm so sorry." Belle wanted to go to her but stayed seated, listening.

"I tried to fight back. I took him to court but lost the lawsuit." She closed her eyes. "That horrible man said in his defense, 'A woman could never design such a sophisticated machine.' Based on his ruling against me, the judge agreed."

"Shameful!" Belle said, popping her fist against the armrest. "But, what about your drawings?"

Abigail shook her head. "Didn't matter." Tears rolled down her cheeks.

Belle sat quietly as Abigail wiped her eyes with her apron. She looked away, down at her cat, busy taking a bath next to the rocker. As Coquina licked an errant stripe back into place, Belle considered that perhaps everyone and everything was constantly trying to manage the disorder of life. It was unavoidable, embedded in the very germ of being.

Abigail let out a long sigh and continued. "I was so enraged and disgusted that I decided to leave Boston and move south. Better weather, a fresh start."

"My, my," Belle said, "that's quite a move. Did you know anyone here?"

Abigail crossed her arms atop her large breasts. "I knew a woman who was hired here as the town's first paid schoolteacher. She wrote me several letters. I guess the way she described the tropical setting and friendly atmosphere gave me the confidence to move. Plus, she mentioned that the boardinghouse was up for sale. Owning my own business appealed to me because I'd worked for someone else since I was twelve years old. I had money saved, enough to buy Baker's, and I quickly taught myself how to make food that would keep the boarders coming back. Cooking is tinkering, and baking is science, right?"

Belle tilted her head to one side. "Abigail, who else knows this about you?"

"No one. Not even Merle." She released her arms. "I'm not one to dwell on the past, especially the painful parts. But"—she looked over at the box—"when I saw that thing working, I had to see it. I wanted you to know its story."

Belle lightly knocked a knuckle on the rocker's armrest. "Well, I still don't."

Abigail slapped her hands on her thighs, as if signaling a shift in mood. She stood and walked to the dresser. With the box in hand, she sat back down on the bed.

"Hmm. It was still on the top shelf when you found it in the shed closet?"

"Yes, but as I said earlier, it was lying on its side with the wires cascading out."

"Uh-huh," Abigail said. "And Coquina was up on the shelf?"

Belle nodded. "She was. Who knows? Maybe she fiddled with the wires . . . like she was playing with strands of yarn."

"Could be." She looked at the cat. "Maybe that rascal is the reason this thing finally works."

Abigail laid the box on the bed. She explained that when Mr. Edison moved in next door, a yearning stirred inside her, a desire to think deeply and tinker again.

"It was as if the passion I'd packed away for so long demanded to see the light of day. It was so powerful that I couldn't focus." She chuckled. "I kept burning food and dropping plates."

Belle smiled. "Unimaginable."

One evening, knowing she was violating the Edisons' privacy, she snuck into the laboratory. She'd seen Boone—and the Edisons during their honeymoon—use a key hidden under a turtle shell on the ground.

"Belle, when I walked into that lab, I nearly fainted. All of the blood rushed to my head, as if the biggest part of my brain had reignited. It was all I could do to leave the machines alone. I wanted to fire them up, see how they worked."

That first trip wasn't her last. She'd snuck back into the lab several more times, again while the family was up north. Careful to leave no trace of her trespasses, she touched nothing. Inhaling the air in the lab was enough to stimulate her mind.

"Well, I have to admit, Abigail, you're a better woman than I." Belle sighed. "I looked through one of his notebooks when I took the Dragons Blood to the lab. It was sitting out on a worktable." She shook her head. "That was very disrespectful of me."

"How can I possibly be better, Belle? I repeatedly visited the lab without permission!" She nodded. "I saw those notebooks, too. The only reason I left them alone was because of what happened to me at the machine shop. Inventors should have the utmost respect for the hard work of another."

Belle shook her head. "There's certainly no risk of me running off with one of Mr. Edison's ideas. Nothing made sense."

"Mmm. I'm sure it was wildly fascinating." Abigail's eyes lit up.

"It truly was," Belle said, "but you're a better artist."

Abigail grinned and then continued.

During what she vowed to herself would be her last visit to the lab, she told Belle how she came across copper wire heaped in a corner. Knowing it was utterly wrong, she smuggled the bundle into Baker's and for weeks pondered its use as an electrical conductor. She barely slept.

"I was exhausted and invigorated at the same time." She twirled a finger around her ear. "The gears in my brain were spinning at high speed. I filled page after page with drawings of a coffee canister equipped with wires, several cogwheels situated along the interior base. The handle would drive the wheels." She tapped the canister. "I painted it black to look more like a machine."

"And, did you know its purpose?"

Abigail picked up the box. "My goal was to create a more compact telephone for use on desks. The user would have easy access while working." Her shoulders slumped. "I *never* meant for it to intercept active phone calls. That's an invention that probably shouldn't exist."

"Well," Belle offered, "I've certainly been the benefactor of your brilliance, Abigail. The conversations I've listened to have been quite enlightening. They're the reason I created the Circle Club."

She cocked her head. "What do you mean?"

"Well, the box somehow connects with a telephone that's being used by a young woman in New York City named Kate Hallock. She's involved with a growing movement up north to encourage women to support one another. The idea is that together women can uplift themselves and their communities."

"Hmm. Interesting," Abigail said. "I'm glad you've found it helpful, Belle, but let me be honest." She picked up the box. "This invention? I put it on that shelf to forget about it. I was so ashamed that I'd stolen from Mr. Edison." She added softly, "I was actually glad it never worked. I deserved that."

"But it *does* work. You created a viable machine, Abigail." She joined Abigail on the bed and put the box in her lap. "Would you like to crank it up?"

Abigail sat quietly for a moment. She then stood and smoothed her apron.

"Under one condition." She held up her finger. "This will be the last time it's used. I want to dismantle it and return the wire to the lab. It's the right thing to do."

Belle stared at Abigail. She did not want to stop using the box. The northern conversations were like getting a glimpse of the future, or at least some exposure to advanced thought. She would miss Kate's march toward meaning. She was certain she could learn much more from her about confidence and optimism. Still, Belle wanted Abigail to be able to forgive herself, to right her wrong. That mattered more.

Belle couldn't help but smile as she watched Abigail crank the handle on her invention. The sight was stunning. It wasn't the whiz next door who'd created the machine, it was the genius on *her* side of the fence!

"I have the best luck when I crank it at about this speed," Belle suggested. She placed her hand over Abigail's, demonstrated the rate, and then let go. She wanted Abigail to bring it to life.

The box was on the dresser. Abigail was standing in front of it, her face at a safe distance from the machine, as advised by Belle.

Within a minute of steady cranking, the show started. Tiny sparks ascended from the box, which began to wobble.

"Is this the process?" Abigail asked, continuing to crank.

"Yes. Keep cranking until we get a few more sparks, and then we should hear voices. That's when you should stop turning the handle."

"Got it."

Belle watched Abigail observing the machine. She wasn't blinking; her mouth was open slightly to accommodate her deep breathing. Belle's skin prickled as she watched the inventor experiencing her working creation for the first time.

". . . the local men's baseball teams."

Laughing. "Are they really outscoring the men?"

Abigail stopped cranking and turned toward Belle. She mouthed, "*Amazing!*"

Belle nodded exuberantly. She grabbed Abigail and hugged her. "*You're* amazing." Belle led Abigail to the rocking chair. "They can't hear us."

Abigail plopped down in the seat. "They can't?" She chuckled. "My brain is already trying to figure out what I did wrong." She tapped her temple with her finger. "Typical inventor."

Perched on the edge of the bed, Belle smiled. "Listen . . . to what you did right."

". . . and the best part is they wear bloomers when they play ball!"

"Well, you're all set then, Katie kid!"

Belle beamed at Abigail. "It's Kate and her friend BB."

Abigail placed a fist under her chin, her elbow resting on her belly. "This *is* quite something."

". . . don't have time to play baseball. But a girl can dream, right?"

"Yes, she can! And this one is dreaming about a proposal from Gerald. What is wrong with that man? I may have to ask *him* to marry me!"

"Now you're catching on, BB. Go after what you want!"

"Oh, for heaven's sake. Next thing you know I'll be swinging a bat and wearing bloomers!"

For the next twenty minutes, two women talked and two women listened. Silently, Belle wished Kate well, and also goodbye.

Chapter 29

Alice was running around the park, wiggling her fingers in the air. The tips of her leather gloves were cut off. She stopped in front of Hazel, who was creating more of the truncated gloves.

"Does your mother know about this?" She flopped down on the ground and stared at Hazel.

"No," she said, and snipped off a glove's pinkie finger. "But if she did . . ." Hazel spread the blades of the scissors and pretended to cut her own throat, complete with a choking noise. Alice smiled.

Members of the Circle Club were dotted across Blevins Park, no chairs, no circle. This afternoon was less about talking and more about creating the gear required to play baseball.

Belle had proposed the idea on the latest postcards, and when the women arrived at the park, each agreed to try to throw and hit a ball. Belle had written in the card that "Baseball could be an enjoyable way to learn to work together for future community projects."

Abigail had once again provided snacks, but this time stayed to help. She was kneeling on the ground, running a plane across a stick of lumber. Curled shavings littered the area around her and stuck to her apron.

Sadie stood nearby. "That's starting to look like a fine bat, Abigail. Keep at it." She slowly rocked a sleeping baby whose tiny fingers were resting atop a baseball. "I'd almost hate to hit this ball, Paulette. It's perfectly clean and white."

Hazel joked, "My mother would approve of that ball."

The others laughed.

"We should definitely use it," Paulette said. She was sitting sidesaddle on a tree stump, peeling an orange. "My sister works at the Spalding plant. She had that ball shipped to me when she first got the job. I can ask her to send more should we need some."

"Now, ladies, let's see how this goes before we inherit a herd of baseballs." Amelia pushed her glasses farther up her nose. She was weaving palm fronds into a makeshift home plate. "I'll bet I don't even see that ball coming at me." Several bottles of elixirs and liniments she'd brought from her apothecary lay beside her, at the ready should there be injuries.

Poppy put her gloved hands on her hips and kicked at her long skirt. "I may trip if I run. We won't be running, will we, Belle?"

Alice spoke first. "Pants." She pointed down at her legs. "They make sense."

Belle laughed and handed Amelia another palm frond for weaving. "You're way ahead of us, Alice."

With a lacy handkerchief, Paulette brushed off pulp stuck to her fingers. "Actually, my sister says women up north are playing baseball in their bloomers."

Belle and Abigail glanced at each other. They smiled and then returned to the business of baseball.

•••

Several men had gathered to watch, arms folded or elbowing each other in the ribs. One man rattled a cowbell. The sight of eight women playing baseball in the park was a first.

"I don't know when I've laughed so hard!" Amelia said, and started laughing again. She was tickled by watching Hazel try to catch her wild throws. The girl was doing her best and seemed to enjoy falling, giggling each time she did.

Belle checked on the baby, sleeping on a blanket far from the action. She waved at Alice, at the ready, waiting to chase hit balls. Alice waved back and then yanked on her fingerless gloves, too big but helpful as padding. Belle looked over at Poppy, pleased they'd made peace since their unnerving conversation about Merle.

Sadie was shouldering the bat, yelling, "Where the hell are the children, Virgil?" She'd spotted her husband standing with the other men.

He yelled back. "Flossie's got 'em. You look good, buttercup!"

Sadie shooed him away with her hand but smiled.

Paulette and Poppy now had the ball and were rolling it back and forth.

"This isn't quite baseball, is it?" Paulette laughed and scooped up Poppy's perfectly straight roll.

"First we roll, then we throw," Poppy answered. She bent one leg back and forth, flexing her knee.

Abigail chose a spot for home base and placed the palm mat there. She then paced out where a pitcher might stand.

When Belle rejoined the group, she said, "What do you say we let Sadie hit, ladies?"

Alice jumped up and down, still standing in what they'd designated as the outfield. "Ready!" She waved her arms over her head.

Belle walked the baseball out to Abigail.

"Go easy on us." She smiled.

Abigail laughed. "I can't stay very long. I've got three pheasants to clean for supper."

Hazel had agreed to play catcher and crouched behind the plate. Sadie held the bat high, her bent arms held to the side. Abigail tossed her an underhanded pitch.

With a *swoosh*, Sadie swung the bat with as much ferocity as someone wielding an ax. The wood nicked the ball, which flew backward and hit Hazel in the lip.

"Ahhhh!" she screamed and fell onto her back. Sadie dropped the bat and showered Hazel with apologies. All but two of the male spectators ran toward her. Amelia got to her first, opening a bottle of witch hazel as she ran.

"Let me have a look, honey." She squatted next to Hazel and inspected her lip. It was split slightly and bleeding. "I'm going to dab your lip. It's going to burn a little." She touched a small cloth to the cut. "Just a little sting."

Hazel winced and stared up at John Parker, son of the well-to-do man who owned Parker's grapefruit grove.

"That ball had it out for you," he said, and smiled. "Are you all right?"

She nodded and attempted to unstick sweaty hair from her forehead.

Virgil reached out his hand to help Hazel up. "Sadie hasn't busted *my* lip yet, but I know she's wanted to."

Hazel started to smile but stopped. "Oww." She took his hand and stood. "Thank you, Virgil."

John took her elbow. "I'll help you over to that tree stump to sit down."

"Oh, thank you, John." She walked with him, adjusting her lopsided ponytail. "I was supposed to catch the ball with my hands, not my mouth."

He laughed and stayed with her after she sat down.

Sadie was at bat again, her expression and stance signaling her desire to smack every bit of the ball this time. Paulette had replaced Hazel as catcher but positioned herself several feet behind home plate.

Abigail removed the ball from her apron pocket, took a deep breath, and lobbed it toward the plate. The pitch was accurate, giving Sadie every chance to connect.

The pop of the ball off the bat started Alice running back and forth, searching the sky for her target.

Belle quickly spotted the baseball and grinned at what she saw happening on the field. Sadie had launched the ball with more speed than height—a real zinger. Just behind the zigzagging Alice was Ida, marching forward, focused on Hazel. Her arms swung back and forth in wide arcs, and she was talking well out of earshot. Belle shielded her eyes from the sun for a better look.

Bam! With a thud, the baseball collided with Ida's massive hat, adorned with a large silk bow and a stuffed bird, front and center, its wings outstretched as if in flight.

"Eeeeeeeeek!" Ida screeched, frozen in place.

The enormous hat careened off her head and flopped to the ground alongside the ball. It landed upside down, the bird's head in the sand. Ida grabbed her head, shocked by the sudden and violent removal of her signature accessory.

Belle covered her mouth with both hands to hide her smile. She glanced over at Hazel, who had stood up but made no move toward her mother. No one did. Sadie leaned on the bat.

"I don't see any blood," Amelia said to Poppy.

"And the bird was already dead," Poppy added.

Abigail walked toward home plate, her back to the incident, grinning at Sadie.

Ida balled her hands into tight fists. She spun around toward Alice, who was giggling.

"Pick up my hat," she hissed. "Do it now."

Alice slowly made her way toward the hat. Once there, she bent over and picked up the ball next to it. As she passed by Ida, she said, "You're not very nice."

Furious, Ida stamped her foot in the sand. She picked up her hat and headed for the tree stump, where the women and some of the men had formed a small group around Hazel. Ida was shaking her head as she approached. Her hair was disheveled and her finger was jabbing at the air. "First of all, I was just almost killed by a farmer's wife." She glared at Sadie.

Virgil tugged at his earlobe, long immune to Ida's condescension. "Calm down, Ida. Your store is filled with food from this *lowly* farmer's field." He put his arm around Sadie.

Ida continued. "And *then*, I have to hear from Mrs. Randolph in Cravin's that *my* daughter is playing a man's game with other women." She glared at Belle. "I *knew* you were up to no good with this club."

Belle was pleasantly surprised by her calmly delivered response. "You don't know anything about me, Ida."

"I know enough," she snapped back. She turned back to her daughter and leaned in toward her busted lip. "Have you been fighting? This is outrageous!" She noticed John Parker for the first time. Her tone softened. "I am so sorry you have to see Hazel behaving like an impious, indelicate, impure hoodlum, John. I did *not* raise this."

John looked down at his boots and back up at Ida.

"Well, that's interesting, Ida. I was just thinking how much I didn't expect this from Hazel."

Ida pursed her lips so tightly that they disappeared. She nodded at him in agreement.

He continued. "In fact, I was surprised to see her out here, running around and even falling to the ground."

Hazel hugged her body and looked down.

"What's most eye-opening, though," John said, "is that I *never* imagined that a daughter of yours, Ida, would allow herself to have so much fun."

Ida stopped nodding and glared at John.

He turned toward Hazel.

"I'd like to court you, Hazel. I've always found you beautiful, and now you've surprised me with your aplomb."

Alice declared, "Hooray for a plum!"

"Now, now. We'll see about that," Ida snapped. "We'll just see."

Hazel spoke, her voice strong. "I'd be honored to accept, John Parker." She crossed her arms and pushed her chin forward. "Go home, Mother. That's where you say a woman belongs."

The other club members began to nod and clap.

Ida stamped her foot again and jammed the hat back on her head. Sand sprinkled down from the bird's bent wings. She stormed across the park, her busy finger continuing its tirade toward no one.

Belle clapped too as she thought of Kate, sharing her day up north with women testing the shifting winds like dancing kites. She looked around at her fellow club mates.

I'm surrounded by women who dare to long for more.

How proud Kate would be of every member of the Circle Club. In the weeks and months ahead, they would laugh and listen and learn . . . together.

Chapter 30

The headlines in the *Press* that morning discussed the arrest of a ring of fruit thieves, impending bridge repairs, and the possibility of a town bank. Nothing was written about Belle's dream finally coming true.

The Edison gardens were finished and in peak form, active with butterflies and hummingbirds. Busy bees dined on a golden banquet of pollen. From front to back, flowers bloomed in a mesmerizing wave of color families. Even the varied leaf patterns were engaging. Belle surveyed the gardens, and for a moment, she lived there too, covered in dermal tissue, not skin. She stood firm as if roots had been dispatched from her soles. How grateful she was. Not only was the project a success, but she, too, had grown in the process.

The clinking of silverware and laughter drew her back to this balmy March afternoon where a lawn party was almost under way. Decker had made a rare exception to allow for an outdoor lunch in the Edisons' backyard.

"This never happened. Understand?" he'd grumbled to Boone, but handed him one of the Edisons' silver cake cutters engraved with wildflowers.

Word had come that the family would not be visiting. Newspaper reports around the country revealed one major reason: a bitter split between Edison and two of his most trusted business partners—Ezra Gilliland, his dear friend who owned the guesthouse at Seminole Lodge, and his longtime attorney, John Tomlinson. Edison claimed that both defrauded him in a deal made to raise capital to market phonographs. The headlines raged: "EDISON OUT $250,000." "GOUGING EDISON." An impending legal battle would mean a winter without the Edisons in Fort Myers. The fact that Mina would soon give birth further sealed the decision to stay up north.

The *Press* tried valiantly to soothe the town's disappointment and frustration with inked optimism: "All that is required is putting up the poles and stringing the wires for electricity. Fort Myers will be a lively place next winter!"

With news of the Edisons' canceled trip, Merle, Abigail, and Boone teamed up to organize a special lunch for Belle to celebrate her completed gardens and her twenty-sixth birthday.

"We're almost ready, Belley," Merle called out from behind her. She turned to see him and Boone standing beside an elegant setup. Both were dressed in their cleanest clothes with the fewest patches, and no hats. She blew them a kiss, which they pretended to battle for, elbowing each other, grabbing for it. Abigail approached from the Baker's side of the yard, balancing a tray of food in one hand, gripping the handle of a coffeepot with the other. Merle moved to help her while Boone pulled out a chair for Belle.

The table was set for a formal meal—ecru tablecloth and napkins, china ringed with a wheat motif, dainty cups for coffee. The gardens were on full display from the table's chosen location in the center of the yard. Abigail set out covered pots and bowls, the feast unfolding as they all sat down.

"Oh yes," Merle said, peeking under a lid. "Mr. Ridley's smoked venison?"

"Of course," Abigail said, and patted her bun.

Boone peeked, too. "Biscuits and giblet gravy, mustard greens with bacon." He shook his head. "Can you please teach Decker how to cook, Abigail?"

Merle answered for her. "You can't teach artistry to a numbers man."

Belle smiled. "Please bring him a plate when we're through, Boone, for allowing this. He said he's too busy to join us, but he's certainly missing out. This is just perfect."

"More eating, less talking," Abigail commanded.

Everyone laughed, happy to obey such a mouthwatering order.

•••

When they finished eating, Boone reached into his pants pocket and pulled out a leather pouch. Merle and Abigail glanced at each other. Boone presented it to Belle. "For you on your special day, from me."

She smiled and accepted the gift. "Thank you, Boone."

As she lifted the flap on the pouch, Boone warned, "Don't reach in. Dump what's inside onto the table."

She turned the bag upside down and shook it. Her eyes widened as two items dropped out.

"Oh, Boone!"

She stood and went to him. She bent over and wrapped her arms around his neck. "I love them!" When she pulled back to kiss his cheek, he turned his head so her lips landed on his. Merle and Abigail laughed and clapped.

Belle laughed, too, and returned to her seat to study her gifts: two unique fishing lures.

"I found them in the river when I was pulling up water lettuce," Boone explained. "They were caught in the roots."

Belle decided to first examine the spoon lure. Its treble hook dangled in the air, a kidney-shaped metal spoon hanging above it.

She tilted her head and held the lure closer. Stamped diagonally across the polished spoon was "CHAPMAN & SON." Directly under those words: "THERESA, N.Y." The number "1" was pressed into the metal at the top of the spoon. She shook the little lure as if it were a bell, the sound of metal on metal barely audible. Belle imagined it flashing through the water, beckoning a fish to eat its words and hooks. She laid it down and picked up the second lure.

"You're a beauty," she said, as she studied the detailed creation.

This one also featured a treble hook, but a fish was lured by something trickier than a shiny spoon. The designer had crafted the bait in the shape of an insect, a combination of a bee and a fly. The bug had four wings, spread in flight, complete with dimension lines pounded into the metal. Two large mounds on each side of the head served as eyes, antennae atop those. Small dots were indented in the thorax, and five black horizontal stripes ringed the copper-colored abdomen.

Belle shook her head. "I wouldn't blame any fish for mistaking this for a meal." She put down the lure. "Thank you again, Boone. I know right where I'm going to put them on my hat."

"Well, I can't think of a better place for them . . . except inside a grouper's mouth." He smiled.

"Good work, Boone," Abigail said, then excused herself to put the coffee back on. Merle followed her with a tray of dirty dishes.

Alone at the table, Boone and Belle shared a longer kiss. When they parted, Boone sat back in his seat.

"You look beautiful."

Belle was getting better at accepting his compliments. "Why, thank you."

"I have one more surprise for you."

She reached her hand out to him. "I don't need anything more."

He squeezed her hand. "You can't say no to this. I told Decker I'd finish the landscaping by myself if he'd allow it . . . and he did."

"Well, now I'm intrigued," Belle said.

Boone smiled, and they both turned their heads to watch Merle and Abigail returning. She was carrying a large white cake; he held a stack of small plates.

Belle shook her head. "Coconut cake? You didn't, Abigail." Belle had seen her create the cake before, hammer and chisel in hand. Cracking eggs was far easier than cracking open a coconut.

"Of course I did. It's your birthday, and your gardens look beautiful." She set down a flawless double-layer cake with white frosting. Grated coconut on its top and sides made the cake look dressed for a party. Merle cut the cake with the Edisons' silver knife and served up slices. The table was quiet as they indulged in the moist, sweet dessert. Belle took one more bite, then stood and raised her cup.

"I want to offer my thanks." She looked around the table. "You have all saved me. I hope you know how much I love and appreciate each of you."

"We love you, too, Belley." Merle reached forward and clinked his cup on hers. Abigail and Boone joined in.

Belle sat back down and realized her napkin had fallen from her lap when she'd stood up. She bent over to pick it up and froze midgrab. Merle and Abigail were holding hands under the table! Smiling, she nearly bumped her head on the way back up. She sat motionless and let the image of their clasped hands sink in. *Finally!*

"Time for a quick spin," Boone announced. He stood and walked behind Belle's chair. "Up you go."

Belle tipped her head backward to look up at him, then glanced over at Abigail. "You didn't tell me he was so bossy."

"What *are* you up to, Boone?" Abigail said.

He led Belle to the bottom of the Edisons' porch steps, book-ended by Belle's gardens.

"Stay here." He walked up the stairs and disappeared into the house.

Belle turned and shrugged her shoulders at Merle and Abigail.

Boone soon walked out, grinning and carrying a phonograph, its large horn yawning open like an oversized angel's-trumpet blossom.

Belle lightly gasped and covered her mouth with both hands.

From the table, Merle said, "Now *this* I want to see."

"You mean hear," Abigail said, and patted his arm.

Boone bent down and set the phonograph on the porch. "Are you ready?"

She nodded, dropping her hands and sweeping her long hair off her shoulders.

Boone cranked the handle on the side of the rectangular wooden box.

Another magic box, Belle thought.

As Boone walked down the porch steps, music began to play, a small wax cylinder rotating on a rod.

"Come to me," Boone said softly, his upturned palm awaiting hers.

She took a deep breath and tucked herself against his frame. She smiled up at him, one hand on his back. "This is very special."

With his arm slipped around her waist, holding her raised hand, he began to sway, turning her slowly in a circle. "The Lost Chord" featured a trumpet melody accompanied by piano, the most prominent sound the rhythmic churning of the rolling cylinder.

"I can't believe this," Belle murmured into Boone's chest. She laid her cheek against him and closed her eyes.

Boone hummed softly, out of tune. "I like you right here," he whispered, and gently pulled her closer.

The music ended after two minutes, well before the pair was ready to part. The sound of Merle and Abigail clapping drew them away from each other.

"You two are next," Belle said as they approached the table.

Merle looked at Abigail. "Shall we?"

"We shall," Abigail said, and slid her chair back through the sand.

Belle caught Merle's eye and made her eyebrows dance up and down. He smiled and led his dance partner toward the porch. After more cranking, the phonograph again came to life, serenading the next couple to enjoy Edison's remarkable, perfected invention. Merle and Abigail laughed throughout the song, especially when she spun him as he squatted below her raised arm.

At a small, round table in the middle of a yard, beside a river, on a clear afternoon, Belle was certain she was happy. Her body was strong, her heart was open, and for the first time she could imagine what life could offer, not take away. Once unrecognizable, hope now showed itself daily with the rising sun, a fresh start to do battle with whatever challenge came her way. Belle was ready—she'd proved herself a warrior.

"I'm very glad the Edisons have agreed to your staying at the cottage," Boone said. He leaned forward and crossed his arms on the table. "I want you near me."

She tapped her finger on the table. "We'll see how long they'll keep me on."

Boone pretended to slip something into his shirt pocket. "Maybe I'll just carry you around in my pocket." He gently patted his chest.

Belle smiled and lightly shrugged. "You never know. Sometimes precious things are tucked away in the strangest places."

Epilogue

Driving north on I-75, Kate looked down at the clock in the rental car. They were making good progress from the airport and would have plenty of time to wander around the property.

"Do you need a snack, honey?" Kate reached over and touched her daughter's arm.

"I'm tired, Mommy." The little girl leaned her head against the stuffed manatee in her arms. Kate had bought it for her in the airport gift shop. The five-year-old chose it from a shelf filled with stuffed alligators, flamingos, and dolphins.

"I know you are, honey. I thought you might sleep on the airplane."

The child's eyes were closed. She was wearing a pink sundress with capped sleeves, dotted with bright images of lemons and limes. Halfway through the drive, she'd kicked off her pink Chuck Taylors.

"You rest. We'll be there in a little bit."

Kate had waited to make the trip from New York to Florida until Andi was old enough to enjoy Disney World. The plan was to spend the day and night in Fort Myers, then tomorrow make the less-than-three-hour drive inland. The flight to Fort Myers was cheaper than flying direct into Orlando, so the decision to land here made perfect sense. Maybe the other reason didn't, but she didn't care. She just wanted to see where a woman named Belle once wrote a letter to her very distant relative.

Kate veered off I-75 North and took exit 138 toward Fort Myers. Her heart began to beat a bit faster. Why the adrenaline? *It could be the divorce,* she thought. Her little family of three had been recently pared down to two. She'd found a secret phone in her husband's gym bag filled with bad decisions. He admitted to everything and wanted nothing, except to remain in Andi's life. They'd worked that part out. The rest was messy, at least for her. She was still rearranging living room furniture, not to mention emotions. Anger here, sorrow over there. *Where the hell do I put loneliness?* That was a pesky one. Maybe this stop in Fort Myers was her way of searching for a connection with someone, even the "friend" of a long-dead relative.

Weeks ago, as she was sorting through her father's belongings, she came across a box labeled "family stuff." He'd always been interested in genealogy, poring over faded photographs or studying family-tree charts, his parents' names, Andrew William Hallock and Kate Ann Robertson, always underscored in red ink. In one file folder, a letter dated 1888 had caught her eye. After reading it, she remembered that her family called it the "odd" letter, referencing a word used by Belle, the writer, and also because some of the content was indeed odd. When she and her brother were young, her parents would encourage them to take turns guessing at what Belle was concealing and why, and what the long-ago Kate must have thought when she read the letter. Over the years, "family stuff" was talked about less and less until finally her father was the only one still interested, which Kate now regretted. She'd kept the letter, wishing she could discuss it—and everything—with her dad. Losing him on the heels of the divorce was an unexpected second blow that knocked her into a corner where she wanted to stay forever. And if not for her precious little girl, she would have. Someone had to be present for Andi, full-time and full of joy, even if she faked the last part. On days when despair pummeled her resolve, she'd reread the letter, left lying out on her desk. Even though Belle wrote the note more than a century earlier, Kate found her words of hope timeless:

April 5, 1888
Fort Myers, Fl.
Dear friend to the north,

Do forgive my penmanship! My hand is better served sketching than writing, but I'm compelled to continue and will trust that my words are discernable enough. I must begin by introducing myself, as you don't know me or even that I exist. My name is Belle Carson, and I live many miles south of you in the state of Florida in a small river town called Fort Myers. Perhaps you've heard of it because of our famous winter visitor, Thomas Edison. We are quite proud to claim him and his family, although neither has found time to soak up our sunshine of late. More about them in a bit.

I should say straightaway, Kate, that my letter may confuse you. I know things about your life, which will seem quite odd since we've never met. I don't understand it myself. But none of that matters. Somehow your enthusiastic words reached me, and for that I am grateful. I learned from you that the northern winds are shifting for women, and that you and others are testing them, as if you're a bevy of kites! I must say, the opinions of your mother (who no doubt loves you) must feel like scissors constantly snipping at your kite's string. The way you stay the course and command even more string is inspiring. You're flying higher and higher! One day, you will bump right into your dreams.

The reason I'm writing is to thank you, Kate. Because of you, I formed a women's club in my little town, the first and only of its kind. I'd been trying to open my heart to more meaningful relationships, and then, I heard yours, longing for more. So I took a chance, and it paid off. Our club is now eight women strong! Our purpose is yet to be determined, but each time we meet there is laughter and candor and fellowship. Perhaps those are reasons enough for all of us to gather. I know they are for me.

And that brings me back to the Edisons, Mina in particular. When she kindly hired me to create a set of gardens on their property, I moved into a pretty cottage right next door. I don't know how to fully capture the setting except to say that there seems to be some sort of magic in the air, a potential for everything and everyone to grow in unexpected ways. I'm pleased to say that both gardens are flourishing, and if I do say so myself, they're quite beautiful. I chose a variety of flowers for the beds, but there is one in particular that I want to share with you. There's a plant called a pink rain lily, quite a stunner. It features vibrant pink blooms with bright-yellow stamens that beckon the bees. But what makes this lily so special is when it chooses to bloom, to showcase its best and brightest. It waits and endures, and then explodes with blossoms after a storm, after the howling wind and driving rain finally relent. I find that so hopeful! We can all bloom, after the rain. I feel that I am doing just that, and I can sense that you will, too, when a challenge comes your way. Something we can share, Kate, is faith that the strongest storms in our lives will fling us into the arms of goodness. We must hold on tight, waiting and trusting.

I will finish now with a hint of sadness that we will never meet. I won't soon forget you, and I offer my well wishes for your road ahead. Keep writing and laughing and inspiring those of us who need a glimpse of fearlessness to begin our own search for it. To find where it may lie within us.

Your grateful friend to the south,
Belle

Kate had Belle's letter with her, tucked in her suitcase in a Ziploc bag. Perhaps she would read it again tonight after their day of exploring. The sentiment that most moved her—*We must hold on tight, waiting and trusting.* Yes, she must.

Andi was awake by the time they arrived at their destination. Kate helped her daughter put on her sneakers in the parking lot. The March day was gorgeous—warm but dry. Before they'd parked, Kate had checked to see what was on either side of the expansive property where Belle once lived. One side was a private property she couldn't access; the other side housed a large church. But no "pretty cottage right next door." Of course a dozen decades of progress had erased Belle's footprint. Of course, but alas. The twenty acres she was about to explore would have to suffice.

Mother and daughter walked hand in hand toward the property's main office. Kate's membership and Andi's age allowed for a free tour. She'd been happy to pay for a membership, to support such a special and important piece of American history—the Edison and Ford Winter Estates.

"Mommy, look at all of those arms!"

Andi was pointing at a huge tree with countless thick, woody shafts that extended down from the branches, creating a forest of trunks that covered an acre.

"Isn't that neat, honey? It's called a banyan tree."

Kate had browsed the Edison-Ford website when she bought the membership. She recalled seeing a photo of the tree, both magnificent and bizarre. Apparently, Henry Ford gave it to Edison in 1925.

"Here, honey—stand next to Mr. Edison."

Kate walked backward and snapped a shot of her daughter next to a cast-aluminum statue of Edison that stood in front of the massive banyan.

Preferring to simply wander and enjoy the sights, Kate declined self-guided tour headsets and instead picked up a map. She would keep an eye out for Belle's special pink blooms.

They started off at the Edison laboratory. The wooden structure was filled with long tables topped with beakers, mortars and pestles, scales, and plastic tubing. Glass cabinets housed shelves packed with corked bottles. Large machines with various functions were showcased throughout the expansive room. Andi reached up for Kate's hand. The space was somewhat dark and perhaps a bit intimidating to her forty-two-inch-tall daughter. Not much would look familiar to her.

"This is a laboratory, honey. See all of the tools and instruments? This is where Mr. Edison invented things."

"What things?" Andi asked, hugging her stuffed animal to her chest.

"Well, things like the light bulb and the record player. People used to listen to music on record players."

"Did he live here?"

"Nope. He just worked in here. We're going to cross the street and see where he and Mr. Ford lived. Mr. Ford invented a car called the Model T."

The two left the lab, walked past various plants for sale near the information booth, and crossed McGregor Boulevard. They were now on the main property that included both the Edison and Ford estates. Kate decided to head for the river. The map showed a lily pond she thought Andi would like. On the way, Kate pointed out a long line of old wooden pilings sticking up in the river. A sign indicated they were looking at where Edison had a long wharf built.

"This used to be Mr. Edison's dock, honey. Isn't the river pretty?"

Andi nodded and pointed at several gulls drifting overhead.

"We see those at home . . ."

"We sure do . . . by the river."

They continued to the lily pond where they could also see a long, rectangular swimming pool.

"Look, diving boards!" Kate said. "I'll bet the Edisons had fun living here."

"Can we see where he lived?" Andi skipped along the pathway away from the pool area.

"Yep. There's a main house and a guesthouse."

They passed by a bubbling fountain and walked toward the residences. Majestic seventy-foot palm trees stood guard in a long row in front of the homes. A plaque explained that the structures were restored to appear as they did circa 1929, forty years after Belle lived next door. *Too bad,* Kate thought.

"Do you want to peek inside, honey?" Kate hoped she'd say no. That way they could see more of the property before the little girl pooped out.

"Let's just go up on the pretty porch." Andi ran for the steps.

Where were Belle's gardens? Kate pulled out a photo of pink rain lilies that she'd Googled. No sign of them. Again—of course the flowers weren't there. Time had churned through countless generations of plants and people that once inhabited the space. She climbed the stairs and, from the sprawling porch of the guesthouse, spotted the neighboring Ford property.

"Over there is where Mr. Ford lived with his family. He and Mr. Edison were good friends. They spent a lot of their winters here."

"Why?" Andi asked.

"Because it doesn't snow here. It's warm, not freezing cold like where we live and they lived, too. Let's walk over to Mr. Ford's yard, okay? I'll bet he has some cars in his garage."

They joined other visitors inside a structure that housed several vintage cars, including a Model T. The cars were roped off, but Kate snapped a cute photo of Andi pretending to hold a steering wheel.

She guessed that her daughter had another twenty minutes in her, so they wandered the property, a botanical haven. Andi seemed drawn to the exotic orchids.

"That's the frilliest, Mommy." Then she'd find a frillier one.

Kate had no idea which species were growing in 1888 but was amazed by the current, well-marked array: a giant Mysore fig, an African sausage tree, trees that produced everything from bananas to avocados, star fruit, and jackfruit.

"Let's go see the coconut grove, honey."

The shady area along the river featured a half-dozen bent trunks. The trees' swaying palm fronds gathered the breeze and tickled each other. Below, Kate studied the photo again. She looked over at Andi, petting a coconut and smiling.

"It's so hairy, Mommy!"

"It sure is!"

Andi began to roll the coconut around the ground, giving Kate a chance to search for lilies in the grove. She squatted down to get a closer look. Nothing at all appeared to be the plant, with or without blooms.

"What are you doing, Mommy?" Andi stood next to her.

She sighed. "I was hoping to get a photo of these pretty flowers for a friend, but I can't find them." She showed her daughter the printout.

"What friend?" Andi asked, and traced a pink bloom with her finger.

"You've never met her, sweet girl."

"Oh." Andi took the paper. "Maybe I can find them for you, Mommy." She skipped off, clutching the image.

Kate sat down on a bench to watch her resilient daughter look for the lilies. She seemed curious and happy despite her parents' breakup late last year. How adorable she looked, her little pink shoes darting from place to place. She stayed in sight but searched a wide area, turning back to smile and wave between stops. Kate briefly closed her eyes. She let the streaming sun soak into her winter-pale skin. The breeze off the river danced across her neck and then moved along. Maybe she would be okay. Maybe soon the hurt would lift. She slowly opened her eyes and marveled at the rich setting. Rough trunks rising from the smooth sand, vibrant bursts of color, gentle waves. *You were right about this place, Belle.* Kate could almost see magic sparkling around the edges of every little thing.

Dear Reader,

My fascination with the Edison property began thirty years ago when I worked as a television reporter and anchor at WINK-TV in Fort Myers, Florida. I was hired as the *Backroads* reporter, tasked with finding unique regional characters and sharing their compelling stories with viewers. I was lucky to work for a news director who valued human-interest stories and to be in the industry at a time when good news was still allowed on the rundown. The beat would become my favorite in the course of a thirteen-year career in broadcast television.

One of the stories I chose to cover for *Backroads* was shadowing a horticulturist who cared for the expansive gardens at the Edison winter estate. (The current name of the destination is the Edison and Ford Winter Estates, listed on the National Register of Historic Places.) I wandered the lush gardens with my skilled guide, captivated by the countless specimens, from all over the world, and the reasons Edison chose them. Some were for research, like goldenrod, grown for its latex content and possible role as a domestic source for rubber. Others were selected for fruit, to attract birds and butterflies, or for privacy. Specific details from that day are vague, but I recall the horticulturist discussing the pollination process of prehistoric cycads. Remarkable!

Perhaps the overall setting so appealed to me because I grew up in a family interested in tinkering, building, gardening, birding, creating, and learning. Whatever the case, my time in the gardens planted a seed that lay dormant for three decades. But when I was considering venues for my first novel, that little seed sprouted in my brain.

I chose to place the story during a year the Edisons did *not* visit so I could showcase the folks you met on the pages of this book. (The family resumed their seasonal visits in 1901 and vacationed regularly at Seminole Lodge for decades.) In 1898, twelve years after Edison's promise to the town, electricity arrived for all in Fort Myers. The town finally had lights and, eventually, additional superstars of industry: Henry Ford, Harvey Firestone, and Edison spent many winters enjoying each other's company in southwest Florida.

Concerning the mix of fact and fiction, I took great delight in researching Belle's dot on history's timeline, when the only thing stored in a cloud was rain. I studied the region, the infrastructure, the Edisons, what was and wasn't available in 1888. I wore out the internet and well-footnoted books that identified, for instance, shipping invoices outlining the Edisons' belongings Boone describes being unloaded at the estates. The words Mrs. Abbott exchanges with the elderly Seminole woman are derived from research on the tribe's Mikasuki language. *The Dixie Cook-Book* (revised 1885 edition) guided me on what to cook, bake, and serve. I took some poetic license on dates—within a year or several—just to make sure you met people I thought you'd enjoy.

I made some small discoveries, like a map of Fort Myers hand-drawn in 1886. I pored over the location and variety of businesses and residences that formed the town that year. The *ding-ding* discovery turned out to be the labor of love that is the Thomas A. Edison Papers Project, a research center at Rutgers School of Arts and Sciences. For four decades, editors and scholars have been wrangling millions of documents related to Edison's personal and professional life and compiling them into an organized look-see for the public. Because of this incredible resource, I had access to a vast and varied set of facts during the time stamp of my story—clippings from the *Fort Myers Press*, letters Edison wrote to his caretaker at Seminole Lodge, his illustrated notebooks from the laboratory in Fort Myers. I am extremely grateful for the hard work of others that made mine easier.

Along with the Edisons, characters in the book who retained their real names are (in order of appearance) Ezra Gilliland, Professor James Ricalton, Edward Weston, Nellie Bly, William H. Wood, and John Tomlinson. Abigail's character is based on Margaret Knight, a prolific American inventor known as the "woman Edison" of her time. When fellow inventor Charles Annan stole and patented her design for a flat-bottom bag machine, she sued him for patent interference. Knight won the lawsuit and was granted a patent for her invention in 1871. You may be interested to know that in 1889, prominent New York journalist Jane Cunningham Croly organized a conference to gather delegates from women's clubs around the country. The following year, the General Federation of Women's Clubs was founded with sixty-three clubs, its mission to promote the viewpoints of women and community enhancement. Shortly after, a motto was adopted: "We look for unity, but unity in diversity." Today, the GFWC estimates a membership of eighty thousand representing women from more than twenty-five hundred clubs around the world.

If you did, I appreciate you embracing the spirit of wonder regarding the black contraption Belle found in the shed. The box was rooted in my desire to see what Belle would do with an opportunity, with a chance to be inspired by "women testing the shifting winds like a bevy of kites." Heck, I guess I got caught up in the magic of the Edison property, too.

If you ever have the chance to visit the Edison and Ford Winter Estates in person, I encourage you to make the trip. Of course, thanks to the internet, a visit is possible day or night. I've included the website below.

Finally, I offer my heartfelt thanks to you, the reader, for giving me a reason to share my writing. I truly hope *After the Rain* was meaningful to you in some way.

With gratitude,

Jane

For more information, visit *edisonfordwinterestates.org.*

Acknowledgments

My beloved parents and sisters can't help but be a part of this book—they're a part of me. If you find a lovely quality in something or someone herein, that's from them.

Hoda, remember when we were running in Florida and I was sharing an idea I had for a copyediting service? You stopped in your tracks and said, "Janie, you're not a copyeditor. You're a writer." You've always believed in my relationship with words, and for that—and for a million other things about you—I'm grateful. And beyond lucky.

A smooch to Jim, who kept reminding me that I had a story idea worth sharing. Your strong belief in the concept (and me) bolstered mine, especially when that gray cloud of doubt showed up. You took my hand and walked me toward the blue patch.

Christine Pride, editor-extraordinaire who gave me the road map to Fictiontown when I was completely and utterly lost. I will never forget who showed me the way, C. You so kindly told me, after reading my epically crappy manuscript, "Every project has hope." (Thanks for Christine, Kerri!)

Two Janes are better than one, Jane Rosenman. Your astute editing is outmatched only by your powerfully positive attitude.

I'm very grateful Jake led me to you, and I'll always remember our email sign-offs: TOJ (The Other Jane).

Adri Trigiani—you're a force of nature who willingly and generously blows life into other people's dreams. Thanks so very much for championing mine. And for the path to Jake and Jane.

To the team at Girl Friday Productions: thank you for guiding this girl! Christina Henry de Tessan, Alexander Rigby, and Emilie Sandoz-Voyer—you answered my endless questions with patience and grace. Paul Barrett—from your creative brain to my book cover. It's beautiful, and I thank you. Amara Holstein—I'm so lucky you were my developmental editor. You truly cared about my characters and gave me all the right problems to solve. I so loved hanging out in 1888 with you! To the eagle eyes, thank you, Carrie Wicks, for copyediting, and Sharon Turner Mulvihill for proofreading. I'm indebted to you both and the entire GFP team.

Thank you to my not-so-secret reader, Sharon Miller. Your early and ongoing input energized me. I value any chance to hear your insightful thoughts . . . about anything, friend.

My childhood pals—Christine, Amy, and Laurie—thank you for your astute eyeballs, and even more valuable, your five decades of friendship.

Susan Chapman, my thanks to you for identifying gaps and for loving my tale. Nicki Dangleis, you had no time to read, but you did it anyway, for me. Thanks, John McCoy, for reading while riding the rails to work. Your extensive and valuable critique was worthy of an invoice.

John Emmert—thank you for hiring me to explore the lesser-known pockets of southwest Florida. Because of you, my time at WINK-TV and on the back roads was the very best of my career.

Thank you to all my beautiful friends, near and far, who cheer me on and hold me dear. I feel like I have pockets full of rabbits' feet.

And finally, to the alphabet—I love you.

About the Author

© David Boyer

Jane Lorenzini spent thirteen years as a television news anchor and reporter. Jane went on to cowrite two *New York Times* bestselling books, *Hoda: How I Survived War Zones, Bad Hair, Cancer, and Kathie Lee* and *Ten Years Later: Six People Who Faced Adversity and Transformed Their Lives*, plus a third book, *Where We Belong: Journeys That Show Us the Way*, with *Today* coanchor and dear friend Hoda Kotb. *After the Rain* is Jane's first novel. She lives in Tennessee and writes everywhere.

CPSIA information can be obtained
at www.ICGtesting.com
Printed in the USA
LVHW051349060119
602927LV00004B/635/P